Praise for *The Lost Letters of Rose Carey*

'This novel is such an accomplished feat. The reverberation between the two protagonists, separated in time, is masterful. At its core though, it is a novel which exemplifies female power. A tour de force of female agency.'
Meg Keneally, author of *Fled*

'*The Lost Letters of Rose Carey* is a beautifully written, expertly entwined story of two women, 100 years apart, who ultimately share a stunning connection. Part mystery, part love story, this dazzling novel completely captivated me, and I absolutely fell in love with both Julie Bennett's modern day and historical heroines.'
Jillian Cantor, author of *Half Life*

'I was instantly captured by Emma Quinn and her struggle to conceive a child with her wife Lauren, but it was Bennett's ability to seamlessly sew a century old mystery into the narrative through Rose Carey's letters that saw me lose my heart to this book. A compelling story of love, loss and the true meaning of family, *The Lost Letters of Rose Carey* grabbed me on page one and I'm not sure it will ever truly let me go!'
Nina D. Campbell, author of *Daughters of Eve*

The LOST LETTERS *of* ROSE CAREY

JULIE BENNETT

SIMON &
SCHUSTER

London · New York · Sydney · Toronto · New Delhi

For my darling Mum, who made me believe
I could achieve anything.

And for my favourite people,
Bruce, Chris, and Lachlan.

THE LOST LETTERS OF ROSE CAREY
First published in Australia in 2024 by
Simon & Schuster (Australia) Pty Limited
Suite 19A, Level 1, Building C, 450 Miller Street, Cammeray, NSW 2062

10 9 8 7 6 5 4 3 2 1

Simon & Schuster: Celebrating 100 Years of Publishing in 2024.
Sydney New York London Toronto New Delhi
Visit our website at www.simonandschuster.com.au

A catalogue record for this book is available from the National Library of Australia

ISBN: 9781760858551
Cover design: Christabella Designs
Cover image: © Nina Masic/Trevillion Images
Typeset by Midland Typesetters, Australia
Printed and bound in Australia by Griffin Press

The paper this book is printed on is certified against the Forest Stewardship Council® Standards. Griffin Press holds chain of custody certification SCS-COC-001185. FSC® promotes environmentally responsible, socially beneficial and economically viable management of the world's forests.

Just for a moment, I thought it was you . . .
And there we were again,
sitting in the long grass, threading daisy chains.
But it wasn't you,
just someone who had stolen your name.

1

Emma
Blue Mountains, 2024

My right leg vibrates. The rule on set is all phones off. Not just silent – off. But I've been waiting for this message all morning and there was no way I'd risk missing it. I want to read it straight away, but I honestly can't while the cameras are rolling and I'm behind one of them. I shift my weight silently from one leg to the other in nervous anticipation, and wait.

I do the calculations again in my head. Thirteen eggs (mine) at retrieval, five viable embryos (ours) after insemination, four frozen, one transferred, no pregnancy. Next phase – two frozen embryos thawed and transferred at different times, one unsuccessful, the other resulting in pregnancy, then miscarriage. Did our chances go up or down? This is our last shot – two frozen embryos thawed, one that didn't make it and the other transferred. Has the number thirteen proven lucky for us? The answer waits on my mobile phone, which now feels like it's burning an imprint on my leg.

Focus, Emma, I tell myself.

I lift my head from the view finder of the camera to the set. We have repurposed the library of the Carrington Hotel, Katoomba for the shoot. Its old wood-panelled walls and thick tartan-style carpet make for effective sound-deadeners, and the room, like the hotel itself, is very atmospheric.

It's an unusual shoot for Hammer and Tongs, which, increasingly, has been working with agricultural companies to produce corporate videos. My boss, Johnno, is particularly interested in work that demonstrates how companies are dealing with environmental concerns. Like me, he's a bit of a greenie.

But he also has a policy of exploring every lead, hence this gig. It's a policy that has seen the video production company he started some years ago grow to a company that now has serious runs on the board and both a Sydney and Melbourne presence.

It seems fitting that we're talking to an expert about the role of the Blue Mountains as an area for convalescence during the TB epidemic here.

'From the late 1800s, early 1900s, until well into the middle of the century, people suffering from tuberculosis, predominantly, came to the Blue Mountains to convalesce. The high altitude and clear air were considered very healthy. A series of sanitoria were ultimately built in what were then fairly remote areas in the mountains. It was also a popular tourism destination. By the 1930s, it had a reputation as the "honeymoon capital" of Australia. People flocked to hotels like the Carrington, which were considered the very height of luxury.'

Although I promised Lauren I wouldn't, I do the other maths. It was most expensive in the beginning. Wait a minute. Who am I kidding? It's been expensive all the way through, despite the rebates.

I stare back down at the camera, watching the action on set through the viewing pane. 'People also quietly convalesced in private homes in the mountains. Back in those days, you see, it was not only horrible to have diseases like TB, it was also socially unacceptable. It was primarily a working-class illness, contracted by people exposed to places like the mines. If you caught it, you certainly didn't want anybody to know about it, and if you could afford it, which most people couldn't, you'd get as far away as possible from those sorts of environments.'

Everything comes at a cost, especially health.

We could have – should have? – been more financially sensible about family planning. We could have gone to a publicly supported clinic. We could have gone about it the 'old-fashioned' way – but just the thought of it offends me and anyway, our options were limited. I could have suggested my brother for her, but not in this lifetime. I would call him a homophobic twat, but he'd probably take it as a compliment. We talked long and loud about Simon, my best friend from university and also, as it happens, Lauren's friend. He might have been okay with it, back when we were still at uni, but his relationship with his partner had been quite new when we started on our IVF journey and I hadn't been game to ask him. I mean, what would I have said?

Hey, Si, can you do me a favour?

Hey Si, we've been friends for yonks now, so I hope you don't mind me asking, but . . .

But what?

Can we please fuck, so we can maybe/maybe not make a baby?

Worse still: *Can you please fuck my girlfriend?*

Wife, I correct myself.

'The fresh mountain air was just what the doctor ordered for people suffering from respiratory illnesses,' the historian goes on.

Fresh mountain air. That's an understatement. We started setting up for the shoot at seven this morning and it was barely two degrees. The company has paid for accommodation, right here in the hotel, but I had to jog to the car to get my phone charger this morning and if I'd had balls, they would have frozen off.

I'm in a traditional room with a private bathroom at the end of what seems, in the middle of the night, to be a long hallway. But it's beautifully carpeted, and both the bedroom and the bathroom have been sympathetically renovated. I can almost imagine what it might have been like to stay here, back in the hotel's heyday.

I wish Lauren were here.

Simon's relationship with Tabitha had been so new, it had also prevented me from asking him for a turkey-baster solution, which on reflection seems a shame. I think his genes would produce great kids.

But I'd also had other reservations. Simon's such a great guy he'd probably want to be involved in the kid's life, and Lauren and I had decided we didn't want that. So, we'd chosen what the clinic called a de-identified sperm donor, affectionately referred to by us as DSD. We know the colour of his hair and eyes, his ethnicity, how tall he is, things like that. If our so-far imaginary kids want to know more, they can look him up themselves when they turn eighteen.

And so, I allow myself to dream. A little girl with dark hair and brown eyes like mine, and a skip in her step, like Lauren. Or perhaps no skip. If Lauren has my baby girl, there won't be any genetic similarities to her, none of those characteristics that I love so much about my wife. The little smile that plays at the corner of her mouth, the way she arches one eyebrow when she is quizzical or cross. Our little girl would be only me – and DSD.

This pierces my heart in a way that it shouldn't. Lauren will be doing the most difficult part – carrying our baby, going through childbirth, nursing her, or him. Things I'd thought too hard for me.

Ah, but who am I kidding? Those are not the only reasons we chose me to provide the eggs and her to carry them. As a teacher, Lauren has a job she can perhaps return to part-time, and more family-friendly hours than me.

'We're heading out,' Johnno says, as we break for lunch. 'Coming?'

As the boss, he's not usually on every shoot, but this one has clearly appealed to him. I shake my head and give him a lopsided smile. 'Got some things to catch up on.'

He nods, looks briefly like he might ask me what things, then obviously thinks better of it. 'No worries, mate, catch ya later.'

I switch off the camera, tidy some cords, make sure things are occupationally safe. Now that I have a chance to look at my phone, it is a dead weight in my pocket. I have an overwhelming feeling that I already know what her text will say. If it had been good news, she would have phoned – more than once.

But maybe not. Lauren knows I can't take calls on a shoot. She knows I can't be distracted. And besides, she's at work herself, she'd have sent the text during recess. She'll be back in the classroom now, watching the clock, counting down the minutes until lunchtime.

My heart pounding, I pull out the phone, wait interminable seconds for the screen to light up, then slide my thumb across the glass.

We don't have the money to try again. Covid bit too hard into my income, into our savings. More than that, we don't have the heart – do we?

I breathe in deeply, exhale slowly, bite down hard on my lip. The message contains only one word.

Negative.

I spend my lunch break aimlessly wandering the corridors. I haven't found the courage yet to call Lauren. She needs me to be strong. I should have texted right away, but I don't know what to say anymore. I don't know how to comfort her. Not what I've said every other time – 'We've got this, babe', 'We just gotta give it another go', 'It'll happen.' I know what she'll want to do, and I'm not sure I'm up for it. I'm not sure I have the guts.

I think back to the hormone injections, the tiredness, the headaches, the bloating – and that was the best of it. I hate injections, and I hated the way I felt after them. It was like PMS on steroids. I don't want to go through it again.

I wander through the hotel, not sure where I'm going. There was all that pre stuff and then there was 'retrieval'. Hours waiting around in day surgery, Lauren by my side, until she couldn't be. Anaesthetic, nausea, pain. Waking up to see the number on the back of my hand. Thirteen. As unlucky as it has ever been. I so want to be everything I can be for Lauren. I so want to give her everything she wants, but I have failed, yet again. I know that love means forgiving each other for the things we cannot do, but will she forgive me for this? And if she pushes me into trying again, and we fail again, will I be able to forgive her?

At the end of the hallway there's a door. I open it, flick a switch, and a yellow light fills the space. It's a storage room. There is a small table in the centre, and wooden filing cabinets crowd the back wall. I pull out the old maroon leather chair that's pushed under the table. I need to sit for a few moments, gather my thoughts.

The trouble with the twenty-first century, I think, as I put my phone face down on the table, is you can never disconnect from it.

I met Lauren six and a half years ago. It was *Destiny*, both figuratively and literally – she was helping with costume and wardrobe on an amateur production of a new play of the same name, at The Genesian in Kent Street, Sydney. Simon had dragged me along.

The theatre has had many previous lives – as a church, and a poor school, and a home for lost souls. We'd met after the show, at the cramped foyer bar.

'I'll have a Scotch on the rocks,' Lauren had said, nudging in beside me. I'd assumed she was speaking to the guy behind the bar, but when I glanced at her, I saw she was looking straight at me. 'Please,' she added, with a smile that pushed her eyebrows up under her ridiculous blonde corkscrew curls.

But she couldn't be talking to me because I'd never met her, never even laid eyes on her. There was no photo of her on the program, either; I'd scoured it at interval.

'Sorry?'

'Come on, you know you want to.'

She had a way about her that I shouldn't like. She was too sassy, too forward, not my type. But as I attempted to stare her down, I knew she was right.

'Scotch on the rocks,' I said to the guy behind the bar. 'Actually, make it two.'

He nodded, and when he set the glasses on the sticky wooden counter in front of us, he laughed. 'Watch out for her,' he said, as I waved my phone over the machine. But his warning was already a heartbeat too late.

'I think people are attracted to people, not genders,' she volunteered later, unasked, as we squeezed into the back corner of the foyer.

'Spoken like a straight woman keen to be seen as an ally.' All right, I was fishing, but I had to.

She laughed, tapping her plastic glass against mine and wasting a thimbleful of ice-affected whisky in the process. 'I'm not straight,' she said.

'You're not gay either.'

She shrugged. 'Like I said, I think people are attracted to people, not genders.'

'You've slept with men.' I had to know.

'Sure. But so have you.' She gave me a coy look over the top of her glass.

'Not the same. I didn't like it, you did.'

'True,' she agreed. 'But if you're asking me about preference . . .'

I wasn't. Was I?

'Well then, I'd have to say women.'

Even then, I worried about her use of the plural. Already, I didn't want to hear about her previous conquests, didn't want the image of her with anyone else in my head. But of course we spent the night together. It was the first time I'd gone home with someone right after meeting them, and it bothered me the next morning.

'I don't do casual,' I said over toast and cappuccino at La Taza, downstairs from her Pyrmont apartment.

She let out a long, exaggerated sigh. 'Pity,' she said, swiping a smudge of vegemite from the corner of her lip with a paper napkin. 'Because I really value my freedom. But if you don't do casual, well then, you'd better move in.'

I didn't know if she was bunny-boiler serious or if she was teasing me, but I realised at that moment I didn't care. I liked her – which was something just as good, but quite different from how I'd felt about her the night before, when my head was between her thighs.

'Well,' I said, surprising myself, 'I guess I'd better.'

It wasn't quite as fast as that. We dated for three months and made no promises to each other, although we did lay down some ground rules. We were free to date other people. We'd practise safe sex. We wouldn't make unreasonable demands, and we'd wait before introducing one another to the significant others in our lives.

'Si is different though, right?' she'd said, straight after we'd agreed to those rules. 'I mean, he already knows both of us and he already knows about us.'

'How would he already know about us, Lauren?'

'Oh. Because I told him.'

That's the thing about her, she's incorrigible. It's what I love most, and least, about her.

But now, my wife is a hundred or so kilometres down the mountain, dealing with the fact that she will certainly not be a mother anytime soon, and I can't find the courage to comfort her, not even via text. I pick up the phone and open the messenger app, then put it back down again.

I look about the room. There's an old lamp with a broken green glass shade in a box in the corner, and a group of framed prints leaning against one of the filing cabinets. Several rugs, rolled into dusty bollards and tied with rope, are propped against a tower of cardboard boxes. A piece of paper with the words 'Pick-up: Rick's' written in heavy black texta is taped to the front of the box tower.

Another quick glance at my phone tells me it's time to head back to work. As I head for the door I see a large, wooden crate with a hinged lid sitting all alone on a side table. I don't know why I stop to look at it. I tug on the lid, half expecting that it won't open, but it does. Inside are yellowing photographs and newspaper clippings, a bundle of letters tied in fading ribbon, an ancient camera, and a large, odd-shaped octangular metal container. Just like the rugs and the framed prints, this strange assortment of things are past their use-by date.

I pick up a photograph. Today we might call it a tasteful nude, but in the early days of the twentieth century, when it must surely have been taken, it might have been scandalous. There are several more photos, all similar, all of the same woman. Her face is always turned slightly away from the camera. She has long, dark, wavy hair and an athletic figure. Beautiful, I suppose.

I put the photos down on the table and reach into the box for the odd-shaped canister. It's heavy, made of steel or galvanised iron, perhaps. I lift it out with some effort and pull on the metal, D-shaped ring on the lid. Again, I half expect it not to open, but after bit of a struggle, I'm able to prise it off. The lid clatters to the floor, and I inspect the contents. Film reels, I realise, each packed in its own individual can. What a curious find.

I check the outside of the canister. There are no markings on it, no labels, nothing to identify it at all. I pick the lid up and examine it. Nothing on that either, inside or out. I pull out one of the individual cans. Like the canister, it is metal, oxidised with age. As I pick it up my fingers are coated with reddish dust. Again, there's nothing to identify it. I'm no film expert, but shouldn't there be some kind of label on something, somewhere?

As I worry the lid open and reach in to pull out the first reel, an unexpected shiver of something like excitement runs through me. The first few centimetres of film unravel, and I hold it up to the light. It feels slightly sticky, as if the years it has spent in the can have caused it to slowly melt away.

But perhaps it's not as old as I thought – the first few frames appear to be in colour. Limited colour, I correct myself. For the most part, they contain stylised illustrations of sea nymphs and other creatures, in shades of green and – as corny as it sounds – gold. On this title sequence, the words 'Carey & Ryan Corp. presents' appear in a modest curved text at the top, followed by the name 'ROSE CAREY' in large, Art Deco stylised font. On the next line, in the same font and size, are the words, 'THE SEA PRINCESS OF THE SOUTH PACIFIC'. It's a feature film, I realise. A very old feature film.

The name Rose Carey strikes a chord. Isn't there a ferry or something named after her? I make a mental note to google her later.

I return the reel to its can, put it back in the canister, and jam the lid on. I brush my hands together, trying to rid myself of the dust and dirt, then give up and wipe them on the back of my pants.

Finally, I pick up the camera. It's a still camera and it looks like a pretty ancient relic. I trace my fingertip over the manufacturer's name, engraved into the metal lens cap: *Leica*. And then I stop. Also engraved on the lens cap, outlined in white paint for effect, are three initials.

E.M.Q.

Exactly the same as mine.

2

Rose
Sydney, 1923

'Oh, let's *do* something,'

It's my favourite catchcry, especially when I'm feeling a bit blue, as I am today. We'd had an enthusiastic welcome when the ship ferrying us from Auckland berthed in Sydney the other day – hundreds, if not a thousand fans, mostly women, all flocking together for my autograph, as they do wherever I go. But the truth of it is, I've not been quite myself since the incident in New Zealand.

If I don't focus on it, I can almost believe it didn't happen, but every now and then, something reminds me of it. I'm not quite sure what it is that's reminded me today.

'All right,' says Bell, getting up off the chaise lounge where all morning she's been listening to me mourn the fact that we've finished filming. 'Let's explore!'

Bell is as Australian as me, but we first met in London, through Alec. She was a typewriter girl working in an office.

She'd studied shorthand and bookkeeping. I'd just arrived in the mother country, eager to further my acting career. We both had a few lean years but later, after I'd made it big in America, she became my secretary, then my costumier, then my friend. Now, she is all three.

I link arms with her as we set out for the garden. We are almost the same height – that is, not very tall – and so we can walk together quite comfortably, neither of us craning or cricking our neck to address the other.

'"House" is really an understatement, isn't it?' I say, as we step out onto the lawn. We are staying in a Point Piper mansion courtesy of Mr Duxton, the merchant king, and his wife. They have lent us their home for our stay in Sydney, which could be a week, or a month, or longer, depending . . . Mr and Mrs D are off visiting family in the Blue Mountains. They are such an entrenched part of society here, there's even mention of their trip in *The Sydney Examiner.*

Mr and Mrs Duxton, of Fairview, *Point Piper, are visiting Mrs Duxton's brother and his wife in Leura for an extended stay.*

It always makes me giggle that such domestic things make it into the newspapers.

We walk down through the terraced garden, which has a view right out over the harbour. We pass by beds of pink and blue hydrangeas in late flower, hedges pruned within an inch of their lives and stands of exotic palms with long fronds waving at the ground.

'It certainly is an understatement,' Bell agrees. She wears her hair longer than mine, although it is a similar colour, and she has it pulled back in a loose roll at her neck. 'I mean, Point Piper is not Golden Bay,' she continues with an ironic twist to her mouth, 'but it has its compensations.'

She pauses for a moment to watch a willie wagtail dance along the branch of a shrub, singing a sweet song to itself.

'Case in point,' she says as the bird fans out its tail and wags it. She unhooks her arm from mine and reaches out her hand. The willie wagtail hops so nonchalantly up onto it that I wouldn't be at all surprised if the two were formerly acquainted. 'Look at him, Rose,' she says, almost as though she's talking to herself. 'That tail, it's perfect. When he spreads his wings, you'll see they are also fans.'

She waits until it hops down off her hand to resume its walk along the branch before reaching into her pocket and pulling out a notebook and pencil. I watch as she sketches the bird's tail feathers.

'Sleeves, I think,' she mutters to herself, and right there before my eyes she sketches the bodice of a dress with fan-like pleated sleeves that drift down towards each elbow.

'Beautiful,' I say, when she holds it up for my inspection.

'Perhaps in black and white, like the bird?' She eyes me up as she always does when she's contemplating a new design.

I nod. 'Oh, yes.'

She puts the notepad and pencil back in her pocket and we resume our walk.

'I suppose it's back to proper business now,' I say.

I'm missing the life we have just left behind on the South Island of New Zealand. Glorious months of frenetic busyness on location, while living simply as we filmed what is to be our very first independent moving picture. We had been as close as cards in the hand of a poker player: Alec, Bell, Walter, Eddie and me, swimming Golden Bay every day, rain, hail or shine. It had been particularly wonderful to work with Alec. He is an Australasian Olympic swimming and diving champion and was once my childhood sweetheart, many years before he realised he was not my way inclined.

I smile, remembering our innocent trysts in the little garden behind the School of Music my parents had established in their home in Macquarie Street, Sydney. Mother was briefly a concert pianist, before marriage and me. All my sweetest memories of her are of listening to her play.

But unlike my parents, I was no musician, and neither was Alec. He came along to the Saturday afternoon recitals with his father and mother, but we'd team up to slip past the rows of patrons, all straight-backed in their wooden chairs, and out the door before the cellist even opened his score.

I put up a hand now to brush my hair back from my forehead. It is always curling into silly brown bangs, no matter what I do to straighten it. It's one of the reasons I favour hats. I'm not convinced a bob was the right way to go, but it's all the rage. I shade my eyes. The sun is splintering the lapis lazuli of the water into crystals. 'I think we go ahead with our plans, Bell, I really do, despite . . . everything.'

'Everything' is the fact that – somewhat outrageously, in my opinion – we don't appear to have a lot of ready cash. I've always taken a hands-on, intelligent approach to financial affairs, but I've never really worried about them. Walter has been my manager since I first started in films in America ten years ago, and he's always done such a good job of managing the money, I've never had much cause to worry. After years of playing the game with the major studios, we recently formed our own entertainment company. It made sense. I am about to commit that ultimate Hollywood sin – turn thirty-five – and we need to, in Walter's words, 'diversify'. He is a native-born American, which does go such a long way in the States, and he has all the right contacts. He is also an astute negotiator and, most importantly, such a great friend.

'Do you think the extravaganza will do the trick?' I ask. The idea had been born after we finished filming, and oh, I do so hope it succeeds. After all, we have already ordered a brand new crystal tank – an enormous glass-walled aquarium of some 10,000 gallons, bigger and better than we used for the film in New Zealand. This one is being made from Belgian glass, to our exact specifications and measurements. I was intimately involved in its design. We need to begin rehearsing in the tank as soon as possible. But Bell seems doubtful, which makes me worry. She knows our business almost as well as I do.

'Remember, what I have planned is not really about films,' I hurry on, 'or putting on shows. It will be something quite extraordinary . . . Daring diving feats, things audiences haven't really seen before, in water and out of it – and you know Alec is on board.'

I glance at her, but she still doesn't comment. 'I want to do a world tour, starting right here, in Sydney, and ending in America, perhaps LA.'

'Yes,' she says, but she doesn't sound terribly enthusiastic.

I'm good at reinvention, I remind myself. After all, I've successfully transitioned from Australian vaudeville player, to London theatre actress, to Hollywood movie star. 'All we need is a strategy.' I frown, thinking about it. I'm good at strategising, too. 'We need publicity, lots of it, if we're going to attract the funding we need. We must have an offer that truly excites investors, and we need to put it into action very quickly.'

'Yes.' If she's cottoned on to what I'm thinking, she doesn't say so.

I look out at the sailing boats, bobbing and bowing in the early autumn breeze. 'We'll start tomorrow. We'll put it all down on paper.'

'Yes,' she says again.

'But it's such a nice day, let's not think too hard on it right now.'

That will give me tonight to find the right way to pitch it to Walter.

'Explain again what you mean by "extravaganza", Rose.'

I've called a meeting for the five of us and we are all in the library.

'A theatrical act, Walter,' I say, patiently for me, 'only on water.'

I hear him draw in a deep breath, so I quickly go on. 'Do you think you could sketch something, Bell, while I describe it?'

She nods and takes her notebook and pencil from her pocket. I sit down on Walter's desk. He moves some papers to make more room for me and rolls his chair back from it.

'It will be like *The Sea Princess of the South Pacific*, except of course we will write something new, a new scenario. What I'm imagining would be performed live, in front of an audience. We would have not only artistic swimming but exciting acts such as . . .' I pause. 'High diving.'

Walter exhales that pent-up breath.

I glance at Alec for support.

'We all know she's an excellent swimmer, and dancer,' he says, right on cue. 'She's had plenty of experience – why she's already performed many artistic dives, and she's in top physical form. She'd be a natural. Of course, we'd need to get into training right away.'

I give him a grateful smile before swivelling on the desk top to gauge Walter's reaction. I think I catch a look of something in his eyes . . . Trepidation?

'I'm so glad we decided to order the deeper crystal tank. Alec says it will give us the depth to train for just this sort of thing.'

Walter's eyes narrow. 'You've been planning this all along, haven't you?'

'Well, of course,' I agree. 'You know I have. It was the whole point of ordering the new tank.'

'It was not the whole point,' he corrects, 'or if it was, you failed to inform me.' The trepidation has been replaced by a steely look of disapproval.

I sniff. We are equal partners in this business, but it is sometimes a tussle. He is right. It wasn't what I'd sold to him in order to get him onboard to commission the new tank. What I'd said at the time was the one we'd used for *Sea Princess* was on its last legs, having served us very well in New Zealand. I'd convinced him that the freight cost wasn't worth the effort.

The real reason I'd wanted a new tank was because Alec had said we needed a depth of at least fifteen feet in order to practise high diving. I slide off the desk, because that look in Walter's eyes is making me feel just a little dishonest.

'Please just hear me out,' I say.

'All right,' he says reluctantly.

I begin pacing the room. 'So, I'm imagining a tale of a beautiful young woman, one of – let's see – seven sisters, all wonderfully talented, of course. We can plan beautiful artistic swimming around all that. Then the seven sisters are threatened by someone or something. Perhaps a wicked stepmother. No, I've had enough of wicked stepmothers, grossly unfair to them I think.'

'Wicked stepfather?' Bell offers.

'No,' I say, thinking about it. 'Let's stop casting step-parents as wicked. A bully of some sort, could be male or female. The villain feels threatened by the sisters and all but one of them goes into hiding, in a faraway place located near the bottom of a treacherous waterfall or something, from which, it is said, it is impossible to return. The star of the show decides to stay and fight it out with the villain. Although she loves to swim, she has no wish to live isolated from the rest of the world at the bottom of a waterfall. She meets a handsome hero,' I throw Alec a glance, 'who teaches her the diving skills she will ultimately need to rescue her sisters. The star then pretends to befriend the villain by telling him or her that surely it is not enough that the sisters are in exile, never to return; surely they must be killed. She lures the villain over the waterfall, the villain dies, and the star rescues her sisters. Of course, the handsome hero is overcome by the star's love and loyalty for her sisters and her extreme courage, athleticism and beauty, and falls madly in love.'

'And they live happily ever after,' Eddie, our chief cameraman and trusted friend, supplies dryly.

'And they live happily ever after,' I repeat with a laugh.

Bell looks up from her sketchpad and shows the page to us. She has captured the scenario beautifully, exactly as I imagined it. A swimming pool in front of the stage, a bevy of swimming beauties, a high diving tower to stand in for the waterfall and me standing at the top of it in a glittering bathing costume. I know she is now itching to design it.

'And the size of this cast?'

'I think we could keep it comfortably to fewer than a hundred.'

'A hundred,' he repeats. But it is considerably smaller than the ten or so thousand people who appeared on the last studio film I starred in, and half the number we had in New Zealand, so I'm not quite sure what he is going on about.

'Perhaps fewer,' I say with a shrug.

'And where do you propose to stage such an event?'

I wave my hand. 'Details, Walter,' I say. 'Perhaps we will create our own space—' I stop, sensing he is about to bluster about that idea.

His concerns are valid. It will be horrendously expensive, as the entertainment business tends to be, and we are only a small independent company. But I've found that, in this business, there are always ways and means. The universe often conspires to help things happen and with big risks come potentially bigger returns. The important thing is to make a start.

'Perhaps we will negotiate with aquariums and baths around the world. The Hippodrome in New York, for example. For now, what I want—' I pause again, searching for less demanding words. 'What I would like to do is start serious diving training with Alec, if, of course, you are agreeable . . .'

There is a long, stretched silence. Eddie begins to tap the floor with his toe, a nervous habit I've lately begun to notice.

'As if I could stop you,' Walter says finally, standing up from the desk.

'Thank you, darling. I'll take that as a yes.'

I navigate down the series of terraced gardens that back *Fairview*, and over the rocks to the water's edge. I'm on my own this time, wearing one of the bathing suits Bell designed, with a blue and white striped knee-length cape over the top. It has become so popular in America, it's been dubbed the 'Rosie Cape'. Almost every woman has one.

How can we be short of money? We sold this design to a clothing manufacturer.

'We have to be judicious,' Walter had said gravely after the meeting yesterday.

I looked up at him, so much taller than me, so much more reserved, and I was concerned to see something like worry on his face. Was he trying to spare me from something? I would have demanded to know what it was immediately, but Eddie was still in the room. Eddie doesn't have quite the same insight into our affairs; we wouldn't talk intimately about money in front of him.

I pull my bathing cap from a cape pocket and tuck my hair up into it. Then I lay the cape on a rock and stand for a moment to stare out across the water. Bell is right, it's not Golden Bay, but is there any harbour in the world more beautiful? I step in and swim out a little way. When I can no longer feel rocks or sand beneath my feet, I tuck my head down and dive. Thanks to Alec, I have learned to hold my breath for more than three minutes.

The water strokes my skin, as warm as milk. Remaining beneath the surface, I swim further out, until I'm certain of the depth and then I perform the tumble he taught me, the one that became part of my underwater routine for the film. 'Make every movement part of a pattern,' he'd said. 'Turn it into a habit, a routine. Practise, practise, practise.'

I swim down and find the rock floor, stand on it; first with both feet, then on just my right. I slide my left foot up my right leg and point it at my knee. Retiré. I bounce off my right leg, tumble into a slow somersault, then glide back up to break the surface of the water. This is my invention. The ballet I have always included in my acts modified to underwater performance.

But even in the water, I feel a frisson skitter down my spine. I see the road winding around the gorge ahead of me, hear the gravel crunch and crackle beneath the tyres. I feel the hard wooden rim of the steering wheel under my gloved hand, the sun beating down on my motoring cap, the wind annoying my scarf . . .

It had been a near thing, that incident in New Zealand.

I sprint back up the stairs and across the multiple terraces, my cape over my arm, my towel around my neck. When I reach the top terrace, I find Bell and Walter sitting at the wrought iron table, having drinks in the setting sun.

'Oh, that does look lovely,' I say, eyeing the whisky in his old-fashioned glass.

'I'd make you one, only . . .' His eyes crinkle at the corners. His face is so tanned by the Australasian sun that his eyes suddenly seem to be an even more brilliant blue. The look in them catches me for a moment, the way the sun is sometimes captured in the depths of a diamond, and I find myself momentarily forgiving him for the fact that he's wearing a white shirt, with a tie. I wish he weren't so buttoned-up. I'd like to see what I know, from our New Zealand swims, lies beneath that shirt and tie more often.

The thought takes me by surprise. I can't remember wanting such a thing before. 'I'll change, and pour my own poison,' I say quickly, in an attempt to smother the unexpected hankering. He smiles faintly at my joke, knowing I don't drink. 'Back in a jiffy.'

When I rejoin them fifteen minutes later, I have the oddest feeling that I have interrupted a conversation. 'What was that?' I ask, stepping out the French doors and onto the patio, the humidity applying a thin layer of moisture to my upper lip.

'I was just reminding Walter that you are the most perfect woman in the world,' Bell says. Had there been the slightest pause before she answered?

'Oh, stop it.' I swipe her with the top of my paper fan. 'It's still the most ghastly thing I've ever been called.' I mean it. I'd been given the dubious title after I became the first woman to appear naked on film. All in good taste, I might add. However, it's caused me no end of trouble, mostly with other women who assume I must now have quite a high opinion of myself. I suppose I do. But I think all women should.

'Oh yes, poor you,' says Bell. She's smiling, but for the first time I think I hear a slight edge to her voice.

In a way, she's correct. However much I disliked it, we did rather milk the ridiculous title for all it was worth. After all, if the newspapers could use it in their write-ups, why shouldn't we?

'The question is,' I say, as Walter stands up to drag another chair over, 'why isn't my "perfect woman" title helping us now?'

Walter's hands are on the back of the chair. I feel as if he is weighing his words.

'Come on,' I say, sitting down. 'You clearly have an opinion. Out with it.'

'Perhaps . . . Alec.'

'Alec?' I repeat incredulously. 'What about him?'

Another little silence. He moves back to his own chair and sits down. I wait.

'People are talking,' he says eventually.

'Good heavens,' I say, catching on. 'About Alec and me? There's nothing going on. You both know that . . .'

Walter is a man of the world, but I can see he's – what? Embarrassed? Annoyed?

'That's not what it looks like.' He has a low, well-modulated, deeply masculine voice. In this very Australian setting, on this very Australian evening, looking through the treetops to the harbour, it also sounds so very . . . what is the word I'm looking for? *American.*

I put my glass down on the table between us. I promised myself I wouldn't think of our troubles today, but he's not giving me much choice. 'As if I give two hoots what it looks like,' I say. 'We all know there is nothing but friendship between Alec and me – between the five of us, come to that – and everyone in our circle must know it too.'

Walter expels a long sigh and shakes his head. 'If there hadn't been that business back home, Rose, we might have been able to ride it out, but this rumour, coupled with that rumour . . .'

It hadn't been a rumour, it had been a very public outing. A scandal, I suppose. All I can say in my defence is that I'd had no idea Tom Jackson, my refreshingly ordinary lover, was married until he'd been forced to confess. If I'm to be brutally honest with myself, which I try hard to be, that was another reason we'd had to form our own company and start making our own films here, on the other side of the world.

'I don't see what I can do about it,' I say. 'Except start something new, something so breathtakingly different they simply won't care.'

The two of them sit again in silence for a moment. I'm starting to feel outnumbered. 'We've just been talking about that,' Walter says slowly.

'The extravaganza, as we discussed,' I remind him. 'A series of spectacular pageants that we take all around the world.'

Another pause.

'Rose, it's a brilliant idea, but as you know, we will need backers if we are to do it properly, particularly on the scale you are considering . . .'

'Yes. That's exactly why we need something daringly different, to garner their support.'

Before I can further expand on the idea, he says, 'And therein lies the problem.'

'You think a little unfounded gossip about Alec and me is going to stop people from investing in us?' I can feel indignant outrage rising within me.

He sighs, shaking his head. 'It doesn't help, Rose. But the bigger problem is that I fear we may already have pushed our business friendships a little too far.'

'What do you mean?'

The evening is so beautiful and blue, so full of birdsong. It's a sin to contaminate it with the image that floats instantly into my head, of the heavy ledgers on the oak desk in the borrowed library down the hallway.

'There's not much interest in . . . us. I have put feelers out.'

I sip my water, trying not to frown. Frown lines are the harbingers of wrinkles. 'Why ever not? They have no idea yet about how very successful our movie will be, the rewards they will reap.'

'Exactly.' He turns the cut crystal whisky glass in a circle on the tabletop, between his thumb and third finger. The black onyx signet ring on his right hand chimes against the glass. 'The New Zealand backers are waiting to see a return on their motion picture investment before committing funding to any more of our ventures.'

I sit up a little straighter. 'Right, well then, we'll just have to find ourselves some new business friendships here in Australia.'

He nods, but it's an unconvincing gesture. 'Not easy,' he says. 'We have been away from Australia for a little while, and you know the old sibling rivalry.'

He's referring to the fact that it's New Zealand that features in our movie, New Zealand that will be on show in picture palaces all over the western world later in the year, and it is therefore New Zealand businesses and New Zealand itself that will benefit from the exposure. Australian feathers may have been ruffled, and they will likely be further ruffled if the picture is the success we expect it to be.

'Leave it to me,' I say, with far greater confidence than I feel. 'I am very good at making friends.'

3

Emma
Blue Mountains, 2024

So, here's the thing. There are reasons why I'm behind a camera and not in front of it, lots of them. But among the top ten is that I don't like talking to talent. Not in person, anyway. I'm good on the phone and online. It's not personal – I'm sure they're nice people, and some of them are very interesting. I'm just not good at small talk.

My mother used to call me 'painfully shy', but my father preferred the term 'guarded', and he was closer to the truth. Apart from one obvious exception – Lauren – I prefer to get to know someone before entering into anything as dangerous as, say, a conversation.

But shortly after returning to my position behind the camera, I realise I'm going to have to make another exception because for some reason, I'm compelled to find out more about the contents of that box. I can't stop thinking about it. Perhaps it's the initials on the camera – my initials – that have me so intrigued. Who was E.M.Q.? And who, exactly, was Rose Carey?

So, I make an exception and, much to the surprise of the rest of the crew, I walk over to the historian after her mic's been removed at the end of the shoot.

'That was a really interesting interview,' I say.

She looks up at me. 'Well, thank you,' she says, but I can tell she's not interested in me. She glances over at Johnno, who is busy on the other side of the room, and I sense she's trying to escape.

I cut to the chase. 'Do you know anything about the box of vintage postcards and stuff in the storeroom?' I'd planned my words carefully. I could have asked her directly about the camera, or the reels, but she's an historian, not a camera expert or a film archivist. I'd deliberately described the photos as 'vintage postcards' because I figured the description would pique her interest.

She stops looking for Johnno.

'Vintage postcards?' she says, tilting her head to one side.

Success!

'I found them, along with some other stuff, in a box in a storeroom down the hall. I thought you might know something about them.'

'I'm very curious,' she says. 'Are you with the hotel?'

She obviously hadn't spotted me behind the camera. That's okay. We have a kind of informal black uniform on shoots. I always choose black trousers, a black T-shirt and, when it's cold, as it is today, a black fleece jumper, an outfit that blends with my dark hair and pretty much everything else around me. Between my intentionally invisible wardrobe and the lights that were trained on her, I'm not surprised she didn't see me.

But this is a bit embarrassing. I'm not hotel staff, so I don't really have an excuse for nosing around in storerooms. There's nothing for it but the truth. 'No, I'm one of the crew.' I gesture to the camera behind me, still set up on the tripod.

'Oh, I see.' She's frowning, trying to put two and two together.

'I took a wrong turn at lunchtime and found myself in the storeroom,' I explain with what I hope is a wry smile. 'There's a box of . . . stuff . . . photos,' I slip the truth in carefully, 'and letters, and so on.'

'Oh,' she repeats, and now I'm not sure her interest is genuine. I mean, she must get asked about old stuff all the time.

'Vintage photos,' I put in quickly, cringing at my overuse of the adjective.

She actually looks away.

'Erotic.' It's not so far from the truth.

Her head snaps back.

'They're all of the same woman. I wonder if that's unusual?'

She's frowning in concentration. 'I'm not sure unusual is the right word,' she says slowly. 'It's certainly interesting. In the storeroom, you said?'

'Yes, yes. I thought you might be interested, that's all.' But I'm not done yet. I give a half-laugh. 'The thing is, there's also an old camera in the box. There are initials on it and – this is the weird thing – they're the same as mine.'

Saying the words out loud makes them sound as ridiculous as I suppose they are. So what if the initials match mine? It's not like I have copyright on them. For someone who spent half an hour working out how to start this conversation, I'm making a mess of it.

She looks me up and down, which is something of an effort – although I'm only average height, I'm at least a head taller than her. Nevertheless, the look somehow makes me feel small. 'I'm sorry, I don't really understand what you're telling me. Are you saying that you took the, um, erotic photos?'

'What? No! How could I have taken them? I wasn't even born. They're old, very old – from the 1920s, I think, maybe even earlier.'

'Right.' I can almost feel her bristling. 'Well, I'm sorry, I don't know anything about that.'

She doesn't believe me. Worse, she now has me pegged as something I'm not. I'm not into naughty old photos. I'm not into naughty photos, period. I'm about to try and explain myself when Johnno ambles over, 'Thank you, Louise, terrific stuff.'

I start to move away, but she stops me and hands me a business card. I read that she offers 'genealogical services at competitive rates'. Obviously, she's not going to let the assumption that I'm some kind of vintage voyeur stand in the way of potential new business.

'If you ever need help with your family tree, please feel free to give me a call.'

I suspect she's already forgotten about the box and its contents, but I take the card anyway and put it in my back pocket, where it will no doubt be rendered illegible by the heavy-duty cycle on the washing machine.

It's well after four now; Lauren will be home. I dial her number, but it goes straight to voicemail. *Sorry I can't answer your call right now. If you leave your name and number, I'll get back to you as soon as I can. Actually, don't bother, I never listen to voice messages anymore. But I do respond to missed calls. Usually.* Then her little laugh.

I ignore her advice and leave the only message I can under these circumstances.

'I love you.'

Quinn is not the world's most common surname. Q is such a lonely letter, so far down the alphabet it made roll call at school seem interminable. I contemplate the initials on the camera, wondering how many names actually start with the letter 'Q'. Probably more than I realise.

I get up from the single bed I'm sitting on and walk to the window. The pane is bubbled in a fashion from the same era as the hotel, late nineteenth or early twentieth century, making it impossible to see out. I raise it as far as it will go – not far – and put my nose out. Grey is slating the afternoon; the day is already packing it in. A cold gust of wind smacks me, blowing the hair that has escaped my ponytail about my face. When I lower the window again, the wind comes after me through a small gap under the sash. I push it until it fully closes.

I wonder how common cameras were way back in the early 1900s, long before Motorola put them into our back pockets. Who might have owned one? And who might have cared so much about one that they'd engrave their initials on it?

I pull my own camera/mobile phone out of my back pocket to consult Google, but it rings before I have the opportunity. Hardly anybody phones anymore, it's always messages or texts; it can only be Lauren. At last. I'm as reluctant to answer the call as I am to let it go to voicemail, but the need to comfort her overwhelms all else.

'Hello, darling,' I say. 'Are you okay?'

I'm still by the window. It rattles in its ancient frame.

The sound of her weeping comes to me from a hundred kilometres away.

'You've made it just in time,' I say as we exit Katoomba railway station, enveloped in our winter coats. 'It'll snow overnight.'

She nods. She's not a sulker, but she's said nothing since stepping off the train and into my arms, almost as if she doesn't trust herself to speak.

'I think you'll like the Carrington, it's gorgeous,' I prattle as we step out onto the street. We finished filming today and I'm now officially on leave for a couple of weeks. We'd always planned for her to come up and spend the weekend, regardless of the pregnancy test outcome. We need the time together and the Carrington was able to extend my stay. It's true that the hotel is gorgeous, in a not-too-renovated way. Lauren loves gorgeous things, especially old buildings, and antique stores, of which Katoomba has many.

She's dragging her favourite teal blue carry-on, an exact match for her winter coat. The coat fits her perfectly, as it should. She made it herself, from a highly-prized bolt of boiled wool. It shouldn't be called boiled wool, I muse. The fabric is too beautiful for such a description, its colour too vibrant. It is also, as she pointed out to me when pinning the pattern to it, lightweight, warm, and wonderfully wind and rain resistant – perfect for this weather.

'I hope you also have a beanie and gloves in that trunk of yours – you're going to need them.'

She shakes her head, and in my peripheral vision I see the cold breeze pick up her blonde hair and pull it away from her face.

'Well, don't worry about it, because this place is arts-and-crafts central. We're sure to find you something.'

I'm aware that my voice has the kind of forced cheer w both loathe, but I can't go on walking in silence, so I keep filling it with nonsense, my breath steaming the air about us.

'I moved rooms at the hotel so we have a nice king. If it's not too cold tomorrow, I thought we might go for a bit of a hike. If it really does snow, we might even find somewhere we can double toboggan.'

She stops, and the wheels of her bag ricochet to a halt behind her. I haven't been game to look directly at her, but I can't avoid it now. She's wearing make-up, but no amount of concealer can hide the dark circles under her eyes. She also looks very thin around the face.

'I don't think I'm up for a hike, Emmie, much less a toboggan.' She says the word 'toboggan' in the same way she might say 'wrestling match'.

Of course she isn't. I'm an idiot. 'All right, we'll do a retail walk, in and out of little shops. If you're up to it,' I add hastily. I bite my lip. What is the right thing to say? I can't add to her pain by revealing my own. I know it cannot match hers, for all that it sometimes feels unbearable.

'Tonight, we can just sit by the fire with a hot chocolate if you like. I have a bit of a story to tell you.'

Diversion, always my go-to. But I see a flicker of interest in her green eyes. She's a great one for stories. She always said if she hadn't become a teacher she'd have been a librarian. In the next breath she'd added, 'Except I'm too talkative, I'd make too much noise.'

'I think that's a fallacy,' I'd told her. 'I've known plenty of garrulous librarians.'

Later that night, we're in front of the fire in the main lounge, as I promised. After a long afternoon spent hugging and crying, I'm desperate to talk about something else.

She listens to the story of the photos, and the letters, and the film reels, and the camera, and then she says, 'Quintal.'

'What?'

'There was a kid in my class last year named Quintal. He came from Norfolk Island for a term. His mother was ill and had to be medevac'd to a Sydney hospital. The family stayed on in Sydney while she convalesced.'

'Right.'

'There's also Quincy, Quigley, Quinlivan.'

'You've had kids in your class called Quinlivan, have you?' I say, raising my eyebrows.

'There's also the Mc's and Mac's – McQueen, McQuoid, McQuade.'

'They start with M.'

She shrugs. 'You said the initials are the same as yours.'

'Yes.'

'E.M.Q. The M and Q could represent a Mc or Mac surname. The camera could have belonged to someone named, say, Emma McQuiggin, or McQuilty, or McQuirk. There are probably dozens of others.'

Why hadn't I thought of that? 'I suppose so.' I feel a bit crestfallen at the possibility.

'And what makes you think it belonged to someone with an English surname? Didn't you say the make of the camera was something foreign?'

'German.'

'Right – so maybe it belonged to someone with a German surname.'

'Do you know any German surnames starting with Q?'

'No, but there might be some. Or it might have been another European name, like, like . . .' Her forehead wrinkles into a frown. 'Quixote.'

I laugh. 'You think the camera was owned by Don Quixote?'

'Well, obviously not,' she says, slightly huffy. 'All I'm saying is there are plenty of other possibilities. To be honest, I think you're making a big deal out of nothing.'

All the fun that had begun to creep into our conversation seeps out again. 'Okay,' I say, and to cover up the unexpected wound her words cause, I sit forward and pick up my mug of hot chocolate from the table in front of us.

'You don't honestly think the camera was owned by someone called Quinn, do you? And even if by some strange, mysterious coincidence it was, so what?'

'Quite right,' I agree.

There's a pause as she realises she's hurt me. 'But,' she says, hurrying to repair any damage, 'if you really want to know, I think it would actually be very easy to find out.'

I take a sip from my mug and put it back down on the table in front of us. 'How?'

'You just need to find out who the woman in the photos was. Once you know her identity, you'll probably be able to work out who owned the camera. Do you have any idea?'

'I don't know for sure, but I held one of the film reels up to the light and took a quick look, and I think the woman in the photos is the same woman in those reels. The title sequence had the name Rose Carey. Maybe she was some kind of early Australian film star. Have you heard of anyone called Rose Carey?'

'No. Did you take any photos?'

She knows me well. I probably shouldn't have – nothing in that box belonged to me – but of course, I did.

'Yes.' I scroll through the images on my phone. I'm not sure how looking at photos of the contents of the box is going to bring us any closer to unravelling the mystery, but I pass the phone over to her.

She scrolls through them with a practised thumb, frowning. 'Not photos of the camera and the reels,' she says with an exasperated sigh. 'Photos of the woman.'

'Oh . . . I didn't take a photo of her.' How stupid. I should have taken photos of everything in that box. Except possibly the letters; the letters were too personal.

She peals with laughter. 'Darling, there's a box of naughty pictures of a nude lady and you didn't take photos? Looks like I'm safe.'

Her laughter fills me with fresh hope.

'As houses,' I agree.

4

Rose
Sydney, 1923

It's one little word in *The Chronicle* that sets me off.

'Seasoned,' I complain to Bell. 'They are calling me seasoned.'

'Well, you are,' she says, through a mouthful of pins. 'What's so bad about that?'

We are on the bottom floor of the house, in a large room that is officially the ballroom. At the mirrored end, near the grand piano, I have installed – with Mr and Mrs D's permission – a temporary barre where I do my warm-up and ballet exercises. I love to dance, on set and off, professionally and privately. Walter has often been my partner at society events across the States. We have even choreographed our own waltz routine.

At the other end of the room, Bell has set up the treadle sewing machine she brought with her from America, and a trestle table to lay out her fabrics. She also has a little desk in the corner, where I am now standing, reading from the newspaper.

'Seasoned indeed,' I mutter. 'I am not a turkey.' I check the author's byline: Harry Beames. 'He doesn't mean it as a compliment. He means I'm old.'

Bell removes the pins from her mouth, pushing them into the pincushion bracelet about her wrist. 'I'm sure he doesn't, Rose,' she says gently. 'I'm sure he means experienced.'

I stab the offending paper with my forefinger. 'No, he doesn't,' I insist. 'Listen to this: *Seen about town – seasoned Hollywood star, Rose Carey, who has returned from a year's filming in New Zealand* . . . blah, blah, blah. And then this: *Miss Carey first left our shores to pursue her acting career over fifteen years ago, at the tender age of only eighteen.* It tells everybody I'm well into my thirties.'

'In fact,' Bell points out, bending over the table to smooth the paper pattern onto the fabric, 'he's made you sound slightly younger than you are, hence, it is a compliment.'

'I am not old,' I say, almost to myself, 'I am physically fit.' I turn to the mirrored wall to confirm this. 'I don't look my age.' It's not conceit that makes me say these things, it's the simple truth. I know how much our fortunes depend on my agility and my looks, and so I protect them.

'I know,' she says gently, from behind me. 'But . . .'

'But what?'

I'm surprised by how my heart hammers in my chest as I wait for her next words. 'But you are right to be thinking about how to hedge your bets.'

I slump down on the bentwood chair at her desk which is, as always, neat and tidy. There is a stack of the thank you cards we send in response to fan mail, waiting for my signature. My favourite fountain pen sits beside them, next to a small bottle of indigo ink. I know that the ledger we use to record our incidental spending, and the cheque book we need to pay for it all, will be neatly placed in the top drawer. Bell's time working in a London office has stood us in very good stead. Not just for this, but also when I wrote my book on women's health, beauty and fitness.

For no particular reason, the memory of our first meeting comes flooding back to me.

Alec had introduced us at his swimming debut at the Westminster Baths in London. He knew Bell from Cavill's Baths in Farm Cove on Sydney Harbour, where they'd both learned to swim. When she arrived in England shortly after him, he'd said she was very keen to meet me, and on introducing us, he'd called us 'birds of a feather' and laughed, as if that were very funny.

I stare at Bell for a moment now, remembering the way she'd extended her right hand and said, 'Bell Procter, without an "e".' She had what I still think of as a capable hand, the kind I equated with my father.

'Without an "e"?'

'B-e-l-l, not B-e-l-l-e,' she said, spelling it out for me.

'Oh, I see.' How unusual. What was it short for, I wondered. I hadn't asked her then, and it never came up again.

Alec, of course, had gone on to compete in swimming and diving at the 1920 Olympic Games in Antwerp, winning silver, along with his teammates, in the men's freestyle relay. When Walter and I started our own film company, I knew we needed to make a name for ourselves. The idea came to me to film an underwater epic in the Southern Hemisphere, so, naturally, Alec was one of the first people I called on.

'I need someone to help me refine my swimming skills,' I'd said, because of course I would star in it. We were having dinner at the time. I'd just finished working on my latest feature film and Alec was in town to 'fill his theatrical cup', as he called it, and 'visit my famous friends'.

'I'm your man,' he'd said with a wicked wink.

Of course he was my man, for that purpose anyway. He'd spent years perfecting the skills he'd first learned in Farm Cove, and had studied advanced diving techniques in Northern Europe. But he was well over thirty and had ruled himself out of contention for the 1924 Olympic team and so was keen to carve out a new career as an exhibition diver and stunt coach.

I explained my idea for the film over our dinner – just a salad for me, broiled veal kidneys for him. At the end of my pitch, which I must admit to having rehearsed a little, he said, 'Well, it's as good a gig as any, and as you know, I'm heading back down under next month.'

The timing was exactly right. I'd sat back in my chair, pleased and relieved. 'I hear that a boatload of the lovely ladies who escorted your ship to Sydney Heads might still be lolling about in the harbour, awaiting your return.'

He laughed. 'If only it were a boatload of charming chaps.'

We all met up again in the Southern Hemisphere, where Walter worked his magic, conjuring up backers in New Zealand. We were a company of over two hundred in all, counting the locals employed as extras and assistants. But we were a tight team at the top – Alec as stunt manager, Bell as secretary and wardrobe mistress, and Eddie as chief cameraman.

Eddie is also an asset. He'd first learned photography during the war, from none other than Captain Frank Hurley, Australia's most famous photographer and adventurer. Eddie had been wounded in Flanders and now walks with a bit of a limp. Cinematographer, I remind myself, that's what Eddie prefers to be called. And fair enough, he is the one creating cinema through his lens.

'Bell's helped me draw up a list of people to connect with in Sydney, and a calendar of must-attend events,' I say to Walter, pouring tea into the bone china cups set on the low table in front of us. She is playing a romantic waltz my mother wrote on the grand piano in the ballroom downstairs, and the sound reaches us all the way here in the morning room, carrying with it the memory of my beautiful mother. Bell plays the piece with almost exactly the same light and shade as my mother did. It makes me miss her.

Walter doesn't answer; all his attention is focused on the newspaper in his hands. I haven't read it this morning. I sense that whatever he is reading is bothering him, but I don't press him on it. He'll spill the beans sooner or later. 'We've scheduled several events,' I continue. 'The very first thing I'm going to do is invite some reporters in for interviews.'

'It looks like you've already been talking to reporters,' he says at last, folding the paper and putting it down on the table. Then he looks over at me, and for a moment it's like watching the tide pull back from the shore. I can't look away.

Then I shake my head briskly, breaking his gaze. It's just the Walter effect, I remind myself. The way he looks at people, it captivates them. I've seen the Walter effect in action many times before, in particular with ladies, on first meeting him.

'No,' I correct him, my voice a little sharp. 'They have been talking *about* me, and not always in the most flattering light.'

There had been a veritable flotilla of reporters to meet me off the boat when we'd first arrived back in Australia, and they've been hanging about ever since. I've made it my business to be seen at various places around town, taking part in afternoon teas, going to the tennis and so on. Harry Beames might think my star is fading, but I'm still a famous daughter of Australia, and *The Chronicle* is not the only newspaper in town. There's always reports of my comings and goings.

But it's no longer enough.

'I need to be hinting that we have ambitious plans,' I say, almost to myself. 'I can pretend we're starting with something slightly smaller, like . . . pageants, yes, pageants. That covers a multitude of possibilities.' I look back at him. 'You know, we could kick off our worldwide extravaganza right here.'

He fixes me with those blue eyes of his and there's that magnetic pull again. 'No, Rose. We need to go back to America. Now. We need this production in the bag, and we need to start the publicity machine for it. There can be no "extravaganza", no pageants, no anything if this film is not a success.'

We are in for a battle of wills. Rather than enter the fray now, I feign retreat. 'Oh, of course, you're right, darling,' I say, patting his arm. 'But we both know it will be a roaring success. How can it not be? So . . . let's stay, just a little longer.'

He's shaking his head, but I plough on. 'Bell had a marvellous idea. She suggested we invite the newspapers in to interview me while I'm doing my morning exercises. Isn't that brilliant? We can't just let journalists keep writing any old thing they want about me. We'll start by dropping little hints that the exercises are in preparation for something wildly exciting, and that all will be revealed—' I catch the resistant look in his eye, 'later . . . in due course. After the film is done and dusted, of course.'

I stand up and stretch. A quick arm exercise, feet shoulder-width apart, hands to first position in front of me, elbows to either side, fingertips not quite touching. I stand tall, neck extended, and then slowly reach my arms out to either side in second position. In and out for the count of ten. When I sit down again, Walter's lips are drawn in a thin line. I pick up my teacup and hold it in both hands, blowing across the steam.

'I've invited Bonnie Spark to come along on Tuesday,' I say, quickly adding, 'She's a female reporter from *Life & Times*. I'll talk up the film.'

I'm not being bull-headed about this. The simple truth is that although I don't see it, the world thinks I will soon be too long in the tooth to star in movies. Therefore, I genuinely believe our future depends on our ability to pull something spectacular out of the bag. But underneath all that, if I'm being truly honest with myself, I simply don't want to go back to America yet. I didn't plan to still be here either, but I hadn't factored in how magnificent the weather would be, or the fact that the Duxtons would give us the run of this mansion for the entire time they are in the Blue Mountains. Those things combined make it very difficult for me to leave.

'You do understand,' Walter continues, 'that we have no backers for the kind of thing you are imagining. We have not even the vaguest interest.'

I sniff. 'But we haven't really tried yet, have we? And we both know these things take time. I'm sorry I haven't been more proactive, but as you can see,' I sweep my hand in the direction of his closed newspaper, 'I have been getting out and about.'

'We do not have the time for that, and more importantly, as I think I explained to you not so long ago, we do not have the money.'

My words have no impact on him. He's always been with me on almost anything I suggest, so now I'm concerned. If we cannot afford to at least begin planning and resourcing the extravaganza, then perhaps we have a bigger problem than I have wanted to admit.

'All right.' There are clearly facts to be faced, and much as I don't want to, I'm going to have to face them. 'How bad is it?'

'Very bad,' he says. 'We need to go back to America to fully investigate. But there's no money in our accounts here, either. I went to the Bank of New South Wales the other day and the balance is at odds with my reckoning.'

I relax back into the chair. 'Oh, the Bank of New South Wales,' I say with much relief. The Australian account is one we keep for when we are in this hemisphere, it's not a primary account. I'm not sure why Walter is even bothered much about it. 'I thought you meant all our accounts.'

'Rose, this is serious.'

'How can it be?' There is a sharp, thin edge to my voice that even I don't like the sound of.

'There is no money left in it.'

'That's impossible,' I snap. 'We were drawing on it in New Zealand. There was plenty of money in it then.'

'Well, apparently there wasn't and now it's all but empty.'

I'm frantically trying to do the maths in my head, but it's a wasted effort. I haven't looked at the account for ages. I'd left everything to Walter, consumed, as I always am, by production matters.

But I don't blame Walter. It had been difficult to be watchful of our account balances there. We'd spent a lot of time shooting out at Golden Bay. We'd camped there, as a company, only going into town when it was truly necessary. We'd bought and carried supplies to the Bay so we didn't need to make that trek over and over again.

'How much is missing?'

When he tells me the number, I begin patting my chest with my hand. 'No, that really cannot be true.'

'It is true. I'm going to have to wire money just to pay for our living expenses and our return. We are going to need every last cent we can garner, just to get back to the States.'

I'm horrified. 'How has this happened? When did this come to your attention?'

'I only noticed it last week. There is something going on, Rose. Something's not right. We must be frugal until I uncover what it is, and that is why we must get on the first boat back to America. That's where the money is to be made anyway.'

He stands up. Alec once said that Walter has the physique of a rower. He does. For the briefest moment, I see him as I saw him on the white sands of Golden Bay, in just his swimming trunks. He had stretched his arms above his head, then rolled his shoulders in preparation for the swim. I want to see those naked shoulders again. I want to see the muscles rippling down the length of his back. Once again, the thoughts have come to me before I can stop them.

'We must stop playing in this little pond,' he says, 'and get back to serious work.'

And with those words, my unexpected desire to see him naked turns cold.

5

Rose
Sydney, 1923

'He had me onboard until he called Australia – and New Zealand, I suppose – a "little pond",' I say to Bell on our morning trek down to the water. 'Little pond, indeed. There is so much untapped opportunity here, if only he could see it.'

It's warm and I'm already perspiring, partly due to the heat of the day and partly because, despite my harsh criticism of Walter, my concern has only magnified since our conversation. 'I'm not sure how we are going to be frugal, with all that I want to do.'

Bell is quiet, letting me vent my frustrations without comment.

'This is very embarrassing,' I finally mutter.

'Not really, not unless people find out,' she says. 'And how will they?'

'The Ball,' I say bluntly.

Yesterday hadn't seemed quite the right moment to tell Walter all that I have promised for the Olympic Ball. It is a much-needed event, raising funds to send our athletes to the games in Paris next year. I hadn't thought twice about pledging what I thought was quite a modest donation for people of our means, but now I understand there is no readily available money to give, perhaps no money at all.

I stop for a moment to stretch my neck, trying to ward off the uncomfortable feeling that threatens to creep down my spine. 'The most embarrassing thing is that I've already put my hand up to help organise the entertainment.'

I'm actually on the official committee, and of course we've pledged to have our own set. In fact, we will be leading the parade into the Town Hall, where we will perform a themed dance routine. I had naively thought it would be a wonderful opportunity to contribute to something I am passionate about, and the perfect lead-up to our extravaganza.

Bell puts a brief, reassuring arm around my shoulders. 'We have to provide everything for our set,' I say with a sideways glance at her. 'Props, costumes, dancers . . . How are we going to do all that now?'

'At the very least, they'll expect you to be there . . .' she agrees. 'But Rose, we do have an out . . .'

I exhale a long, sad sigh. 'Yes, we do . . .' The out is that the Ball is months away. We could return to America. We could cite pressing business, and we wouldn't even be stretching the truth.

We resume our trek, zigzagging our way down through each terrace of the garden.

'But,' she says, with a determined edge to her voice, 'for the moment, I think we just take one step at a time and see where it leads us.'

'Hmmm. Next week, it leads us to a committee meeting, where I'm expected to hand over a large cheque.'

She grimaces, and for a little while there is only the sound of us tramping along the gravel path, then she says, 'You don't have to contribute money, do you? Can't you contribute something else?'

'Like what?' Concern has roughened my throat, made the words sound harsher than I mean them. I stop tramping again for a moment to hear her out.

'What about suggesting a further money-raising idea instead?'

'Such as?'

She thinks for a moment. 'A fundraising auction. Everybody could donate something to it. You could do it on the pretext that it will likely raise much more than you could ever give.'

'Oh, clever girl! I could donate something of my own, some interesting prop from one of my acts.'

She nods. 'There'll be something in the Tivoli storeroom. I'll go tomorrow.'

The Tivoli storeroom is where we house our props whenever we are on this continent.

'Why didn't I think of that? Bell, we'll not only be able to use those props for the Ball, we'll be able to use them for the extravaganza . . . you know, that thing Walter says we can't do.'

We both laugh, and as she comes in for my hug, I wonder, for the umpteenth time, where I'd be without her.

The Tivoli storeroom is in Surry Hills, which is not Sydney's most auspicious address. I haven't visited it since we were last in town, en route to New Zealand, to choose what we'd take to Golden Bay. Given my unexpected and what I've decided are temporary financial limitations, it does seem the best way to source something appropriate for the auction.

It's drizzling with warm rain as Eddie drives us from Point Piper to Brumby Street. He wasn't enthusiastic about doing it, and I feel a moment of guilt, wondering if using the clutch bothers his wounded leg. But since 'the incident', I've been reluctant to drive myself and since his role in my rescue, I've leaned on him for this kind of thing a bit. I will get over my silly fears, I'm sure, probably once we are back in America where, as strange as it sounds, I'm more familiar with the roads.

Eddie parks the car on the corner of Elizabeth, outside the True Briton hotel, then walks us down the narrow laneway, holding a large umbrella over me. There's room for Bell under the canopy too, but she won't have a bar of it.

'No, thank you,' she says pointedly when he offers, opening her own umbrella. I can't decide whether she's being feminist, or if it's something to do with the fact that it's Eddie doing the offering. There has been an odd tension between them since New Zealand.

'Do you know what this building used to be?' Bell asks as we arrive at the storeroom.

'No, what did it used to be?'

She shakes rain off her umbrella, then tips it briefly in the direction of the building in front of us.

'An aeroplane factory. George Taylor rented it from about . . .' she thinks on it for a moment, '1909, and used it as an aeroplane factory.'

I give it the once-over. It's a two-storey terrace, almost indistinguishable from its neighbours. 'It's not a factory.'

She shrugs. 'It wasn't built as a storeroom either, but that's what it is now. George constructed his biplane glider here, flew it about a hundred yards on Narrabeen Beach. I went there to watch. He and Florrie, his wife, took twenty-nine flights in it that day. They're quite a pair. You'd like them, Rose.

He's the sweetest man, generous to a fault. His brother is Captain Penfold.'

'The balloonist?'

'The balloonist,' she confirms.

'And how do you know all this?'

She turns to me with a half-smile. 'I used to live here.'

'What?' I'm shocked. Like I said, it is not the city's most salubrious suburb, and not the most salubrious street. 'Right here?'

'No, across the road.' She looks it up and down, nodding towards a building at the opposite end. 'That was Lloyds,' she says, and when she sees that once more, I don't know what she's talking about, she adds, 'Pub – until they delicensed it a couple of years ago. There'll be more to go. The True Briton will be next, mark my words.'

She's referring to the work of the Licences Reduction Board, which you might say was a victory for the Women's Christian Temperance Union. Bell shakes her head, but I'm not convinced it's in disapproval.

With all that she's told me, I'd like to inspect the street more closely, but the rain is growing persistent, and Eddie's umbrella is less effective against it, so I march up to the door instead.

Mr Randolph himself answers my knock.

'Miss Carey,' he says with a warm smile, ushering the three of us inside. 'How lovely to see you.' He nods a greeting to Bell and Eddie.

'Thank you, Mr Randolph, likewise. I think Miss Procter explained what we're here for on the phone.'

'Yes.' He ushers us to his desk and pulls a large bunch of keys on a wire loop from a board behind it. 'We've been keeping your props in the storeroom below. Please come with me.'

I find myself looking for evidence that the house was once an aeroplane factory, but the hallway looks much like the hallway in my Sydney childhood home.

'Do you recall offhand what we have stored here, Mr Randolph?' I ask.

'Well, we keep your properties locked up in a discrete area, Miss Carey. There's only the one key, and I've never had cause to open it since the day you left them in our care. There is an inventory, of course, but if you're asking me off the top of my head, well, let me think . . .'

We're walking two abreast down the hallway. He opens a door at the end, flicks the electric switch to light our way and guides me down a set of stairs towards a cavernous room, Bell and Eddie in our wake. Ah, now this area could certainly have been an aeroplane factory.

'If I remember correctly, there are at least eight chariots and pony heads, a few plaster urns, plinths and matching columns . . . among many other things, of course.'

'Ah.' I laugh. 'The last days of the Roman Empire. That was quite a sketch. Do you think they could be put to use for the Olympic Ball, Bell?'

She tilts her head, considering it. 'Well, the Games were first held in Ancient Greece, but if my memory serves me correctly, they continued to be held when Greece came under Roman rule, so maybe?'

Mr Randolph smiles, shepherding us to a large, sectioned-off area fitted with walls and a locked door. The words 'Carey & Ryan Corp.' are painted in freehand on the door. He fits a brass key to the lock and turns it. I expect it to grate, given it hasn't been used in some time, but it seems to have been well oiled and the door opens without a sound. He flicks another switch, and a warm, yellow light floods the walls and floor.

The space is empty.

'Right, then.'

Bell gives me an odd look, as if she expected me to say or do something more dramatic. I shake my head. She should know me better than that.

'Please inform the police, Mr Randolph,' I say, opening my handbag and retrieving my grey gloves. I pull them on with a ferocity they don't deserve.

'Of course, of course.'

His words end with a clearing of his throat. I look back up at him and study his horrified face. Although I don't think he had anything to do with the disappearance of our property, it was left in his keeping, and as he had previously admitted, only authorised personnel had access to the keys.

'Miss Carey, I can only say that I am dumbfounded and I will naturally be interrogating every member of staff—'

I nod. 'I know you will, Mr Randolph. Please keep me informed of your progress – or lack of it.'

'Yes, yes, of course.'

I exit the way we came, marching down the stairs and up the street, not even bothering with an umbrella this time – a little rain won't kill me. Bell and Eddie are in my wake.

'I'll also start my own investigations,' Eddie says, struggling to keep up with me on his wounded leg.

I'm so lost in my own thoughts, so busy trying to put together pieces that don't fit, that his words take me by surprise. I stare at him. When we'd left America, it was in the grip of winter, and he'd been wearing the army great coat he'd souvenired from the war. He looks different here somehow, without it . . . smaller and – what is the word? Gnarled.

'Thank you. And please also check on the crystal tank.'

'I don't see how the tank could be stolen,' Eddie ventures. 'We haven't even taken delivery of it yet.'

'That's true, but check on it anyway, see if you can get a delivery date. If you don't mind. Please,' I add, as an afterthought.

'All right,' he says, a strange tone to his voice. After a short pause he says, 'The way I see it, the theft of the props must have been undertaken by a rival company.'

I can't imagine what a rival company would do with them. Roman chariots are Roman chariots and, by definition, very distinctive. If they popped up on stage anywhere between here and Timbuktu, we'd know about it. No company would be so brazen. Of course, they could repurpose them, theatrical companies are very resourceful like that. But it's a lot of trouble to go to.

'I don't think so,' I say sharply.

'Then who?' Bell says from behind me.

'I have no idea.'

I march on, my boots splashing in little puddles that are gathering on the pavement.

'A rival company wouldn't necessarily use them,' Eddie continues after a moment's silence, reading my mind.

I stop in my tracks to look at him. 'Well then, what would they do with them, Eddie?'

He thinks about it for a moment. 'It could be a malicious theft.'

'All thefts are malicious,' I snap, but I'm mulling it over. Walter had said we have no money. If anybody were aware of that, they would know that the theft of our props would impact our ability to put on any kind of future production – stage, screen, or pageant. They may have stolen them not because they want to use them, or repurpose them, or even because they want to sell them, but to further handicap us. But even this seems a very strange thing to do because the fact of the matter is that, aside from the Olympic Ball, we have not made our future plans, at least for Australia and New Zealand, widely known. My extravaganza idea has so far been a closely held secret. I haven't even begun to drop the hints I'd discussed with Walter.

I start walking back up the street. Who might know about our apparent money problem? Although, unlike Walter, I am convinced it is only temporary, there's no denying it is a nuisance. It has also arisen at a most inconvenient time, given my promises to the Olympic Ball committee. But, I resolve, I'm not going to let it impact, inconvenience or embarrass us, I'm going to press ahead. It's what I always do, no matter what. I'm just not sure exactly how.

'We need to get our act together.'

I glance at Bell in time to see her forehead crease with worry, but she doesn't contradict me. Instead, she follows my lead. 'And something to auction.' She says this as we reach the car. Eddie shakes rain off the umbrella and hooks the curved handle over his arm before opening the door.

'My parasol,' I say, looking at the umbrella. 'I don't know why I didn't think of it before.'

'The black and white ribbon one with the onyx handle?'

I press Bell's hand. Like so many other things in my wardrobe, she made it for me. 'I'm not giving it away,' I remind her gently. 'I'm auctioning it for a great cause. Will you make me another, Bell?'

She nods and smiles, but I catch something wistful in her eyes before I step into the car and slide along the leather seat to make room for her.

Eddie closes the door on us both and goes around the car to get into the driver's seat.

'But this is ridiculous . . .'

I don't realise I have said the words until Bell says, 'What's ridiculous?'

'Relying on Eddie to drive us everywhere.'

She doesn't say a word to that; in fact, she presses her lips together as if to stop herself from speaking. It's not fair. All Bell – and many others – could think when it happened was that I'd previously been bothered by the police for speeding in America, and even hauled before a judge.

'The New Zealand incident was not my fault,' I say now, emphatically. 'The investigation proved that.'

She nods, but like everyone else, I don't think she believes me.

I'd asked Walter to arrange cars for the five of us. Before the others had even finished packing, I'd taken the Packard convertible, a high-powered machine. I wasn't concerned about that. I was an experienced driver; I'd driven many high-powered machines in America.

I was driving too fast, I know that. I always drive too fast. It doesn't account for what happened. It doesn't account for it at all.

6

Emma
Blue Mountains, 2024

By Sunday the snowfalls, such as they were, have moved on. We check out at ten.

'Do you want to go straight home, or shall we take the scenic route?'

She considers it. 'Scenic route.'

I bring the car around and she throws her cabin bag onto the back seat. As she moves to get into the passenger seat, I pick up the bag and stow it in the boot.

'I saw that,' she says as I open my door.

'You're welcome,' I say, and I'm rewarded with a smile.

Then I pause. Just to the right of where we're parked is a ute, the words 'Rick's Rubbish Removal & Recycling' emblazoned across its panels. A guy in hi-vis is picking boxes up off a trolley and throwing them into the ute. Off to the side is the wooden crate I discovered in the storeroom yesterday. I close the car door and wander over to him.

'G'day.'

He gives me a nod, but doesn't stop what he's doing.

'Are you taking these to the tip?'

'Yep.'

I feel myself begin to sweat, and not just because I hate the thought of anything going to landfill. We are such wasteful creatures. 'Even this one?' I glance briefly at the crate.

'Yep.'

I just can't allow it. Knowing its contents, it seems criminal to throw it away. There's also the fact that I want it.

'Do you mind if I take it?'

He stops what he's doing for a moment to check me out.

'I've been working on a shoot,' I say – after all, it's the truth. 'We've been filming the hotel.'

'So, you need the crate? Is that what you're telling me?'

I can see I've confused him and, for my sins, I decide to press my advantage. 'Yes.' I mean, I haven't said what I need it for, so it's not actually a lie.

He puts his hands on his hips. 'I wish you people would make up your bloody minds,' he says. 'I was told it was all to go to the tip.'

I'm trying very hard to formulate a response, but he doesn't seem to need one.

'Left hand doesn't talk to the right hand, does it?' He doesn't wait for me to answer. 'Just this one?' He indicates the crate with a jerk of his head.

'That's right.'

'Well, you'd better take it, or you'll never see it again.'

'Great, thanks.'

It's heavy so he helps me load it into the boot. I thank him and get into the car. Once in the driver's seat, I wonder if I should double-check with the manager and also ask Johnno if it's appropriate for me to just take it.

But the ute guy had said he'd been told to dispose of everything and there had been a queue at reception, so double-checking might take some time. As for Johnno, he and the rest of the crew had checked out yesterday.

If I don't take the crate now, it will be lost forever. The ute guy had just said so. Lauren gives me a long, questioning look.

'What's the prob?'

I shake my head. 'Nothing. Echo Point?'

She laughs. 'Sure. Why not!'

The one-hour parking up at Echo Point is not cheap but, the signs tell us, the money goes towards keeping the infrastructure spick and span, which I'm totally onboard with, so I refrain from trawling the streets in search of a free and less convenient spot.

We walk down broad, paved steps past the Visitor Information Centre, to the architecturally designed lookout.

The sky is an eye-smarting blue, and we have a clear view of the Three Sisters and all the way down and across the Jamison Valley to Mount Solitary, several kilometres away.

'How far do you think we can see?' Lauren asks.

'As far as a light year away,' I say gravely, 'perhaps more.'

She laughs. 'What, so more than nine trillion kilometres?'

'At least.'

From way up here, the eucalypt and wattle trees that cover the floor of the giant valley look like a blanket of grey-green moss, somewhere God might sit down for a picnic, if, in the scheme of things, there were a god. It is hemmed, as far as the eye can see, by walls of mountains – not all that high by world standards, but long and broad. The curving spine opposite us is part of the Great Dividing Range.

The wind up here is so strong it drives a part through the back of my hair, where my mother used to divide it into two long dark plaits. Then suddenly, it seems to pause for breath for a moment and there's only the unmistakable sound of a pair of crimson rosellas singing to each other and the crunching of crisps from some tourists behind us.

'You've been here before, right?' I pull my hair back into a ponytail and secure it with a black elastic band I habitually wear on my wrist.

'Yes,' she agrees, 'but it gets you every time, doesn't it?'

'Sure does. Are you up to walking to the Three Sisters?' I nod in the general direction of the three giant sandstone rock formations ahead of us, each rising almost a kilometre from the valley floor. It's a fairly easy walk around to them, but still, I have to ask. She pauses as she wraps her scarf about her neck more securely and investigates the sensible shoes on her feet. Then she looks me in the eye, and nods.

I smile and take her hand.

En route to the first guidepost, Oreades Lookout, we encounter a spider web. I put out a hand to break it, but Lauren stops me. 'Don't,' she says, and then, very gently and very delicately, she lifts one small silken thread and re-anchors it to a bush to our right. She does this a few more times until the web has been safely relocated to the bush, out of harm's way.

'You,' I say, with a little kiss on her nose, 'are completely amazing.'

'I know.' She smiles and kisses me on the cheek in return.

We continue on to Lady Game Lookout, gaze out at the vista again, take the requisite selfies, and then descend the first set of steep stairs – more like a ladder – of the Giant Stairway.

'Honeymoon Bridge,' I say as we cross it, a little further along the way.

When we reach the first sandstone sister, she turns back to me. 'So, what's the story with the Three Sisters again? Something like Lot's wife?'

'Lot's wife was turned into a pillar of salt,' I remind her, 'so no. There's a couple of Dreamtime stories. The one I've heard most often is a classic boy-meets-girl-but-their-families-don't-approve story.'

'Sounds familiar.'

'Yeah, I guess so. In this case, there was a tribal war about it, and the sisters were turned to stone for their own protection. However, the elder who performed the magic was killed in battle, so he couldn't turn them back, and here they remain for all eternity.'

We walk as far around the rock formation as safety measures allow.

'I wonder if anyone has ever fallen off,' she muses.

'Several people, I think. There's a memorial cross to a rock climber on the other side of the third sister.'

'We should go and see it, pay our respects.' She heads purposefully towards the second sister. 'Oh, but it's roped off from here. I'll have to take your word for it.'

We head back and climb up the ladders. We're somewhere between Lady Game and Oreades when I notice it. Later, I'm not even sure why I did. Perhaps I slipped on a damp leaf, perhaps a skink skittered across my path. Set back in the undergrowth, I see something that looks like a plaque and come to an abrupt stop. Lauren is several steps ahead of me before she notices.

'What is it?' she calls back. 'Another spider's web?'

'No.' I crouch down beside it, wipe its face with my sleeve.

In loving memory of our Quinnie.
d. 4 September, 1924

Lauren comes to stand beside me, bends down, and reads the words aloud.

'It's a memorial,' she says.

'They had my name.'

'It's to someone called Quinnie,' she corrects. 'Your name is Quinn.'

'True. Still, it's curious, isn't it?'

'I guess,' she says with a slight shrug, standing up again.

I don't know much about my father's family. I wonder if it has anything to do with them.

Lauren and I live on the top floor of the apartment building. There are only two apartments on this floor, and our living areas face east, towards the city.

Except it's not really our apartment. It belongs to Lauren's sister, Allie, who rents it to us for half the going rate. I frown, wishing, for about the hundredth time, that we could afford it in our own right. I don't like feeling beholden to Allie.

There is a large, U-shaped deck that also offers a view north, through the London plane trees, which at the moment are winter bare, and across Johnston Bay towards North Sydney. On the southern side, we look out over a courtyard of square blue and white umbrella canopies, to neighbouring apartment blocks and the tower of the Victorian Italianate building that once served as Pyrmont's local school. The creamy facades and canopied courtyard couple up to remind me, vaguely, of Florence.

Built into the southern brick wall of our apartment, accessible only via the deck, is a double door that opens into a smallish, windowless, concrete-floored storage area. It's the perfect place to securely store those important items we seem to be able to live without from day to day, but can never find the courage to dispose of properly.

It's here I've put the crate containing the camera, the photos, the letters and the film canister. Now that I'm on leave I have some time to go through it. I put the crate on a trestle table, pull out a folding chair and begin unpacking.

It's the odd-shaped metal canister that's grabbed my attention today. I take the lid off, and reach inside for the contents. Each reel fits neatly into the can, with no room to spare, so if I were a betting person, I'd say I have a complete set. That's nice. I've never studied film – all our camerawork is digital, has been for my entire working life. But I'm pretty sure that even if these reels are from the earliest days of film, they, like the camera, are unlikely to be worth anything. They'd probably only be of interest to somewhere like a museum or an archive and, being mostly government bodies, they are probably not flush with funds. This thought makes me feel better about stealing the crate from the Carrington.

I didn't steal it, I remind myself. I saved it from landfill.

I put the first reel, the one I briefly inspected at the hotel, on the table, then pull out the second and unravel the strip. More washed-out pictures of octopi, seaweed, rocks, and some kind of tropical fish. I've had a grand total of one deep sea diving experience in my life. Although I'm a fairly strong swimmer, I was unexpectedly gripped by terror and had to hold the hand of the instructor the entire time. That experience, however, leads me to suspect this was staged. The fish, a dusky brown-black with a pinkish tail, is definitely an inhabitant of a reef somewhere, perhaps even the Great Barrier, scene of my underwater terror, but the shots are picture-perfect.

I hold a few more frames up to the light. A close-up of an oversized goldfish, freckled with silver, hovering above a bleached-out seabed. The sea life is followed by another close-up, this time of a woman, presumably Miss Carey, with long strands of pearls floating around her from a close-fitting pearl encrusted cap. The strands are captured at her wrist in a bracelet.

The odd thing about these frames is that Miss Carey is filtered entirely in green. As I spool through the film, it goes from strange shades of colour to black and white, to colour and then back to black and white. My suspicions become firmer now – although I'm convinced Miss Carey is underwater, I suspect she may be in some kind of large, specially planted glass tank.

I'm very curious. This film screams 1920s to me, and yet it's partly in colour. There is more of Rose Carey swimming, without any kind of breathing apparatus, through the reef garden, not a diving instructor in sight.

I remove the remaining cans and place them on the table in front of me. They are oxidised, and my hands are growing filthier by the minute. I promise myself that next time I inspect them, I'll wear gloves.

I pick up an old rag and carefully wipe the surface of one of them. As I move the cloth, I realise that it's not oxidisation causing the brown stains on my fingers, it's paint. The cans must have originally been painted brown, and now the paint is disintegrating, exposing the steel underneath. In the process of cleaning this particular can, I've inadvertently removed something that may have helped identify the film.

I'd originally thought there was nothing to identify the cans, but now I realise that words had once been etched into the paintwork. I reach for the next can, to see if there are any identifying marks on it, but before I can inspect it closely, the double doors screech open behind me. 'Lunchtime,' Lauren announces.

'Oh, okay, thanks.' I feel mildly disappointed to have been interrupted. 'These are fascinating,' I add, with a wave of my hand.

She gives them a cursory glance, raising her eyebrows. 'Uh-huh.'

'No, really,' I insist.

'My homemade fish burger awaits.'

A nice lunch. I feel a slump settle on my shoulders. Nice lunches always preface difficult conversations. 'Great. I'll be right there,' I say, trying to mask my tension.

She bends to kiss me lightly on the neck, then disappears through the unoiled doors.

I let out a long sigh as I return the cans to their proper place. I go to put them back in the crate, but the letters, tied with fading blue satin ribbon, are in the way.

I take them out and put them down on the table. They are unenveloped, the fine pages of each individual missive folded horizontally into three. I slip one from the bundle and examine the handwriting. It's small and neat. I can make out the word 'Dear . . .' but I can't read the next word. Dear Who?

I try again. Does that say *Dear Birdy*? If so, then perhaps they are not letters *to* Rose, perhaps they are letters *from* her, to someone called Birdy? If that's the case, why didn't she send them?

I frown, trying to make sense of it. Was Birdy a nickname? I skip to the bottom of the letter, searching for the signature. But it's simply signed, '*Me.*'

I badly want to read the whole letter, but the paper is thin. I can't risk damaging it, so I slide it carefully back under the ribbon. Then I return the bundle and the cans to the crate and head inside.

'Elephants and rooms,' says Lauren, as I knew she would.

'No elephant, no room,' I respond, as I usually do.

She lets out an exaggerated sigh. 'Come on,' she mutters, not quite under her breath.

'Lauren, we already discussed this, before the fact.' She's lightly fried a thin fillet of fish in lemon butter and put it on a bread roll with baby spinach, thin slices of avocado, cucumber and tomato, a sprinkling of capers, and a little garnish of dill from the planter box on the deck. Exactly how I like it. I use my knife to carefully cut it into two.

'I know.' She sits down opposite me. At least she's honest about it. She has served herself a plate of salad and will therefore be hungry until dinner time. I want to tell her she should eat what she wants, when she wants, but on the subject of diet, she's never paid me much attention.

She draws a deep breath, and I know she's about to tell me something I'm going to oppose. 'So, Allie says she'll support another round.'

'*No!*' I'd expected something I wouldn't like, but this is beyond the pale. We are already indebted to Allie.

But she's brave, my wife. She takes my outburst on the chin. 'Look, I know what you think, Emmie . . . but . . . you have eggs, we can get more sperm, we have me, and we both want a baby, right? All we need is the money and . . . that's what she has.'

I pick up one half of the fish burger and the cucumber slides off it, landing on the simulated marble of the dining room table. 'Number one,' I say with careful politeness, picking it up and eating it, 'I thought we'd agreed that we wouldn't discuss baby-making with Allie.' Saint Fucking Allie is what I privately call her. Always riding to the rescue, big noting herself in the process. Nothing Allie does is without fanfare. She also helped pay for our wedding. Even though we'd explained that we wanted to keep it very private, she thought paying for it gave her the right to post wedding photos and her own version of our love story all over her socials, for her one-million-and-counting followers to fawn over. I've wanted nothing to do with her ever since.

Lauren sighs again and slumps in her chair. 'I know, but . . .'

'Number two,' I go on, 'we said we'd give it our best shot, and we did.'

'One round though, Emmie, it's not enough. I looked it up – hardly anybody gets pregnant after only one go.'

This line of argument makes me furious. For a start, we knew the odds going in, we were spoon-fed the data. In our mid-thirties, we think of ourselves as quite young, but in terms of baby-making, we are bordering on geriatric – or, as it's now more euphemistically termed, of 'advanced maternal age'. Our overall chance of having a baby was less than forty per cent and we'd said that, given the fact that we're only getting older, and the state of our finances, we'd only do the one round.

'Number three,' I say, 'we both agreed that if we were unsuccessful, we would plan for a different life, and it would be no less meaningful. The only thing I think we need to discuss now is that alternative life.'

It's too soon. I know it's too soon and I know she'll explode. I bite down on my burger, but it might as well be made of sand.

'Number one,' she says furiously, standing up so quickly the chair slides back across the faux timber floor and almost hits the wall, 'I'll talk to whoever I damn well want to about what's bothering me, *especially my own sister*.'

There's nothing I can say to interrupt what I know will be a tirade, so I don't try.

'Number two, one go is not our best shot, it's *one shot*.'

I resist the impulse to correct her. It was not 'one go' or 'one shot', it was one *round*. One round in which four embryos had been transferred, on separate occasions, all of which had failed.

I take another bite of my fish sandwich, try to focus on the texture, the taste. Sand whiting, wild caught, from the fish markets.

'Number three, I don't want a different life, I want a baby.'

I swallow. 'And there we have it,' I say quietly. But I don't look at her. I knew all of this, all along. She was never going to settle for one round. She will never be fulfilled until she has a baby, and she was always going to pull out all the stops to get one, including begging her sister for money.

'What do you mean, there we have it?' Her words are still laced with fury.

'You lied to me, all along, on all three counts.'

She has no answer to this because she knows it's true. But I also know I'm being unfair, because we both knew she was lying.

Now I do look at her, and I see immediately that my words have cut her to the quick. Tears rest at the corners of her eyes, somehow magnifying the very dark curl of her over-long lashes. More stupid thoughts come to me as I watch them slip down her cheeks.

I wonder if she knows she doesn't need lash extensions to be attractive to me. I would love her even if her lashes fell out, if her eyebrows disappeared, if she were bald as a badger, if she never has my baby.

But for the first time in a long time, I wonder . . . would she say the same for me?

'You okay, Em?'

I glance up from my pale ale to look at Simon. 'Yep.'

'Nope,' he counters.

I smile, but it only reaches one side of my face.

'Woman trouble?'

'In our house, there's no other kind.'

He laughs. 'Okay, spill.'

Lauren is a warts and all kind of girl. If Simon had asked her the same question, she'd have told him everything. Most of the time, I love that she doesn't hold back her emotions, and therefore has little filter around those she loves and trusts. But I'm not like that myself, and I don't want to talk about it.

'It's nothing, really. How's things going with Tabitha?'

He takes the hint and talks nonstop about his lady love instead. Then he says, 'Hey, did you know there's a Tarantino film festival on next month at the Ritz in Randwick?'

'Oh yeah?' I'm a bit of a Tarantino fan, and so is Lauren.

'Double date?'

'Sure, why not. I'll check in with Lauren and get back to you.' It might do us both good. 'On that note, what do you know about film?'

He pauses. 'Tarantino films? I like them, that's about it.'

'No, not Tarantino. I mean the medium.'

'I don't think I getcha.'

I play with a coaster. The cardboard is already a bit worse for wear and it's only nine in the evening.

'Didn't you do the film studies elective at uni?'

'Dropped out,' he said. 'Couldn't see the point.'

I'd felt the same at the time, but now I'm burning to know more about it. I'm letting the contents of an old crate occupy the space in my head that should be devoted to working out how to mend the fissures appearing in my marriage, but for the moment, I can't help it.

'Why do you ask?'

'I found an old film container with some cans in it when I was working on a shoot the other day, rescued it from landfill.'

'Oh yeah?' He's trying to feign interest.

'There are five reels in total. I think it's intact – as in, I think I have the whole movie.'

'Cool.' He looks across the bar and gestures for another round.

'I'd love to watch it,' I say, surprising myself. I hadn't even thought about watching it until this point. 'Do you think I could run it through a projector?'

He shakes his head, pushing his now empty glass back towards the bartender and waving his phone over the machine to pay for the two new beers on the counter. 'I can't pretend to know any more than you, but it depends what you mean by old, I reckon. What are we talking about here? Sixties? Seventies? Is it in good nick?'

'Older, I think. In fact, I reckon it could be from the twenties or thirties.' I wait for him to tell me it could be worth millions, but he doesn't, so I think I'm right about that too. Its only value is historic. 'As for the condition . . . I didn't see any damage to the sprockets or anything like that, which is why I think I might be able to play it. But it's a bit . . . tacky.'

'Well, those early films weren't exactly feted for their storylines, Em.'

I laugh. 'No, no, I don't mean the subject matter. I mean it's a bit tacky to the touch, sticky.'

'Oh. Well, like I said, I don't know much about film, but maybe it's deteriorating. Keep it out of the sun. Could be flammable.'

'It's in a tin can, Simon, in my shed. No light from yonder deck gets in there.'

'Goodo.' He takes a mouthful of beer and manages to swallow a burp.

'It features Rose Carey.' I wait to see if he recognises the name, but he just looks at me blankly.

'The silent film star?' I prompt.

'If you say so.'

'I've done a Google search and there's a filmography, but the film I have isn't listed on it.'

'Bit strange?'

'Yeah . . .'

'Maybe it's not her then.'

'I'm pretty sure it is – I've been able to see the title sequence and her name's on it.'

'Hmm . . . I could ask around if you like.'

'Do you know someone who would know?'

'Someone will know someone who will know something,' he says. 'What about your boss?'

'Haven't had a chance to ask him. I'm still on leave.' Given how I came by the film, I also feel a bit shy about asking him.

'You could always take it to the National Film and Sound Archive.'

Yeah, I could. But I have a feeling they'd try and talk me into surrendering the find to them.

'Nah. Not yet.'

I suddenly feel very protective of Rose Carey.

~

Before making my way upstairs to bed, I go to the shed. I open the crate and pull out the bundle of letters, removing the one

I'd looked at briefly before. I put it down on the desk and gently flatten the fragile paper with the palm of my hand. I'm now almost certain it reads, 'Dear Birdy'.

The Carrington Hotel
Saturday, 3rd November 1923

Dear Birdy,

I had to write because I never had the chance to say goodbye. I didn't want to leave you, you must believe me. I didn't want to leave at all. No, that's a lie, of course I wanted to, I had to, I had to get as far away as possible . . . and for more reasons than one. But I didn't want to leave you behind.

When I think of it all, a dark cloud descends over me. All I can see is blackness. Sometimes I wake in the night, consumed by guilt and grief. I don't know how I will ever redeem myself. I am so terribly afraid you will hate me forever. I never knowingly did a single thing to hurt you, I promise you that.

But, and this is the hardest thing to admit, when I wake in the morning, and find myself in the arms of the one I love, the darkness recedes and I am oddly happy. Is it right to love when I have caused so much unhappiness?

I can't be truly happy until I earn your forgiveness, and I can't do that unless I tell you all that happened. But where to start?

You will see from the marks on the page that I keep stopping and starting this letter. I keep blotting away little pools of ink brought about by my tears. I am desperately sad and yet so desperately happy. And oh, how I miss you.

But I'm being foolish. Of course you hate me. How could you not?

Perhaps if I tell you the whole story, from the very beginning. Not now, I can't bear it. I'll write again, I promise, after I've had time to gather my thoughts properly, and put them down in such a way as you will understand.

I'm sorry.

Love, Me.

7

Rose
Sydney, 1923

The crystal tank has arrived, and is being erected under Walter and Eddie's strict supervision at a warehouse in Mascot. While we await its completion, Alec is coaching me daily at the Domain Baths, affectionately known as 'The Dom', to help me further finesse the skills I honed on location in New Zealand. We are working on a seemingly death-defying dive that will be integral to the extravaganza I have planned, and which I still mean to deliver.

'This is daft,' I say to Alec as we stride along the wooden platform of The Dom. 'I am being impeded at every turn.'

'Oh, if only they knew,' he agrees with a laugh.

'It's not funny, Alec,' I say, pushing a stray curl fiercely back under my rubber swimming cap.

I'm talking about yet another piece of gossip printed in a Sydney newspaper, again insinuating I am the central player in a love triangle, with Alec as one of my paramours and Walter the other. The reporter didn't actually use the word 'scandalous', but he heavily implied it.

'Of course it is,' he says heartily. We have reached the base of the fifty-foot diving tower, and although we have already warmed up, he stops to do a few more calf stretches against it. 'We all know it's not true, therefore it is highly amusing.'

'No,' I say emphatically, taking up position beside him to do some stretches myself. 'It is not.'

'Since when has a little gossip bothered you, Rose? I've heard you say on more than one occasion that you agree with Mr Barnum: there's no such thing as bad publicity.'

I push myself off the tower struts to glower at him. 'Well, maybe I was wrong,' I grump. 'And Mr Barnum ran circuses. Of course he would think that.'

Alec stops stretching and holds my gaze, unflinching. He doesn't favour a bathing cap, and his white-blond hair is parted in the middle and crimped close to his head. 'Put it out of your head for now, we have work to do.'

He's right. We work on my entry, from one of the lower platforms. This work is about form and style, which is so important artistically. Once I'm able to perform the dive to his satisfaction from this level, we will work from a higher level. Whether or not I ever dive from fifty feet, however, remains to be seen.

'We still need to work on your splash,' he says as we exit via the pool gates later. 'Remember, the smaller the splash, the better the dive.'

'Audiences love a big splash,' I protest.

He shakes his head, as he always does. 'The theatrics can come later. We are aiming for perfect execution first. Know the rules before you break them, Rosie.'

'Perfect execution,' I murmur. I think I'm making excellent progress, but I wonder how far I am from perfect and how long I will need to work to achieve it. Patience has never been my strong suit.

'You're doing all right,' he says with a grin, reading my mind.

I laugh. 'Damned with faint praise.'

'No,' he contradicts. 'You *are* doing all right.'

I smile. 'Thank you.'

As we walk up and over the hill into the Botanic Gardens, I return to the topic that has been so troubling me.

'Can I tell you something?' I begin carefully.

'As long as you're not going to carry on again about the gossip.'

I shake my head. 'If it were just the gossip, Alec, I wouldn't be quite so concerned.'

'All right then,' he says, barely breaking his stride. 'Let's have it.'

I still feel some hesitation, but Alec is my longest-standing male friend.

'We've had a theft.'

I spend a moment analysing the look on his face. But Alec wouldn't steal from us – he has no need. He is an Olympian, I remind myself, he served this country in the Great War and, more to the point, he recently inherited a pot of money from his grandmother.

'What kind of theft?'

I let out a long sigh. 'Our props have been stolen from the Tivoli store.'

He frowns, well aware that our livelihood in part depends upon such things. 'It's a loss,' he agrees.

'Yes, and . . .' This is the big admission, the one I can only tell him if I trust him implicitly. 'Money has been disappearing from the company accounts. A lot of it.'

He takes a little while to absorb this information. 'Who do you suspect?' he says finally.

'I don't know.' I'm not a hand wringer, but the words sound needy, even to my own ears.

'Who has access to the accounts?'

'Only Walter . . . and me, of course. But I haven't been actively watching them since we left America.'

He shakes his head. 'It is not Walter,' he says emphatically. 'That would be like stealing from himself. And if it were, he would not have told you about it.'

I exhale another sigh. He has both voiced my deepest concern and invalidated it. Of course it's not Walter.

The trees on either side steeple over us, dappling the pathway ahead.

'I can't shake the feeling that all our recent . . . misfortune, shall we call it, is personal,' I say.

'What do you mean?'

'So much bad luck, over such a short time,' I say. 'All of it affecting me quite personally. It makes me feel like someone has it in for me.'

We walk on for a little while and I sense he is waiting for me to explain further. 'It all began with that business with Tom Jackson, in America. Someone leaked our liaison to the press.'

He laughs at that. 'Someone didn't "leak" it darling, you made no secret of it. You were running all around Hollywood on his arm. Some clever little journalist simply found out and told the world about it.'

'No,' I correct. 'That's not all that clever little journalist did. He also painted me as a scarlet woman.'

He nods. 'The newspapers write stories, Rose. You didn't fit the wronged woman mould.'

'So, I must be a harlot and a homewrecker? Why are women always pigeonholed as saint or sinner and never what we truly are? Human beings, the same as men, and we all make mistakes.'

'I agree, that part was personal. But as you also know, when you step into the spotlight, you must be as prepared for slings and arrows as you are for outrageous fortune.'

He is always borrowing from the Bard. I put it down to his schoolboy education. 'The question, I suppose,' he goes on, 'is why the papers here are reporting stuff and nonsense, when there's no particular evidence of it.'

'Walter is worried. He thinks my tarnished reputation might be what's spoiling negotiations here. But I'm more concerned about the thefts. I think they are also personal. Without the props, the plans I have for the extravaganza are at risk. Without money . . .' I don't need to finish the sentence. 'Even the reporting of the incident in New Zealand,' I say instead. 'It was very unkind towards me.'

He pauses, then he says gently, 'All they said was that you were driving too fast. And you were, Rose.'

'It was an accident,' I snap.

I see it play out again, like a series of frames on film. The only time I have relived those moments was when I was forced to by the authorities, straight after the accident. I have consciously refused to live through them again. But now, I can't seem to stop. It's as if someone has called, *'Action!'*

It started with a bang, like the sound of a gunshot.

A blown front tyre . . . that's what they'd told me.

The car pulled violently to the left, bucking towards the bridge railing. In a panic, I slammed on the brakes, wrestling with a steering wheel that felt like a bucking beast.

The worst thing you could have done, they said, as if I didn't know, as if that wasn't immediately clear.

I hear again the violent flap of rubber disintegrating on road. I feel the car spinning in furious, wide circles across the narrow bridge, then suddenly I am on the opposite side, heading directly for the wooden barricade.

'I thought I would die . . .' I realise I have said the words aloud, because Alec stops us in the dappled sunshine.

A strange calm had come over me. I'd wanted to take my hands off the wheel, but they were stuck there somehow, divorced from the rest of me. I couldn't remember how to release them. It had all happened so fast and yet, time had slowed right down and there was no sound in it. I was in the moment; before it, and after it, time was pliable, like plasticine.

I put my head in my hands now, massaging my temples, and Alec puts a reassuring arm about my waist. If only the gesture would make the kaleidoscope of images stop. But it doesn't. I am replaying every single frame.

The car hit the barricade and I was airborne. When it landed, the two front wheels were hanging over the top railing and the back two were on the ground. Sound returned to me. I heard the crack of the wooden rails, felt them straining under the weight of the car. If the car crashed through it, I would hurtle down the bank and into the river, thirty feet or more below. I would drown. How ironic.

When the car lurched through one railing, I was roused, but I couldn't risk opening the driver's door. Someone wrenched it open. Someone pulled me from my seat. Someone saved me. I didn't save myself.

I turn my head to look at Alec. 'I'm so lucky to have friends like you,' I say, feeling unfamiliar tears sting my eyes.

'And Eddie,' he reminds me.

'And Eddie.'

8

Rose
Sydney, 1923

Alec leaves me at the Government House gates on Macquarie Street. Despite his reassurances, I can't shake the feeling of doom that came over me as I relived the accident. The thefts and the narky press only add to the feeling. Somebody wishes me, and our company, ill. *Who?*

It could be anyone. A competitor – Mayfields, probably. That would make sense. Mayfields has a new American manager, some kind of war hero nobody knows much about yet. Mayfields would know how valuable our props are to us; they might even attempt to use them in their own productions. But how would they steal from our accounts? And this new manager, what was his name? Gray? Griggs? Griffiths? Would he actually go so far as to cause me physical harm?

A shiver runs down the entire length of my body, from the nape of my neck to the tips of my toes. I stumble and have to stop, drawing in deep, shuddering breaths. I must find someone to continue the self-defence classes I had been taking in America. Alec might be able to find someone.

Then I catch myself. This is nonsense. Mayfields doesn't even have a New Zealand presence – how could their manager have had anything to do with the accident? It was just that: an accident. I can't allow myself to be spooked by it.

That just leaves the thefts. Mr Randolph has reported our missing props to the police. Walter has reported the stolen funds to the bank. These two incidents might be crimes, but they are not threats to my person. And the narky press, in and of itself, can't physically harm me. The only damage is to my reputation.

I can fix that, once and for all.

By the time I arrive back at Point Piper, I have reached a momentous decision. It will be the perfect smokescreen, I reason, and a welcome distraction for the press. It's a wonder I hadn't thought of it before. After all, women have been doing it for years.

'Walter,' I call as I enter the hall, pausing only to remove my hat and gloves.

From somewhere in the depths of the house I hear what is possibly the sound of his footsteps finding their way towards me. When we meet, it's in the sitting room, the room that leads out onto the terrace. I pause for a moment. Apart from that curious moment the other day, when I found myself imagining him semi-naked, it might be the first time I've really looked at him, as a man and not a manager, since . . . when? Since we first met in America.

'I have an idea,' I say.

He gets that look in his eye, the one that tells me he assumes I've come up with an impossible suggestion.

I look at him for a moment more, recognising that he is still as he was when I first met him. Or perhaps not quite. In those days, he wore a suit jacket that slid off his shoulders at the slightest shrug. His shoulders are now too broad for that to happen.

The sun, streaming through the unshuttered French doors, is picking out golden highlights in his light brown hair. I have never before noticed what the sunlight does to his hair.

'Do we need drinks for this?' he asks, moving to the sideboard.

'Not at all,' I say, although that's likely a lie. He might need one. I go out onto the terrace, and he follows in my wake. We settle into our customary chairs.

'Now, then,' he says, 'what is your wonderful idea, Rose?

I pat the folds of my dress smooth across my lap. The fabric is a shade that is not quite nude, not quite apricot, with chiffon flutter sleeves and a lace insert trimming the neckline. Now that the moment is upon me, I find it harder than I had anticipated to share my idea. I fancy for a moment that I can hear the clock on the mantel in the room behind us, murdering the silence between tick and tock.

I glance up at him and am momentarily mesmerised by the cornflower blue of his eyes. He is very handsome. I feel, oddly, as if I am coming out of a fog. 'We've always spoken plainly to each other, have we not?'

'We have,' he agrees.

'So, I'm going to just come right out and ask you.' I slap my hand down on my lap, partly to dispel any lingering vapour from that unexpected fog, but mostly so that there can be no doubt about meaning what I have to say next.

As I continue to look him in the eye, I see he has no idea what to expect. I realise I am tapping the pointed toe of one of my kid leather boots on the flagstones underfoot.

Oh, I had rehearsed this so many times after leaving Alec, on the walk up Macquarie Street, and all the way home. I had chosen every word with great care; I had rehearsed them so many times they had become just like lines in a play.

'Marry me,' I blurt, which was not at all how I had rehearsed it.

Walter has a fine, almost olive complexion; even so, the colour fills his face all at once. When the flush washes out of it just as quickly, I panic.

'It makes such good sense,' I say. 'It will close down the rumour mill and it will give the press something positive to write about – a wedding, think of that!'

Still, he says nothing, but having said it, I now can't bear the thought of him turning me down. And so, I go on and on, as I had mapped out in my head. I lay out my terms and put forward my persuasions. I explain all my whys and wherefores. 'It will vastly improve my reputation. Why, I'll be positively respectable,' I say with a little laugh. 'Perhaps for the first time in my life.'

He doesn't laugh with me. 'I can see how good this could be for you,' he says finally. 'But how, exactly, would it benefit me?'

I blink. In all my rehearsing, I had not even thought about how it might personally benefit him.

The silence makes my ears ache. 'It will benefit the company,' I say finally.

'The company?' he says.

'Yes, the company.'

There's a movement at the open French doors. Eddie. 'I'm about to put the car away,' he says. 'Unless you're thinking of taking it out?'

'Oh,' I say with strained politeness. 'No thanks, Eddie.'

Walter shakes his head.

'Right you are then,' Eddie says. 'I'll put her away.' He hovers for a moment, then, sensing the unusual tension between us, disappears.

'It's your company as much as mine,' I say flatly, tapping my fingers on the wrought iron table between us. 'If it suffers, you suffer.'

He sits back in his chair and looks out over the harbour. The sun is slipping lower in the sky, turning the water rose gold.

'If we marry, backers will see that I am not a reputational risk – quite the reverse. I will be a respectable married woman. Think about it strategically, Walter. Think of all the positive publicity our union would garner.'

He shakes his head slightly and I wonder what he is saying no to. I feel my heart begin to patter. Then he turns to look at me, and I can't remember ever seeing such flint in his eyes. 'It is a very interesting proposition, but when I take a wife, I would like her to be a wife, not a business partner, and I would like to be the one doing the asking.'

I am surprised by the look in his eyes, and the tone of his voice. But I am also surprised by other things: that he infers he wants an ordinary life, an ordinary wife. People involved in a theatrical life . . . we are not cut of the same cloth as others. I don't say that from a position of superiority, or from an opposing position, either, but merely as a fact. We have different lives; we want different things.

That gives me the pluck to say, 'Oh fiddlesticks, Walter. An ordinary wife would bore you silly. You need a partner and a friend, just as I do. We would make a perfect couple, and you know it. Why, we practically are one already.'

'Are we, indeed?'

'Of course we are – we do everything together. We work together, we run a company together – why, we're even *living* together.'

He shakes his head. 'We are all living here, except Alec,' he points out. 'But that is only when we're on the road, not back in the States.'

'No, but that doesn't have to be the case, does it? Once we get back to Los Angeles, we could live together there too. We might even buy something . . . something like *Pickfair* in Beverly Hills, and live near Mary and Douglas.' Mary Pickford and I are about the same age, and we already have a nodding acquaintance. 'Think how good that might be for us. Think of the opportunities that might come our way.'

He is still shaking his head, and I realise I'm letting the idea run away with me. I expect him to say that we must find out what's happened to our missing money before we can even think of such a thing. But he doesn't. Instead, he says, 'And what of love, Rose?'

Love? The pace of my pattering heart picks up. I have never been a romantic, and I hadn't thought he was, either. I don't think I even believe in romantic love. I've experienced passion, of course I have. But that is something different. I've never been in love, at least not the way it's played out on the stage and screen. It all seems like make-believe to me. Truth to tell, I never thought I'd love anyone enough to want to marry them – and that is still the case. I only want to marry Walter because, well, it just makes good old-fashioned common sense.

'What of it?'

He shakes his head again, as if he still can't quite believe what I'm suggesting. 'And babies?'

'*Babies?*'

I didn't mean to spit the word, I swear I didn't. I enjoy babies as much as the next person. 'I just don't want them for myself.'

When he nods, I know that I have spoken the words out loud.

He is forcing me to investigate my thoughts on love and marriage and children, but I have seen romances ruin too many careers – women's careers, of course, not men's. I have seen too many women disappear into the arms of men and never return to the stage, or screen. Some of these women, I'm sure, have been perfectly content with their lot. But some of them, I know, have not. Some have even been abandoned, left to bring up children on their own.

'And neither do you,' I say, looking unflinchingly into his eyes. 'Do you?' It's a risk, a gamble. He may very well want children, but I have a hunch he does not. The only thing I don't know are his reasons.

He shakes his head. 'Not children, no,' he agrees.

And then I understand. He had spoken of love, he had spoken of babies, but he means something else. He means sex. I am not surprised. I am not even disappointed.

'Oh . . . and as for that . . . well, if you like we can include it in the arrangement.' I am a grown woman, saying such things doesn't make me blush. But I do have to stop myself from imagining sex with Walter. Walter coming towards me with that look men get in their eyes. Walter undoing his buttons, his gaze never leaving my face. Walter shrugging out of his shirt, baring his chest . . .

I find I have to clear my throat. 'Or find it elsewhere, if you wish. If you are discreet, I can turn a blinder than blind eye.'

'Is that so?'

I pause. 'That is so.'

'And you?'

'What of me?'

'Will you "finding it elsewhere if you wish" also be part of this "arrangement"?'

I frown, confused. 'Well, what's good for the gander,' I say. 'I mean, if that's what we agree on.'

'And you can be discreet about that, can you?' He sounds snappy, annoyed.

'Of course I can,' I say, knowing I sound defensive.

'You don't have a very good track record in that respect.'

I sniff. 'Well, I have learned from my experiences.'

He stands up, and for a moment I think he will simply walk out; he can be quite haughty sometimes. But he doesn't. Instead, he reaches for me and pulls me into his embrace. I surprise myself by going willingly. I want to know what it is like to be wanted by a man like Walter, I realise. I want to know what it is like to be kissed by him. I want to know what kind of lover he is. I turn my face up to his.

His eyes are so glitteringly blue, the look in them so intense. I find myself leaning into him. He is so much taller than me, so much bigger, so much stronger. But I am no shrinking violet either. I am fit and agile and, after years of swimming and dancing and now diving, I too am strong. We are such a good match, even physically.

All these thoughts are running through my head, and I realise that while I am still making an intellectual case for our marriage, Walter is doing something else.

Walter is sliding his hands down my back. He is holding me so close I can feel the rock-solid muscles in his body pressed against me.

Something inside me is melting. I am not usually a passive lover – if I want a man to kiss me, I usually take the initiative myself. But all I want now is to sink into him. I am fixated by his lips, I can't take my eyes off them. I reach my arms up around his neck. 'Please, Walter,' I hear myself say.

And so he does. His lips are tender and passionate all at once. I open my mouth for him, and he tastes me. Rivers of desire run from my lips to the pit of my stomach, and down my legs. My fingers explore the fine cotton of his shirt. I find myself playing with the buttons. I want to know the texture of his skin under my palm. I want to feel the rasp of the hair on his chest. I am suddenly impatient and no longer passive. But as I expose the breadth of his chest, he breaks off the kiss and captures my hand in his. For a moment we can do nothing but stare into each other's eyes. I feel as if I am on the brink of understanding something important. All I can hear is the sound of our ragged breathing.

'Thank you for doing me the honour of asking me to marry you,' he says finally. 'I must think on it.'

Why hadn't I asked Alec?

I'm still outside on the terrace and the evening light is spilling onto the harbour. I am filled with regret. I never thought that Walter might want to consider my proposal. I should just have asked Alec.

I sit back in my chair as the day closes in on me. It's growing cold.

I didn't ask Alec because I couldn't. I know lots of people do it, especially in our trade, to hide their real romantic relationships, but I can't. Partly because it would send the wrong message to those who would otherwise love him, but mostly because I know that, out of loyalty to me, he would say yes.

When I seek Bell out the next day for our early morning swim, she's not in her bedroom. It's fair enough – it's a Sunday. Sundays are for her to spend as she wishes, and I also usually reserve the day for myself. But after my discussion with Walter last night – if that's what it was – I don't feel like being alone.

As I navigate the path down to the harbour, around a particularly prickly grevillea, I hear voices.

They are standing in a clearing. Eddie has set up two tripods. I can't see them in any great detail from my vantage point, but I'm fairly certain one is for a movie camera, the other for stills. He's using the whole shebang; he could be shooting a scene for one of our films. He must have been up early to have set this up already.

Something about the way Bell is looking at him tells me she doesn't really want to be here. I should make a noise. I should make my presence known. If he's compelling her to do something she doesn't want to do, I should step in, do something to stop it. But is he? I'm confused by the little tableau, so I resolve to watch them quietly for just a few more moments.

Eddie says something and Bell puts one foot forward and turns her hips towards the camera. The sheer skirt of her cream dress plays around her knees before settling into soft folds just below them. Contrary to the fashion, the dress is fitted at her slender waist with a ribbon band, and worn with what I can see even from this distance is a pale apricot slip. She designed and made it herself, and she looks well in it. She has a figure almost equal to mine and, if I am being honest about it, a fairer face.

'Right, and put your foot back again. Lean against the tree.' There is no encouragement in his words, he's being very matter-of-fact. He's trying something out, another invention, no doubt. To his credit, Eddie is always tinkering with techniques and apparatus. The camera itself is some sort of pre-production model. His enthusiasm for his medium has stood our films in very good stead. But I'm not convinced Bell is a willing subject, and if that's the truth then I wonder why she has agreed to pose for him at all.

He issues another instruction and Bell turns her body into a different pose. He makes another adjustment. Cameras are still such a mystery to me, but he is ever the inventor, always testing something or modifying it, always searching for better-quality shots. He has so far been unlucky in having any of his inventions patented. Someone has always been there just ahead of him with something a little bit better. But he will get there, I'm sure of it.

'We'll have sound one day,' I hear him say. 'People are already working on it.' But it's almost as if he's talking to himself. Bell says nothing in response, not a single word. 'That'll be the end of subtitles. Nobody will be left guessing, even the illiterate will be able to understand movies.'

He returns to the other camera and issues more instructions. Bell unbuttons her dress and pushes one shoulder through the neck of it. I'm so surprised. I'm not sure why. I don't have any problems with nudity. How could I? I've appeared in film naked myself. And Bell's a long way from being nude, she's simply showing one bare shoulder.

He clicks the button on the camera. 'That's when we'll see what's what.'

I don't know what he means by that, and I don't hang around to find out.

9

Emma
Sydney, 2024

P.S. You know I would never have married him, if not for the accident.

10

Emma
Sydney, 2024

I almost missed that post script.

When I tear myself away from the letter and come inside, Lauren is sitting up in bed with her laptop open.

I sit down on the edge of the mattress and unzip my ankle boots. 'How was your day?' I ask, as I ease my foot out of first one boot and then the other.

She doesn't answer, but I hear the laptop snap shut behind me and the case knock against wood as she puts it onto the bedside table.

'You've been drinking,' she says.

I put my boots onto the rack under the bedside table, next to the slides I wear in place of slippers.

'Yes, I was out with Simon,' I agree. I'd told her where I was going. 'He says hi.'

She sniffs. 'You could have invited me.'

I turn to look at her, but she is staring straight ahead. 'Did you want to come?'

'That's beside the point.'

I laugh, hoping to dispel the black cloud that's surrounding her. 'Well, not really. That is the point. I only want you to do things you want to do.'

She does look at me now and her eyes are fighting green. 'Right. Well, kindly leave decisions about what I might want or not want to do to me.'

I undress, drop my clothes in the laundry basket, then pad back to the bed, taking my nightshirt from under the pillow and putting it on. Then I get into bed, careful not to sit too close to her. She goes back to staring straight ahead. This is the trickiest part of making up. What I want to do is put my arm around her, pull her head down onto my shoulder and kiss her, but that's as likely to deepen her resentment as it is to soften it, and so instead, I just sit next to her, waiting.

'He was my friend before he was yours, remember?' She pushes her hair back from her face as she says it, bringing attention to the scowl between her brows.

I resist the impulse to sigh. 'I think we worked out that we both met him at about the same time, but we didn't know it. Does it really matter?'

She doesn't respond, and the silence between us stretches until I'm forced to break it again. Emboldened by beer, I decide to come right out and say it. 'You know I would give you a flock of children if I could afford to, right? A giggle of them, a colony.'

The tears spring immediately to her eyes and then sit on her lashes, as if she has summoned all her willpower to stop them from trickling down her cheeks. 'Gaggle,' she corrects. 'If you are going to steal a collective noun and apply it to children, make sure it actually is one.'

But her voice breaks on the word 'children' and her willpower trembles.

I do reach out to her then, pull her close to me, lay her head on my shoulder. 'A bunch, then,' I say, stroking her hair and pushing it behind her ears.

'A charm,' she hiccups.

'A family.'

Then she does cry, great big sobs that I can do nothing to stop. The sound of them is difficult enough, but the feel of them shuddering through her body and into mine is the hardest to bear.

I know there is nothing I can say or do to fix this. I also know we will get through it, but it will take time and love and care. I find myself wanting to project us forward to a time when the pain is less raw, a time when we have come to terms with it. But I can't, and so I just hold her, wishing, for the first time in my life, that I had chosen a more lucrative career.

When she is all cried out and lying quietly beside me, not quite sleeping, I go to the curtains over the sliding doors and pull them back. I stand there for a minute looking out across the upstairs balcony into the night. The sky is blue velvet – it never really gets dark here – and the lights of the city are imperfect substitutes for low-hanging, multi-coloured stars. There are a couple of new buildings going up next to the controversial Crown, and one of them is already all lit up, cranes with red lights at each knuckle sitting on top of it.

I have always been a city girl. I'm not even particularly fond of the suburbs. If it were up to me, we'd live here, or perhaps even closer to the CBD, for the rest of our lives. But I had been willing to trade it for a little house on the fringe, somewhere affordable, perhaps at the foot of the Blue Mountains. I would be willing to trade almost everything to give Lauren what she wants.

'What are you doing?' she says.

There is still something left unsaid, so I ignore her question and bring it out from the shadows. 'I know you wanted me to agree to trying again, with or without money.'

She makes an almost inaudible sound.

'I just can't.'

'I know.'

'We have to be able to afford it,' I continue, still looking out at the night.

I expect her to protest, but she surprises me.

'I know,' she says again.

'If we're going to be a family, we have to be able to start it, and then continue to support it.'

'Yes.'

I look down into the street now. A young drunk, singing at the top of his voice, is swinging around the lamp post on the corner, a little way up from the row of terraces that house some of our local restaurants. They are all closed now, and the yellow light from the lamp turns the scene into something from the 1900s. It's a stark contrast to the twenty-first-century vista laid out beyond.

If it were any other goal, I'd say we could make compromises, perhaps even use our credit cards to fund the gaps for more treatment. But this is not a goal we can buy on credit, or time payment. We can't go into parenthood with debt like that. We can't even save up for it. It would take time and time is running out for us.

I almost wish I had been born a man. I say almost, because it's possible that what I really wish is that women's child-bearing years were extended a little longer, that we might enjoy the same long fertility as men – but all I see is women evolving the other way, becoming less fertile, sooner.

'I know all this, Emmie,' she says softly into the darkness. 'And I almost agree with you. I just wonder . . . is money the only reason?'

'What?'

I let the curtain drop back into place and the room falls into soft darkness. I can't see her face anymore.

'Do you actually . . . want children? Or . . . is the lack of money just an excuse?'

There's no venom in her voice – quite the opposite. She asks the question as if she is very afraid of my answer. A prickle of anxiety grips the back of my neck. I cannot pause too long, I cannot consider the question for a moment, and so I don't. 'Of course I want children.'

Oh, but do I? I love Lauren, but I also love our city life. Would the little house in the foothills satisfy me? Or would the long commutes to city gigs wear me down over time, make me resent the move, resent Lauren, resent my family? Am I just a tiny bit relieved that our attempts have been thwarted?

I come back to the bed, lift the covers, and get in beside her again. The truth is, I wanted her to have our children because it would have made her happy.

'If we did have more money . . .' she begins, and I feel myself tense. I hate these speculative beginnings to sentences, because they tell me I'm about to hear something I'll find difficult to answer.

'Yes,' I say warily.

'Would you reconsider?'

'Of course I would, you know that.'

'No, that's not what I mean.'

I prop myself up on my elbow so I can look into her face, even though the darkness shields her expression.

'Well, what do you mean?'

'I mean . . . we've already tried to get me pregnant . . . would you consider trying to get pregnant next time – if we had the money?'

No! I don't want to be pregnant, and I never have. It's not that I'm afraid of it, and I don't think it's disgusting. I'd love to parent, I just don't have a biological urge to use my own body to procreate.

Again, I could lie to her. The fact is, we don't have the money, so this 'what if' scenario is unlikely to be tested. But I won't lie to her. It's morally wrong to pretend I would consider it, even for a minute.

'We talked about this too, darling. You know the answer.'

She doesn't go off again, she just nods in the darkness and lets out a long, shuddering sigh. 'It would be so nice, though . . .' she says quietly.

I smile and lie on my back, pushing out my stomach so that it swells into something resembling early pregnancy. I take her hand and run it over my belly. 'Would it, though?'

She laughs, pushes at my stomach to return it to normal, then settles into my arms. 'Yes,' she says, 'It would.'

There's a buzzing in our quiet bedroom and for a moment, sleep-affected, I can't place it. When I open my eyes, I see Lauren's face in the shadows, close to mine.

'Lipstick,' she says, nibbling at my ear.

I am instantly awake.

I had helped her choose her 'lipstick' from an online store. It had to be realistic, she said, in a shade she might actually wear – 'Love Me Do Red'. It had to be angled, not just so that it faithfully resembled the real deal, but also for practical purposes. A pointed tip for precise stimulation, a wider and a flatter side for more general use. It fits into the palm of her hand, and it is vibrating.

She applies the tip to my lips, outlining them the way she might if she were doing my make-up. My mouth feels instantly swollen. The vibrations run all the way through me, to my breasts, between my legs, to my toes. I open my mouth. She inserts the lipstick into it and I suck.

She turns. She has already discarded the long T-shirt she wears to bed. Did she start before waking me? The thought only turns me on more. She climbs on top of me, her large breasts falling either side of my face. I abandon the lipstick to draw her nipple into my mouth. It hardens as I nip at it. She begins to moan.

But she has invested in the toy and so it's not the end of it. She sits up, grinding against me as she does. She puts it to her own lips, outlining them the same way she had mine. She moistens them with her tongue, and I watch for mind-blowing seconds as she lip fucks it. Then I go to tumble her over, as is our usual practice, but she clenches her thighs together; she won't let me.

This is new.

She tips her head back and her blonde curls fall away from her neck, exposing the white column of her throat, the outline of her collarbone. The moonlight spills its milk into the room and all the way over her naked body as she puts the vibrating tip first to her left areola and then to her right. She is bucking on top of me. Then she crumples and suddenly falls back, discarding the toy in the process.

I rip off my nightshirt and discard my underwear with an efficient flick of my legs. I move below her waist to kiss her, but she stops me. 'Not this time,' she says, and she is suddenly on top of me.

This is not what we do. This is not how we usually do it. I pleasure her first with my mouth, she pleasures me with her hands. That's the way, that's what we do.

But not tonight.

She turns and her face is between my legs, mine between hers.

She fumbles for a moment and then I hear it. She turns up the speed on the lipstick.

~

The next morning, Lauren has gone to an advanced sewing class in Surry Hills. I'd watched her pack her organiser into a nifty, wheeled trolley. It reminds me of a cabin bag but was designed, she'd told me, to house a sewing machine. She's adapted it to fit the organiser, packed with things like scissors, pins and needles, spools of thread, tailor's chalk, measuring tapes and an odd-looking ruler, which I've learned is called a 'French curve'.

'The trolley makes it easier to get to classes on public transport,' she'd said, 'and means I don't forget anything,'

So, I'm at a bit of a loose end. I sit outside on the deck with my iPad and do a little more investigation into the life and times of Rose Carey.

There is plenty of information about her online. She is credited as one of Australia's most popular vaudeville exports, one of our first Hollywood movie stars, perhaps our first ever stunt woman and the first woman in the world to appear nude in a major film.

This last detail is accompanied by a photo of her perched naked in a tree, arms outstretched, a length of chiffon strategically draped over her breasts and lap. It resembles some of the photos in the box in my shed, and I remind myself to check them against this later.

Her filmography is also online. She was in several movies, many of the storylines derived from myths and legends and centring around women saving men from immorality. Some of these she wrote herself. I run my eye quickly down the list of titles, but I can't see the name of the film now in my possession. If I want to know more, I'm going to have to look further than Wikipedia. I'm about to close the browser when my eyes alight on a subheading: 'personal life'. Beneath it, the text lists where she was born, where she died, the names of her parents and details of their careers. But it is the last line that captures my attention. It contains only three words.

Married, no children.

11

Emma
Gold Coast, 2024

Allie is getting married. Correction, Allie is having an engagement party. It remains to be seen whether she and Jaxon will actually make it to the altar. This is the third party I've attended to celebrate her upcoming nuptials, and Jaxon will be the third fiancé I've been introduced to.

There was never any question of not going; we didn't receive an invitation so much as a royal command. Lauren bought the plane tickets months ago in a Jetstar 'fly home free' sale, and we're staying in a beachfront Gold Coast apartment that Allie organised and paid for. Thankfully, we have been accommodated on the ground floor. This not only gives us the best access to the beach, it is also furthest from Allie's penthouse upstairs, the one she owns, where she is now holding court. These are the spoils of a fitness guru who struck gold a few years ago and now has a gazillion followers on Instagram, I think to myself, as I take in the stunning view over Mermaid Beach from the enormous terrace.

The Jetstar sale and the free accommodation meant I could hardly protest that we couldn't afford to go. All this is costing us is our time, and a gift. Regarding the first of those things, I'm beginning to think time is the most valuable thing I own. As for the second, Lauren has made Allie and her fiancé a blue cropped Haori style jacket, lined with hot pink silk and featuring bold white buttons on the left shoulder. Allie doesn't realise it's a piece of art. It's designed to be displayed on a bamboo hanger, preferably on a bare white wall but instead she's wearing it, no doubt thinking she's being incredibly supportive. When I suggested to Lauren that she explain the piece, she just smiled. 'It doesn't matter, Emmie. Art is to be enjoyed and she's enjoying it. That's all I want.'

Allie is walking over to me. Apart from Lauren, Allie and their ever-so-slightly-eccentric Aunty Julia, who is deep in conversation with a gangly-looking fellow in the furthest corner of the balcony, are the only people I know. Unless you count Jaxon, to whom we have just been introduced.

Allie waves a bottle of champagne towards my half-empty glass. 'More bubbles, sweetie?' she asks. I glance at the label. *Ruinart.* I've never heard of it, but it seems appropriate.

'I won't, thank you all the same.'

She is wearing gold-framed, blue-mirrored sunglasses, so I can't see the expression in her eyes.

'Oh, you're probably right,' she says, and her smile reveals perfect white teeth. 'It will go to our heads, and we'll all be plastered before midnight.' She sets the bottle down on the bar table beside me. 'Especially given we're drinking it in the midday sun.'

So much for health and fitness, I think as she pulls her braided straw hat a little further down over her face. 'How are you, anyway, Emma?'

I'm surprised by the question. Allie doesn't usually bother with such niceties. It's always just been the Allie show at these kinds of do's.

'I'm fine, thank you,' I say in my best sister-in-law voice.

She nods. She has draped her long blonde hair over her shoulders to partly cover her beaded white crop top – or is it just a bra? – and tanned midriff.

For a split second she reminds me of someone. Who? The image of the postcard seems to float before my eyes. Rose Carey, I realise, except Rose had dark hair. Or could it be that I am becoming slightly obsessed with Rose?

'And our Lozza?'

I despise the nickname. It sounds so . . . bogan, and Lauren is anything but bogan.

'Lauren is also fine,' I say.

She nods again. 'I'm so sorry about . . . everything,' she says. 'I know that the only help I offered was financial, but I just want to say, if there is anything else I can do, please let me know.' We both look at Lauren. She's standing at the railing with Jaxon, stunning in her white dress, the one with the blue flowers, cap sleeves and plunging V neckline.

'Thank you, I say,' knowing I do not sound at all thankful.

After an uncomfortable pause, Allie says, 'You work for a video production company, right?'

She's known me for six years. She already knows this. 'Yes,' I say.

'I was just wondering . . .' It's at this point that people usually ask if I do weddings, so I brace myself, but she continues with, 'does – what's the name of that company you're with? Sledgehammer or something?'

'Hammer and Tongs,' I correct.

'Yes, right. Do you do anything really creative there? You know, interesting stuff that could go viral on TikTok and other channels?'

I stare at her. *TikTok?* Why is she asking me? When she was in her twenties, she'd gone viral on social media as *GoodGriff!*, the handle being a play on their surname, according to Lauren. Today, Allie, a dedicated gym junkie and former department store beautician, has amassed a small fortune thanks to the devoted followers of her 'refreshingly frank' beauty and fitness tips. I realise I am both envious of her success and annoyed by it, so I bite down on an acerbic response and say mildly, 'Why do you ask?'

She picks up her glass and sips from it. 'Well . . . tell me if I'm stepping out of line here, but there's something going at Hot Rain.'

Hot Rain, the entertainment company that has aided and abetted her rise to fame and fortune.

'Right,' I say.

'There's a new producer on board. He wants to try something . . . different. It's a decent gig, Em, a pretty big contract.'

I want to smack her.

'Right,' I say again. It's all I trust myself to say.

'It's exciting,' she insists. 'I can't say much more at the moment, but they asked me if I knew anyone.'

She doesn't actually think I have exciting ideas, she just thinks I'm related to someone exciting – herself. 'Well, thank you, but—'

Hearing the refusal that's about to leave my lips, she cuts me off. 'How about I just send you the stuff?'

I take a long pause before responding. 'Sure.' But we both know I won't act on it.

She lets out a long sigh as if she's already given up on me and glances back at Lauren. 'Ah, look at her,' she says. 'She'd look so cute with a bubba in her arms.'

This single sentence sends a wave of fury through me. A sensitive person wouldn't flutter a lucrative job offer under my nose and then immediately connect it to the fact that we can't afford to try again. A sensitive person wouldn't mention babies at all. A sensitive person would realise that what we want at the moment is some time to adjust, and a bit of privacy. A sensitive person wouldn't call my wife *cute*, even if she is her sister. I want to tell Allie all that and I open my mouth to do so, but the words don't come out.

Lauren laughs and the sound travels over to where we are standing. Jaxon is smiling down at her.

'What does he do?' I ask bluntly.

'Jax? He's *Jaxonshape*.' Then she laughs, as if it's hilarious that I'd forgotten. *Jaxonshape* is some kind of fitness app that projects what people will look like if they continue to follow the Jaxon exercise regime. He has almost as many social media followers as Allie does. They are the ultimate power couple. How could I have forgotten?

Easily, I remind myself, because the only thing that interests me about Jaxon is what he is saying to make my heartbroken wife laugh like that.

'I don't think I've met him yet – not properly. I'd better go over and say hi.'

'That looks like a very good idea,' she agrees and smiles, as if we are co-conspirators.

I make my way over to the balustrade.

'Emmie,' Lauren says with a little wave of her hand, 'come and say hi to Jax.'

The abbreviation makes him sound sexy, which, I have to concede, he is. He has that rugged, outdoor look I like.

'Hi, Jaxon,' I say, extending my hand.

He shakes it. 'Hi, Emma.' He says it with a warm smile that reminds me of open fields and long grass.

'Congratulations,' I add.

'Thank you – she's a gorgeous girl.'

I suppose he means Allie, but it's hard to tell because as he says the words, he turns back to Lauren. 'I'm a lucky man,' he continues, looking briefly at me. 'I'd say we're both lucky.'

I nod, but I'm not happy.

I don't like the way his eyes sparkle as he says it. I don't like that his summer smile is now all for Lauren. But most of all, I don't like being reminded, for the first time in forever, that when I met her, I had thought my wife was straight.

~

'That was fun,' she says as we get into the lift and head for the ground floor. 'Did you have fun?'

'Not as much fun as you.'

'Oh, don't be like that, Emmie. I don't care what you say about Allie, she does know how to put on a good party, and we get to put our dancing shoes on now.' She simulates a toe-tapping routine around the lift. At least Allie, or Jaxon has put a spring back in her step.

But the thought of kicking on this evening makes me want to draw my toes up into claws. The party in the penthouse was just a warm-up. We are now off to some OTT Gold Coast hotel where Allie has promised, along with dancing, 'top-line entertainment'. Heaven knows what that means.

I watch as Lauren swipes the keycard to our door and pushes it open. She walks along the short corridor in front of me, hips swaying. She's teasing me. We don't have time to do anything other than change our clothes. I'm done in five minutes flat, but Lauren is dancing back and forth between the bedroom and the ensuite in her underwear for a good half hour.

She's very beautiful, but her sister is right. She would look even more beautiful with a baby in her arms. For some reason the thought brings back those three little words at the end of Rose Carey's bio.

Married, no children.

Was it by choice?

I sit on the bed and while I wait for Lauren to do her make-up, I google Rose some more.

By the mid-1920s, after starring in numerous feature films and shorts (documentaries), Carey's film career was effectively over. She then appeared to go through a brief but significant period of financial difficulty.

Well, I can empathise with that. Now I have more questions – was it money that prevented her from having a family? But surely she overcame the financial troubles? Given we've named a ferry after her, she couldn't have fallen into obscurity.

'What do you think?'

Lauren is standing in front of me. If she's Portia de Rossi, then I am Ellen DeGeneres. But this time I'm the one in a dress and she's wearing an electric blue silk jumpsuit she made for this occasion. It also has a plunging neckline, and she's straightened her curls so that her hair falls in shining strands around her face.

'It's the colour of 2024,' she announces, twirling so I can fully appreciate it. Her hair forms a graduated V down her nearly-naked back. 'I just made that up. According to Allie, the colour of the year is peach fuzz. But I think this suits me better. What do you think?'

'You look beautiful, as always.' I stand up and walk over to her.

She captures my hand and slides it inside her cleavage. She's not wearing a bra. I mould my hand to her large, perfect breast. 'No time for that, Emmie,' she says, as if I were the instigator.

'Are you sure?' I ease the fabric over a little to expose her breast and pull her nipple into my mouth.

She laughs again. 'I'm sure.'

Reluctantly, I remove my lips from her skin and she smooths her neckline back into place. Then she lifts her head. 'You look beautiful too.'

I half-smile. I had thought this dress was so gorgeous online, but . . . 'It's not this year's colour. It's probably not even last year's colour.'

She hugs me. 'No, but it's a little black dress. Timeless.'

~

As she promised, the venue Allie has chosen to celebrate her third engagement is 'pumping'. She and Lauren are on the dance floor, as are most of the guests.

Thank God there's an outdoor garden. I'd be happy to spend the night in my own company, drinking cider and talking to the hibiscus but somehow, I find myself outside, in conversation with Aunty Julia.

'I think I'm officially the oldest person here,' she says with a laugh. She is only in her fifties, but even so, she is the only representative of the older generation. Lauren and Allie's father, Julia's older brother, passed away many years ago and their mother is slow-travelling the world, perhaps forever.

I smile. 'If it's any consolation, I feel like the oldest person here.'

Julia is perhaps five feet tall. She wears her hair in a Cleopatra-styled bob, dyed jewel red, and has an eclectic fashion sense that stands out in any crowd, including this one. Tonight, she is wearing long, heavy, gold earrings that reach her shoulders, a purple, beaded yoke cocktail dress and an I-don't-give-a-damn-how-old-I-am attitude.

She laughs in response. 'You underrate yourself, dear Emma.'

'Thank you.' I lean on the fence that sections off the garden from the rest of the hotel grounds. 'You look fabulous, by the way.'

'Thank you.' She smiles, then continues, 'How are things, Emma?'

When Allie had asked the same question earlier, I'd been offended. But somehow, I'm not evenly slightly put out by Julia asking it.

'It's tricky,' is all I trust myself to say.

'Life is,' she agrees.

When I make no comment, she simply pats my hand.

I look about me to avoid making eye contact, afraid her kindness will make me cry, and see Lauren coming into the garden. She is on Jaxon's arm, champagne tumbling out of her glass as she moves towards us. I'm a little bit surprised to see her with a drink in her hand, but then she isn't on IVF treatment any more and there is no chance she could be pregnant.

'There you are. I've been looking all over for you.' She lets go of Jaxon's arm long enough to kiss her Aunty Julia on the cheek. 'What are you two talking about?'

'My birthday,' Julia lies. 'I think I'll have a dinner this year. Can I count the two of you in?'

I hold out my hand to Lauren. She takes it and says, 'Absolutely!' Then she cricks her head towards Jaxon, who's now standing an arm's length away.

'He's very good looking, don't you think, ladies?' She says it in an exaggerated whisper. I wonder if she intends for him to overhear.

Julia laughs. 'Of course he is, darling.'

Lauren gulps from her champagne glass and I'm starting to suspect she's had one too many. 'Smart, too. Designed an app, so he must be a tech-head. Aren't tech-heads very smart?'

'I think it helps,' Julia agrees with an indulgent smile.

Lauren stumbles slightly as one of her stilettos sinks into the soft grass. 'And he seems nice. You've talked to him haven't you, Aunty Juls? Is he nice?'

Julia looks into Jaxon's bemused face and lets out a mischievous laugh. 'Oh yes,' she agrees, 'he's very nice.'

To his credit, Jaxon just smiles, albeit a little self-consciously.

It is possibly time we went home. Lauren is talking about Jaxon as if he can't hear a word she's saying. I'm not terribly worried because I've never seen her more than endearingly tipsy, and I'm sure if she has anything further to say it will be something about how Jaxon's good enough for her sister, and that she sanctions the union – or words to that effect. I'm not about to tell him that she'd sanctioned the union of his predecessors, too.

But she proves me wrong, and I am completely unprepared for the next words that spill, uncensored, from her lips.

'All right then.' She takes a sip of her champagne. 'I think you'll do. Jaxon, if we give it another go, you can be our baby's daddy.'

12

Rose
Sydney, 1923

'Oh, I am so excited, Alec,' I say. The crystal tank is complete at last. They have even constructed a tower with a diving board, not six tiers high like the one at The Dom, where we have been practising every day, but certainly high enough and, by all accounts, almost as solid. The tank is now filled with water heated to seventy-four degrees Fahrenheit and waiting for us to test it. If all goes well – and it must, if I am to get Walter over the line – it will form the centrepiece for our extravaganza.

As we enter the warehouse, I see Walter in consultation with some helpers. Eddie was supposed to be here, but his leg is troubling him and he's laid up. It is an unusually warm day, all the doors of the warehouse are thrown open. Bell is seated on the top row of tiered seating, temporarily erected to provide everyone with a good view of our act. She has her notebook and is busy with her pencil. Alec and I climb the ladder to the surface of the water.

'Ready?' he asks.

He will enter here, at the surface. I will climb further up the ladder and dive in from the diving board.

'As I'll ever be.'

He laughs and slides into the water, then swims to the centre and treads water, waiting while I climb to the diving board above. I wait until everyone is seated with Bell. Then I look down, and Alec waves to signal he's ready. I'm not the nervous type and I've certainly jumped from heights before, and yet I feel a little shiver run through me. I breathe in deeply, exhale, then I gather myself and run seven steps along the board. I touch the end of it with one foot, arc my arms overhead. I leap towards the light and for the briefest moment I am a wingless bird, born of joy. Then I twist, turning mid-flight towards the slate blue below.

I break the surface with my clasped hands. Bubbles effervesce along my arms and through my hair, soda down my sides. Water fills my vision, silences my ears. A piece Mother wrote for the pianoforte dances inexplicably in my head.

Alec is there behind me, just where he should be. He takes my hand, pulls me towards him, lets me out again. I swirl like a top from the ribbon of his outstretched arm. We dance together and apart. The light shafts between us and we are as bright and gay as Mother's music.

He takes me to the bottom, draws me to his waist. I arch my back, curve my spine, my head arcing to greet my toes, I am an inverted crescent moon. His cold lips find my neck. I pretend no interest, breaking away to lead the swim back to the surface, as I must. I scissor and turn. I am swimming upwards and away. He follows in my wake. He is just behind me. Scissor and turn. I feel him in the pull of the water. I break the surface.

But something is not right.

I hear an angry crack and then the water is dragging me back under. It is roaring over me, surging around me. I am tumbling like a barrel over Niagara Falls and then I am pulled down, down, into a spin that is not of my own making.

My lungs are bursting. I can't breathe. The water is staining red. I can't see. Dear God, which way is up? I reach out blindly.

And then, without warning, I am dragged over a fence of sharded glass. My flesh tears, my suit rips. I am taken as if by a giant hand, barrelled over and slammed into the ground.

When I can open my eyes, the world is silent. I pull great gasps of air into my water-logged lungs. After an age, heads circle me, bend down as one to attend me. Words form on lips, I cannot hear them, I don't understand.

I twist my head. Water streams from my mouth. I splutter and cough, but I need an answer to something.

And then I hear the sound of myself screaming, as if from a long way away.

'Alec!'

The Sydney Examiner
Monday, 7th May 1923

DEATH OF ALEXANDER CHARLES GRANTHAM

The Inquest

Finding of Accidental Death

An inquiry into the death of Australasian Olympic swimming champion, Alexander Charles Grantham, on Friday morning before Mr. F.R. Cassidy, coroner.

Rosella Carey, an associate of the deceased, attested that she was a film actress and producer, usually domiciled in USA, but currently living at Fairview, *Point Piper. On Wednesday last, together with Mr Grantham, she was rehearsing an underwater sequence in an aquarium at the Fulham warehouse in Mascot. Miss Carey said she and Mr Grantham were swimming in the newly-constructed glass-walled aquarium, which had a capacity of some 10,000 gallons.*

Miss Carey further attested that the accident happened so quickly she did not immediately understand what was happening but that her manager, Walter Ryan, who was also at the scene, later explained that the sides of the aquarium had burst, and such was the force of the water that she and Mr Grantham were torn over the resultant shattered glass.

Miss Carey was stunned but, other than some superficial lacerations, unharmed. She immediately called out for Mr Grantham, but he did not respond. Mr Carey summoned a doctor, and Dr James Harvey arrived forthwith but found Mr Grantham expired.

DOCTOR'S EVIDENCE

Dr Harvey's evidence, given on the Wednesday of the incident, was produced. Dr Harvey attested that the injuries Mr Grantham received included a ruptured aorta and multiple cuts and abrasions. He noted the shattered remains of the burst aquarium and observed that the floor of the warehouse was awash with bloody water. Dr Harvey found death to have occurred immediately and the cause of death was the ruptured aorta. The injury was consistent with the body having been pulled over the shards of broken glass by the surge of water.

THE CORONER'S FINDING

The coroner found that Alexander Charles Grantham died from the ruptured aorta resulting from accidental injuries sustained when he was pulled over the broken glass sides of an aquarium while rehearsing an underwater swimming sequence with Rosella Carey on Wednesday, 2nd May 1923.

Mr Grantham represented Australasia in swimming and diving at the 1920 Summer Olympic Games in Antwerp. Together with his teammates, he won a silver medal in the four-by-200 metre men's freestyle relay. He is survived by his parents, John and June Grantham, his sister, Florence, and his family, friends, and fellow Olympians.

Other stories are being written about me, other things are being said. People are holding me responsible for Alec's death. A reporter reignites the story of the car accident in New Zealand . . . it reads as though I recklessly put members of our company at risk, when in reality, it was only myself. I was the only person in the car that day. I was the only one who came within a hair's breadth of death.

These stories damn me for being who I am. They damn me for being an actress, for being successful, for being seen on the arms of numerous Hollywood men, for being, the papers imply, a strumpet, a woman not to be trusted. A dangerous woman.

The reports arouse something in Walter I have not seen before. There is a fierce light in his eyes. He says we must stop the gossip in its tracks, at once, and the best way to do that, the only way, is to marry without delay. It will show people that he for one does not fear me, that there is nothing to fear. It will show people that he, my longstanding manager and business partner, believes both incidents were accidents – for who would marry a woman believing she had a hand in a death such as Alec's? And finally, it will show people that the gossip columnists had it all wrong – that it was not Alec I have been in love with all these years, but him.

'If we prove them wrong on that,' he says, 'people will doubt all the rest.'

My eyes fill with tears at his loyalty, and love, I suppose you would call it. He comforts me, pulls my head to his shoulder, wipes tears from my eyes with his monogrammed kerchief. He is so dear to me, the scent of him so reassuringly familiar.

And so, we marry at the Registry Office in Elizabeth Street, Bell and Eddie our only witnesses. I want no publicity, but Walter insists. That is the whole point of getting married, he says. I am so heartbroken and so afraid, his words don't wound as they otherwise might. He is right. We have no sentimental reason to marry, we are simply signalling to the world that we are together, united, in business and in life. It is not just my reputation that is at stake now, and as much as I might, in ordinary circumstances, rail against this fact, I feel at risk. For if people believe I had something to do with the death of one of their favourite sons, might they want to take revenge?

I need Walter's protection.

As my wedding day comes to a close, I go down to the ballroom, still in the sheath of oyster satin Bell had quietly wrapped me in this morning. She had sewn little satin bud roses into the dropped waist, draped tulle over my arms and stitched it in place. It is not the dress I would have worn to the society wedding I might have had, but it is elegant and beautiful. Before we entered the registry this morning, she passed me a little bird made of fabric, stuffed with cotton, and looped with a length of thin blue ribbon. 'It's a willie wagtail,' she whispered. 'For luck.' And our eyes filled with tears as I slipped it on over my wrist.

Now, I turn at the sound of the ballroom door opening. For a moment he just stands in the doorway looking at me, then he says a single word, my name.

I can't think of how to respond. I have no words anymore. He comes to stand by my side, not quite touching me. We watch the light slowly disappear from the sky outside the long windows, and as the room darkens, I hear myself begin to keen. At the very first sound of it, he turns to me. I am sinking, I am crumbling, I am folding into him. I am in his arms, my face wet with tears against his chest.

'Shhh,' he says softly. 'I am here.'

'It's my fault,' I sob. 'It's all my fault.'

'No,' he soothes, lifting my face and framing it in his hands, his thumbs smoothing the path of my tears, 'it is not.'

'How can I go on?' I plead. 'The extravaganza was my idea. I insisted we trial the aquarium with a routine. We should have just tested the waters first, a few practice swims. The newspaper is right . . . I dictated all the specifications. I should have inspected it myself. How can I live with myself? If not for me—'

'You mustn't think like that.' He runs his thumb over my lips as if to stop the words.

'I can't help it,' I hiccup, and my legs give way underneath me.

He gathers me bodily in his arms then, carries me close against his rower's chest, up the three flights of stairs to his bedroom. He lays me on the bed, comes to lie beside me, turns me into him.

'I loved him,' I cry. 'I loved him, loved him, loved him and now he's gone.'

I search his eyes and I believe they are as anguished as mine. 'I know,' he says quietly. 'I'm so sorry, Rose.'

I pull myself close to him, move to wrap my legs around him. I need him, all of him. I need the living, breathing comfort of a man like him.

'No, darling,' he says softly. 'Not like this, not in grief. 'Let me just . . . take care of you.'

Then he pulls my head onto his shoulder and he holds me, all night long, his soft voice in my ear until, exhausted, I sleep.

13

Emma
Sydney, 2024

'I'm sorry,' Lauren says, 'but for the hundredth time, I was drunk.'

It's morning, we are home, and we are both stone cold sober. I get out of our bed without speaking and go to the bathroom. My face in the mirror is tired, furious, ugly. I pull open the bathroom cabinet and find the toothpaste, then squeeze a layer over the bristles of my toothbrush.

My wife fully intends to do another round and/or she wants to fuck her sister's fiancé.

I hunch over the sink, brushing my teeth furiously as my tears fall onto the white porcelain. I don't want her to see me wounded like this.

Julia, bless her, had laughed uproariously, trying to turn Lauren's comment into a huge joke. Jaxon and I knew the best thing to do in the circumstances was to join in the hilarity. But I didn't find it funny. Many a true word is said in jest. And for all that he openly admired Lauren, I don't think Jaxon found it funny either.

'I need some time out,' I say, when I'm finished in the bathroom.

She props herself up on her elbows. 'What does that mean?'

'That means either you go out today or I do. You choose.'

'Fine,' she says, pushing the sheets down with her bare feet and jumping out of bed. 'I'll go.'

Later, after she has left the apartment, I slide open the doors to the balcony and pause for a moment to take in the air. The breeze gathers up the salt from the harbour at the end of the street, making it somehow easier to breathe.

I can't keep worrying the issue; I have to do something to take my mind off it. But what?

Rose Carey's box of tricks.

As I open the door to the shed, I inhale a peculiar smell. I should probably google the cause of that later. Right now, I'm keen to get back to 1923. I switch on the fluoro light and take the box from the shelf, resolving to inspect the photographs first.

They are all of a similar size and shape, faded but in good condition, and all of the same person. I'm not yet an expert on the features and form of Miss Rose Carey, but if I had to guess, these pictures of a naked, thirty-something woman, taken from a respectable distance, are her.

The photos are not lewd, but there is something not quite as tasteful about them as the photo of Rose sitting in a tree with carefully arranged chiffon. Here, there is no attempt to hide her breasts, no attempt to hide anything, in fact, except perhaps her face, which is turned slightly away from the camera, looking over her right shoulder. In one of the photos, the woman is wearing a tall headdress. It looks like part of some kind of theatrical costume. But again, her face is . . . blurred is the only word for it.

I put the photos down and pull a letter out of the bundle. This one is just a single sheet of paper.

The Carrington Hotel
Tuesday, 6th November 1923

Dear Birdy,

Nothing was an accident, we all know that now, but . . .

I should tell you everything. I keep stopping and starting. I don't know what to say, how to explain it all. I can't seem to write the words. I will soon, though. I promise.

For now, just know that I love you.

Me.

On the first Wednesday of every month, I go to a hotel in Darlinghurst with my boss, Johnno. It's a nice old pub, refurbished, and like a lot of places around here, it is laid out over several storeys. On the floor above us there's a rooftop terrace with a pretty decent view of the city. Wednesday night is ten-dollar-margarita night, and while I'm not really into cocktails, for ten dollars, I make an exception.

'Cheers,' Johnno says, clinking his Tooheys New against my glass, after giving my drink the look he thinks it deserves.

'Cheers,' I echo, without much enthusiasm.

But it's our shared interest in environmental issues that brings us here, not the view from the terrace or the cheap margaritas. Once a month, student environmentalists, studying at various campuses around the city, deliver talks on their work. Although still students, Johnno firmly believes that these are the people who will ultimately direct our environmental future and we all need to start listening to what they have to say, as soon as they start saying it. I agree.

'So,' he says, 'which of tonight's topics grabs you?'

I look down at the program. 'They all sound good.'

He nods, pushing the sleeves of his checked shirt up to his elbows. 'You know, I used to wonder if the marine plastic bag thing was real. It all seemed a bit fishy to me, pardon the pun.'

I blink. It's an unusual thing for him to say. 'What are you talking about?'

'Settle down, Em, hear me out.'

I give him a little sniff of disapproval, but cooperate. 'Okay . . .'

'So, back in the day, the supermarkets gave shopping bags away, right? However many you wanted, whenever you wanted. They didn't give a damn.'

'Yeah, so?'

'So, suddenly they about-faced and gave a damn? I don't bloody think so.'

I frown, trying to follow his reasoning. 'You're going to have to do more to catch me up on this one.'

He puts his beer on the counter with an emphatic thud. 'Well, it strikes me that one day they looked at the books and they went, "Hey, these plastic bags are costing us a bloody fortune. Huge cost centre right there. Why are we giving these things away for free?"'

'Ah.'

'Yeah. So, some bright spark says, "Well, we'd better start charging for 'em," right?'

'Right, which is what they did.'

'Actually, that's not entirely what they did.'

'What do you mean? Most supermarkets charge for bags now. Where are you shopping?'

'Well, they're pretty smart in those city offices.' He taps his nose with his forefinger. 'Someone probably said something like, "If we start charging people for something we've been giving away free for donkey's years, on the pretext that we don't want to anymore, all hell is going to break loose."'

He has a point.

'So, what'd they do?' he asks, rocking back a little dangerously on his bar stool.

'They changed the bags and made us pay for them.'

'That's right, but – and here's the sneaky part, or genius, depending on your viewpoint – they told us the reason was concern for the environment. Concern for the environment, my arse.'

He's right, and the fact that he's right puts my blood on a slow boil. 'They turned a cost centre into a profit centre,' I say.

'Boom.' He rocks back to the counter and picks up his drink again. 'Seems like more people should be making more noise about stuff like that, don't you reckon?'

He seems to be making some kind of point, but I don't quite understand what it is. 'Yep,' I agree.

He gets up off his bar stool. 'Come on, the room is filling up. Let's find ourselves a pew.'

Afterwards, we walk down to Central together to catch the light rail home.

'What'd you make of all that?' he asks.

'Enlightening.'

'Yeah.'

'You?'

'Yep, same.'

He pauses to look at me, a speculative look in his eyes. 'We could all be doing better.'

I'm still confused – he already knows we both think that.

'Yes.'

'You'd be on board with that, right?'

Now I'm even more confused. 'Sure. Of course.'

After we part ways, I think about what he's said. We could all certainly do better for the environment. Which makes my decision about the Hot Rain opportunity the right one, I reason.

Allie had sent me the brief for the opportunity, but it had done nothing to whet my appetite. I'd only had the stomach to read the first few paragraphs. Under the heading 'Call for Expressions of Interest' in what I'd call a blocky, radio-inspired font, were the words: *Are you digital and video geniuses, brimming with creative ideas that hit the mark every single time? If that sentence captured your attention, it could be we're looking for you!*

That sentence hadn't captured my attention, unless making me want to vomit counts.

I hadn't even bothered to look for a job description or salary indication before pressing the delete button on the email, because I suspected neither would have been included. As it was a call for expressions of interest, they were more than likely looking for contractors, which means I'd have to set the terms, conditions and pricing. I'm not willing to do that, because I can't afford the level of insecurity that comes with contract work. I'm also pretty certain I wouldn't fit the Hot Rain mould.

I look down at my outfit. There's nothing wrong with it. I'm wearing a bright but simple little dress, a cropped denim jacket and sensible shoes – I knew we would be walking to and from the station. I have slung my satchel-style vegan leather handbag over one shoulder. I think I look good, but not in a Hot Rain kind of way. I don't have even a smidgeon of Cara Reed or Nat Taglieri, two of Hot Rain's hottest, rainiest personalities, about me.

The job was so 'not me' that I didn't even discuss it with Lauren. I stop for a moment under the neon lights of the 7-Eleven to adjust my bra strap. Lauren would think it was an amazing opportunity. Why don't I?

It's not as though Hot Rain has a bad corporate reputation – quite the reverse. Its values which, all right, I'd skipped ahead to read on the brief, didn't raise any red flags with me, and I know, from when Lauren first showed me Allie's Hot Rain profile, that there is an acknowledgement to country on its website. A 'giving back' culture also seems to be encouraged. Those sorts of things are important to me. It's just that overall, Hot Rain seems so, well . . . embarrassingly enthusiastic.

But if I don't want to work at Hot Rain and I can't earn the kind of money I need from the work I'm currently doing, what do I want to do?

I want to do something that makes a difference, I realise. When did I stop focusing on that? Actually, I can probably pinpoint the exact time. It was the moment we started IVF.

It's not good enough, I decide. While it's understandable that I've been focusing my intellectual, not to mention emotional, attention on the process that might one day deliver us the child we dreamed of, I don't think it's been healthy for me.

Hammer and Tongs has, increasingly, been doing more interesting things and tonight, I think Johnno had been hinting at something. Perhaps a potential new gig that he doesn't feel at liberty to discuss yet. I make a mental note to talk to him about it later.

It's late when I arrive home, but Lauren is still up, marking papers in the study. The room is poky; there's only space for the one desk and one chair, which Lauren and I share. She stores her rose-gold MacBook Air in one of the desk drawers, bringing it in and out as required, and I do the same with my laptop, which I connect to the two larger screens on the desk. It's easier for editing.

There is still a little bit of tension between us, fallout from the engagement party. She doesn't look up to say hello, so I decide to make the first move. 'Hi, honey, I'm home.'

She glances at me briefly. My attempt at levity has fallen flat, as I knew it would. Behind her reading glasses, her eyes are frozen green. 'Hi.'

It looks like I'll need an ice pick if I want to chat. 'I'm going to make myself a cuppa – do you want anything?'

'No.' She looks pointedly at her half empty coffee mug. She never drinks caffeine this late unless she's snowed under with work, so perhaps that accounts for the monosyllabic answers.

'Okay, it's just me, then.'

She nods and returns to her marking. It's going to be a long night. I pull off my shoes and throw them into the hall cupboard, then I shut the door, head for the kitchen, and flick on the kettle.

I go to open the fridge door. Stuck to it, secured by a real estate agent's magnetised calendar, is a printout of an email addressed to Lauren.

Hey, How did Em go with the Hot Rain opportunity?

Fuck.

I take the email off the fridge and read it all the way through. She'd folded it so I would read the initial inquiry first. What follows is a long series of predictable questions.

Lauren: *What Hot Rain opportunity?*
Allie: *Oops, sorry, forget I spoke.*
Lauren: *WHAT HOT RAIN OPPORTUNITY?*
Allie: *Sorry, can't share. But maybe ask her?*
Lauren: *When did you send it to her?*
Allie: *After the engagement party.*
Lauren: *Is the opportunity still available?*
Allie: *Talk to her, babe.*

Fuck, fuck, fuck and by the way, fuck.

I go back to stand in the study doorway. 'Well, this is very passive aggressive, Lauren,' I say, waving it at her. I hope she hears what I don't add: *and childish.*

'The alternative,' she says, 'is aggressive aggressive.' She puts her red pen down carefully next to the pile of papers she is marking.

'Right,' I say. *Fuck,* I think again, bracing myself for the onslaught that I know is about to come.

'Were you ever going to discuss it with me?'

'Probably not.' I try to be scrupulously honest with her – even though I recognise that I have been lying by omission.

There's a long silence. 'You've already made up your mind.'

'Yes.' I certainly have made up my mind. I'm just not a Hot Rain person, and I think working for them would make me miserable.

'Did you even read the opportunity?' She picks up her pen again and starts tapping the tip on the desktop. Then she looks back up at me.

Not properly, no, I find myself thinking. *I couldn't get past all the 'brilliant', 'magic', 'peppy' bullshit.*

'Have you?' I prevaricate, playing for time.

She shakes her head. 'She wouldn't send it to me. But whatever it is, it's Hot Rain. It's obviously going to be a brilliant opportunity.'

'Well, if you had been able to read it, you'd realise they're looking for contractors.' I'm saying this so that she will think I've properly considered it. But I'm also saying it because she knows as well as I do that contract work doesn't have the same level of security as a job.

'So what? This is Hot Rain, for fuck's sake, not some start-up. You could probably name your own price, make it worth our while. It's a huge company, you could probably charge a small fortune. But you're not even going to try, are you?'

'Lauren, I can't do this,' I say. My hand is starting to itch and when I look down at it, I see a faint rash.

'What can't you do?'

I step out of the doorway. I can't keep looking into those fierce green eyes of hers. It's not just an emotional reaction, it's a physical one. I lean against the doorway, feeling slightly dizzy and a bit sick, tired and spent. 'It's not the right fit.'

'How would you know it's not the right fit? You haven't even met these people.'

Oh, but I have. They run radio programs like *The Show* with Gina Glamorazzi and *The Best Little Breakfast Gig in Town* with Peaches and Flanno. Glamorazzi, Peaches, Flanno – for heaven's sake, what kind of names are they? And how much more do I need to know in order to recognise that they are not going to be my kind of people?

'I don't have to meet them, do I?' What I mean is, I don't have to meet them to know that it's not the right fit. What she hears is, I don't have to meet them, period.

'No, you do not,' she says, neatening the pile of papers on the desk.

She's furious. I can tell by the way she pulls the lid off the top of the pen and snaps it back on over the tip. But I suspect that part of the reason she is so furious is because she knows I'm right. Hot Rain would be all wrong for me.

14

Rose
Sydney, 1923

'We are going to have to find some money for the Olympic Ball,' I inform Walter. We are in the sitting room, overlooking the harbour. The French doors are partly open and the white lace curtains are rising and falling on a cool breeze.

'Rose,' he says gently. He doesn't want to say no to me, especially given how low I've been since Alec's death, but he shakes his head and smooths his moustache in a gesture I recognise as grave concern, then says it anyway. 'There is no money, and we cannot stay here, certainly not until October.'

'Well.' I sit down next to him on the settee. 'You may say that, but I refuse to be cowed. I refuse to let fear and a lack of funds stop me from doing what I want to do, what I must do, to honour Alec's memory. I mean to do as I say.'

He turns in his seat, dislodging the lace-edged antimacassar draped over the arm of the settee. The look in his eyes is as gentle as his words, but it doesn't prevent him from saying,

'So do I. It is foolish to stay here, Rose, and I believe it is also . . . dangerous.'

I briefly close my eyes. When I open them again, I say, 'Is it foolish and dangerous, Walter, or are we just spooked? Is someone really trying to ruin us, or are we being a little paranoid because we have had such a terrible run of things?'

He pauses before saying, 'I think there are too many "terrible things" for it not to be a concerted effort to ruin us.'

I resolve to do what I always do when I must face my fears. I will dissect them one by one. This time, I will dissect them with him.

I turn towards him. It's a small settee, but our knees don't quite touch. 'First of all,' I say, 'the incident in New Zealand . . . That was my fault.'

I sense he wants to shake his head, but he keeps it rigidly still.

'I've been in trouble in the States for driving too fast and something like that was bound to happen. I could excuse myself, but excusing myself is what would be dangerous.'

The look on his face as I accept responsibility for my actions tells me that either he still doesn't think the responsibility lies with me . . . or he wonders if I have truly learnt my lesson . . . which is it?

I don't want to be the cause of such anxiety for someone I care so much about and so I quickly add, 'I have learned my lesson, Walter, I promise, and as a result, I will be much more careful.'

He shakes his head ever so slightly. 'I know you will, Rose.' But the look on his face does not change one iota.

'Number two,' I say, with less confidence, 'Alec's death was ruled accidental.' I clear my throat. It has been over a month since he died and I wonder whether the pain of it will ever diminish, even a little.

'That is what was ruled,' he says. 'It does not mean that is what it was.'

I bite my lip, but press on. 'As for the lesser things. The gossip in the newspapers against me was just that. Malicious gossip, to be sure, but still just gossip all the same, and our marriage has settled things down a bit, just as we hoped.'

He attempts a smile. 'Is our marriage a lesser thing, Rose?' he queries.

I'm appalled that he would take it that way. 'No,' I say quickly. 'Not at all. It is a very important thing. It has helped us enormously, don't you think?' With those words I feel that I have somehow made things worse.

'Oh yes,' he agrees. 'It's certainly stemmed the worst of the gossip about you.' It's true, yet he doesn't sound sincere. I have the feeling he thinks, as he thought when I proposed to him, that all the benefits of our marriage apply only to me. He's right in one sense. We do not share more than we did before we married. We do not, for example, share the same bed, even though I'm sure he knows I would like to. He has made no conjugal demands of me, no demands at all, really – except for constantly saying that we should return to the States.

'That's what we needed it to do,' I remind him. 'For the sake of the company and for our future.'

'Of course,' he agrees, still with the same pasted-on smile.

I clear my throat again. 'The missing props,' I continue, 'that was theft, pure and simple, perhaps by someone from Mayfields, perhaps not.'

He nods. 'And the funds that have gone missing from our bank account?' he asks. 'What do you make of that, Rose?'

'Well . . . that is the only real mystery,' I say slowly.

He says nothing, he only shakes his head.

I intended to search his face for answers but I find myself distracted. The memory of our first kiss returns to me so suddenly that it floods me with unexpected longing.

'We must carry on,' I say, but my voice sounds whispery soft. I realise I am leaning towards him. We are sitting so closely together that I can smell the bay rum of his aftershave and it is intoxicating.

'We must find out what is going on,' he corrects, and there is nothing breathless or intoxicated about his voice. He is firm and direct. 'I still believe someone is trying to harm you, Rose.'

His words douse the flame that had threatened to spark inside me and I sit back into my corner of the settee. It unsettles me, that all my rationalising has done is convince Walter that I am at risk.

I take a moment to collect myself and then I say, 'It has simply been a bad year.'

He shakes his head again. 'Too many things have happened for it to be merely a bad year,' he says. 'I believe the safest – and smartest – thing to do is to go back to America.'

All the remaining heat ebbs out of me and a cool finger runs down my spine. I stand up and begin pacing the room.

'I've made a promise to the committee, I've made a promise to myself, I've made a promise to—' I don't finish the sentence, but I know he hears the name anyway . . . Alec.

'Circumstances have changed,' he says, his voice now even firmer than before. 'The committee will understand why you can't honour that promise. They may even be a little . . . relieved.'

'What are you saying?' There is a rough edge to my voice as I come to a stop in front of him. 'Are you saying they won't want me on the committee anymore? Are you saying they won't want to be associated with me?'

'No, I'm not saying that.' He stands up and comes towards me, reaching for my hand. It feels both comforting and somehow alarming. It is grief that makes my next words sound so harsh; an anguish so awful, it makes me angry.

'I don't care if circumstances have changed. I don't care if people will understand. I don't care if they want me to disappear. I am a member of the committee, and I will not be usurped. I am also a person of my word. I will not renege on a promise.'

It comes in waves, this fierce thing called grief. I can be travelling along quite nicely and then suddenly I am tossed about and dumped on the shore. Other times, when I least expect it, a single tear will fall from the corner of my eye and roll silently down my cheek. I have to explain it away – a speck of dust, an errant eyelash.

'You know, Rose,' he says slowly, and I am angry too that he sees the grief in me, understands it. 'You have always been so practical, so sensible. I have always greatly admired those qualities.'

'What is that supposed to mean?'

He gives me a long look, but we have always spoken plainly to each other, even in the most difficult of circumstances, and so he continues. 'If you refuse to see the danger to yourself, can you at least see that we cannot afford for you to keep your promise?' He is now stroking circles on the soft flesh of my palm, beneath my thumb. 'There simply is no money for that.'

I'm not sure what disturbs me more – the truth in his words, or his touch. I snatch my hand away and rub at it furiously, as if I might erase the memory of his fingers on my skin. 'Well, speaking *practically*,' I snap, 'people are depending on me. Australia is depending on me. This Ball might mean the difference between our athletes going to the Olympic Games and not – do you realise that?' It desperately matters to me that they go. If Alec were here, he would want that too. If Alec were here . . .

He sighs. 'Rose, that is not your responsibility.'

'Not my responsibility? Of course it's my responsibility.' I begin to pace again.

'I understand that you made a commitment – although I did warn you that we don't have access to our funds, well before Alec's . . .' he can't say the word, I realise, substituting 'death' with 'accident', even though he's just implied he doesn't believe it was one. 'I understand that you feel honour-bound to fulfil that commitment. But someone else will step up—'

Someone else? No, absolutely not, not in a million years. 'Have someone else step in and take my place? I couldn't bear it.'

'You are going to have to bear it,' he says, and his tone is still so firm yet . . . as smooth as silk. He has a beautiful voice I realise, irrelevantly. 'You are going to have to accept that when there is a problem that is not, in fact, your problem, you don't always have to be the person to solve it. We should have gone home weeks ago—'

'Sydney is my home,' I say, staring down at him. 'And I will keep my promise to the committee. I'll use my own money if I have to, the money my father left me.'

It's my final card. The money I'm talking about is in what I think of as an emergency fund, a little account that I have here in Australia. I've never touched it.

His look is long and speculative, and for a moment the ground underneath me seems to shift. 'Are you sure you want to do that, Rose?'

'I'm very sure,' I say, in my surest, most assertive voice. It's the voice I use when I am least sure of anything, but I don't think Walter knows that, not even after all the time he's known me.

'Okay,' he says. For a moment I think he'll return to the library and the company's books, but he pauses for a moment. 'Like it or not, the film does need to go back to the States now – there's work to do. You know that. We can't stay here forever.'

'Go now yourself, if you must,' I say, folding my arms. 'I won't be going with you.'

'At least it's not raining,' says Bell.

True, but after a mild autumn, June has turned suddenly bitter. It is so cold today, I have had to don my blue and black brocade coat with its fox fur collar, and my grey-blue Fifth Avenue cloche hat.

A doorman takes our coats, and our hats at the door of the Cavalier Restaurant on King Street.

'Miss Lewis's meeting is taking place in the Supper Room, madam,' the doorman says. 'Please follow me.'

I brace myself. Will they all welcome me?

But Walter had nothing to fear. Miss April Lewis, the committee chair, had been a friend of my mother's and she makes a great point of greeting me enthusiastically as I enter the room. 'My dear,' she says, taking my face in her hands and kissing me on both cheeks, 'We are all so terribly sorry to hear of your recent terrible . . . sadness.'

I feel my eyes begin to sting with tears. I try to blink them away. She sees my struggle and rescues me. 'But so pleased to hear of your nuptials. I hope you and Mr Ryan will be very happy.'

'Thank you,' I hear myself say.

'Come,' she says, taking my hand and in doing so, sending a clear signal to everyone in the room. There are quite a few women, I note, including Bonnie Spark, the reporter from *Life & Times*.

'Sit next to me. I saved you a place.' She has a seat at the head of the table, which is covered with a starched white cloth, enlivened by a vase of bright yellow and orange Iceland poppies, sprigged with white gypsophila. The place she has saved for me is at her right hand.

I glance at Bell and she gives me a small smile, moving to the opposite end of the table to take her place.

The rest of the esteemed company, most of whom I know, greet me well enough. There is much discussion on the format of the proposed Ball, and who will take on what roles, and then, as a further signal that I am to be treated with respect and kindness, Miss Lewis invites me to put forward my thoughts on entertainment for the Ball.

As I stand up to speak, the door opens. A late entrant enters the room and my hands begin to tremble.

It simply cannot be . . .

Alec.

~

'Oh, Mr Griffin.' April Lewis is gushing, and her words break the spell. 'I am so glad you could join us, and you are just in time. Miss Carey is about to speak. She's agreed to lead the pageant for the Ball. Sit down, sit down, dear man, there is a vacant chair.' She gestures to it.

Now that I understand he is not Alec, I want to leave the room. I'm not sure how I'm expected to go on.

'I apologise for my rudeness, Miss Carey,' he says with what he probably thinks is a disarming grin. 'But better late than never, I hope?'

He runs his words together like a San Franciscan, smashing the last of my illusions to smithereens. Cocky. That's what we'd call him here in Australia.

'Of course, perfectly fine, Mr Griffin. I am just about to begin.' My voice is even and strong.

There's a silence, into which he inserts the scraping of his chair as he sits down.

I pause, and then clear my throat. 'Ladies and gentlemen, what a wonderful thing it is to be Australian. Although I now spend much of my time in America, Australia is unquestionably my home.'

A quiet round of applause. I use it to blank my mind. I must focus.

Oh, but Mr Griffin has reminded me so much of Alec, it's as though he is standing here beside me, hovering like a spectre in the corner.

'We have so much to be proud of.' I marvel that I can still speak with such purpose, with the memories that are starting to collapse over each other in my head. How will I ever go on without him?

'But when it comes to sport, we do have rather the short end of the stick. Our athletes do not have the same access to training or even equipment that other nations enjoy. That is why I believe we must work hard, very hard indeed, on their behalf.'

Another round of hearty applause.

'If we are to compete on the world stage, which I say we must, then we need to put in our very best efforts to raise funds, not just for their passage but for their every need.'

'Hear, hear,' says Miss Lewis, smoothing the serviette she has laid over her side plate.

'They must not have cause to worry about a thing except honing their skills. I firmly believe we can do that with our Olympic Ball. In fact, I will go so far as to say I think tickets will sell out. I look around this table and what do I see? Patriots. Make no mistake, everyday Australians are just as patriotic as we are. They will want to support our athletes in their noble sporting endeavours.'

'Hear, hear,' Miss Lewis says again.

'That said, I would like to move that patriotism be the theme for the Olympic Ball.'

'I second the motion. All in favour say "aye",' says Miss Lewis, and the motion is carried.

'And another order of business, if I may . . .' Walter is right – I cannot fund the entertainment, as I suspect people might be expecting. I cannot afford to purchase props and I have none to loan. I cannot front the cost of musicians or dancers.

'In order to make this event a spectacular visual and fiscal success, I propose we host an auction, to raise the funds to produce it. Any leftover monies could be added to the athletes' purse.'

This motion, too, is unanimously carried. It is agreed the auction will be held in a month's time, some three months before the Ball, which will be held at the Town Hall in early October. The pageant will be a series of sets produced by various groups, organised by each of those present, all official Olympic Ball committee members. Each group will receive some of the fundraising to pay for their entertainment set and will make up any difference themselves. Each member also commits to selling 150 tickets to the Ball, which will total 1500. It's a lofty goal, but I think it's achievable.

'Well done,' says Bonnie Spark as she passes me on her way out.

I smile back at her. 'Thank you,'

'We women, we can conquer the world now, can't we?' she says with a wink.

I laugh. 'We can try.'

With April Lewis's help, I have successfully wooed Sydney's elite, potentially won a newspaper ally, and solved the money question Walter was so concerned about. Perhaps now, he will agree to stay on.

15

Emma
Sydney, 2024

There is no other word for the way I'm feeling about my conversation – or non-conversation, really – with Lauren, than furious. She's clearly going to sit at her desk until she's finished her work, so I wander out to the balcony. I don't even bother to take in the view – I know where I'm headed. In the shed, I open the crate and retrieve a couple more of Rose's letters.

The Carrington Hotel
Saturday, 17th November 1923

Dear Birdy,

I want to tell you how it all began. I want to explain what happened, and even though I know I should begin at the beginning, somehow I can't. The only place I can start is that day at the Cavalier. You must remember it. It was the day we first met Griff.

As we discussed later, when he entered the room, I thought he was Alec . . . But what I didn't tell you was just how much I truly believed he was Alec. I had to bite my lip to stop myself from calling out his name. In that brief, delusional moment, I felt light, the way I used to feel before . . . before everything happened. When we were younger, and life was kinder. Remember those days?

For just that fractured moment, I was convinced that Alec . . . why, he must just have been missing, that's all, the way a soldier is missing sometimes, but then turns up again, unexpectedly. I know how silly that sounds, but we had all heard the war stories, we had read about them in the newspapers, and I so wanted to believe.

It was only a moment.

Then he smiled, and still I was deluded. You can't blame me. After the meeting, you remarked on the likeness yourself . . . He had the same kind of laughter lines about the corners of his eyes, and those eyes . . . they were the same water grey . . .

It was his eyes that brought me to my senses. Water . . . I heard again the cannonball crack of the aquarium exploding and the furious protest of dammed water suddenly set free. Even now, all these months later, I am rendered deaf by the memory of it.

As reality returned to me, I couldn't breathe, I couldn't speak. I couldn't even look away.

Then he said, 'I apologise for my rudeness.' And in that moment, I realised he was not Alec after all, for that was not his voice. There was not the same cadence to it, there was no larrikin lilt. You know Alec had such a way of talking.

I remember gripping my hands together, scratching the backs of them with my fingernails. I remember I wanted to tear my skin, make it bleed. I felt I must, because if I did not, I might do something even more dreadful. I might cry, right there in my place at the table. No, worse than that, I might sob.

I had seen Alec pulled from the crystal tank myself, I had seen the knife of glass in his chest, I had seen the rivers of his blood, the vacant staring of his eyes. How had I fooled myself, even for a moment?

But you see . . . I so desperately wanted to . . .

I remember pleading with God then, as I have pled a thousand times since. Let it not be true. Let it all be a terrible dream. Let me wake up and everything be as it once was. I blamed myself, you see, and I know that later, you blamed me too.

But you must also know that if I could, I would reverse those minutes, just before he took the plunge. I would have raised a warning – I still would, to this very day. Why is it so much to ask of the universe, to reverse those minutes? Who would miss them? I could simply unpick them, you know I could do it without leaving a single mark. Nobody would ever need to know.

I wanted to write it all down tonight, but I find I cannot. I'll write again soon though, tell you the rest of it. I promise.

Love, Me.

The Carrington Hotel
Tuesday, 20th November 1923

Dear Birdy,

I want you to know that when he introduced himself to me, that day at the Cavalier, I wasn't the least bit interested in him personally. I was so distressed by his resemblance to Alec that I didn't want to meet him at all, but he was just so insistent. What could I do anyway? April Lewis had insisted he sit next to me. I remember him extending his right hand and saying, 'John James Griffin – but please call me Griff'.

Whenever I hear his name now, a little thrill runs through me, but not then. Or maybe that's a lie, maybe a little thrill always ran through me. All I remember is I didn't want to shake his hand – but I did, of course. I asked him straight away what he was doing at the Cavalier, but he just laughed and sat back in his chair and said he was there to help with organising the Ball, same as the rest of us. He did have a wicked kind of look in his eye though, when he said it. I remember thinking he had a fine opinion of himself. But why wouldn't he? He's so damn handsome, even you can't say any differently.

I also tried to uncover how he managed to even be in the room, and he said it was all Miss Lewis's doing. I wasn't afraid to ask her about it, you know me, but at that moment she was engrossed in a discussion with Miss Spark, from Life & Times *and I knew she wouldn't be interrupted for love nor money.*

So, I kept on trying to gather more information. I was doing all this for us, that's the honest truth, and remember, I told you all he revealed to me that very day. I asked where he was from and he said San Francisco, although I'd already picked up on that, and then he told me about being a fighter pilot in the war. I have to tell you, I took all that with a grain of salt at the time. Some people say they were war heroes when they were nothing of the kind, as we both now know. But as we both also now know, he wasn't exaggerating. And then I asked him what a San Franciscan war hero was doing in Sydney, and he made this cheeky remark about wanting to rule the theatrical world from Australia, or something like that.

That's when April Lewis's ears pricked up. She said how wonderful it was to have Mayfields and Carey & Ryan working together on the Ball!

It was only then that I realised he was the new manager of Mayfields, our number one rival this side of the equator, and if you remember, I also told you that at the first opportunity. I did not conceal a single detail about that encounter.

Miss Lewis prattled on and on about how wonderful he is, what an asset he would be. Really, she is quite incorrigible, and I don't believe for a moment that she innocently threw us all together.

I believe she did it on purpose – to hedge her bets, if you ask me. Sure, she was nice as pie, but she's shrewd, and I think she invited Griff in case we hightailed it back to the USA, for any reason . . . Do you blame her? I don't know, we might have done the same in her shoes. She wanted the best Ball in the world, she didn't want anything to derail it, and she got what she wanted, didn't she? In the end.

Oh, but even thinking of the Ball makes the anxiety gnaw at my throat . . .

I must go. I will write again soon.

Please remember that I love you.

Me.

These letters are beginning to affect me in a way that the earlier ones hadn't. Reading about the death of somebody that both the letter writer, presumably Rose Carey, and the unknown recipient clearly knew and loved is distressing, and there is a kind of raw angst in the words, as if Rose felt some level of responsibility that she couldn't yet bear to put in words.

I search through the box and lift out the newspaper clippings. I find one with a headline: DEATH OF ALEXANDER CHARLES GRANTHAM, which tells me the cold hard facts. Then I find another, ON WITH THE SHOW FOR ROSE CAREY, and suddenly I understand her gnawing anxiety.

The Sydney Examiner
Wednesday, 13th June 1923

ON WITH THE SHOW FOR ROSE CAREY

Rose Carey has made her first public appearance only weeks after the coroner ruled the death of her former beau and aquatic partner,

Olympic champion Alexander Grantham, accidental, and barely a month since her hasty marriage to her manager, Walter Ryan.

Mr Grantham's heart was pierced by a shard of glass while rehearsing an underwater sequence in an aquarium which inexplicably shattered. The aquarium, only recently installed, had been designed, manufactured and constructed according to Miss Carey's precise specifications.

Before returning to this hemisphere a year and a half ago, Miss Carey had been a household name in Hollywood. She starred in several moving pictures and was regularly seen in the company of numerous escorts, including a married man.

Her friendship with Mr Grantham, which began right here in Sydney when they were children, reportedly blossomed into love after the pair met up again in America several years ago, and since arriving 'down under' they had been widely rumoured to marry.

Demonstrating a commendable 'show must go on' mentality, Miss Carey said, when asked by your reporter, that she will be working with the Olympic Ball committee, as it is more important to her now 'than anything in the world'.

'I know that my good friend, Alec, would have wanted me to put my every effort into raising funds for the Olympic Ball, so that our sportsmen and women can compete as he did,' she said. 'My commitment to the Ball is in memory of him.'

She would not, however, answer any questions relating to Mr Grantham's fatal accident or how it came to be that the aquarium, so carefully constructed to her own design, might have exploded.

Miss Carey has had more than her fair share of troubles lately. Inquiries into her affairs by your reporter have revealed that while on location in New Zealand last year, Miss Carey, driving at speed, caused a company loan car to crash off a bridge in the South Island, narrowly avoiding tragedy.

What did actually happen back in 1923, I wonder?

I pick up the letters and the clippings, bundle them in my arms and take them inside. The shed isn't exposed to the elements, but I suddenly feel an urge to better protect them.

16

Rose
Sydney, 1923

Bell gets into the seat beside me in the Cadillac. I turn the key and for a moment I sit there, trying to calm my nerves. It is the first time I have sat in the driver's seat since the car accident.

I replay the moment again, as I have replayed it a thousand times. Every time, it is soundless. The tyre blows, the car sways violently to the left, hits the guard rail . . .

'Are you all right?' she says gently.

I turn and stare at her. For a moment I'd forgotten she was here, I'd forgotten everything, except that loose metal road. When they pulled the car from the river, they found a bolt wedged in the rubber. I must have run over it somewhere. I wasn't surprised. Those roads were not great.

'I'm fine.' I press my foot on the clutch, shift the car into gear, and we drive off. It's not very far, I remind myself, and this is Mr and Mrs D's car. It is meticulously maintained, and Eddie himself checks the tyres every day. It had been raining earlier, but it's stopped now, and the road here is infinitely better than the roads around Nelson.

We travel at what for me is a moderate pace, and in an attempt to steer the bad memories away, I say, 'Isn't it time you had a beau, Bell?' The moment the words are out, I realise the truth of them. To my knowledge, she has not had a beau in a long time. I take my eyes briefly off the road to look at her. She presses her lips together in a thin line, staring straight ahead. 'No.'

I look back at the road. I would have to say that Bell is my best friend. She has been by my side through thick and thin. She has sewn my clothes and sorted my paperwork. She has listened tirelessly to my triumphs and my tragedies and given me her honest advice and unwavering support. But I now realise I know very little about her private life.

Because she doesn't have one.

'You don't want a beau?'

'No,' she repeats emphatically.

I could make light of that remark, tell her she's a smart woman, but something makes me ask an even more probing question. 'Have you ever been in love?'

In my peripheral vision, I see her look away from me and out the window.

It's then I realise something else – I've never heard her talk about her family. In fact, the most information she's ever revealed was the day we'd visited the Tivoli storeroom in Surry Hills, and she talked about once living across the road.

'I don't believe so.'

She cranks the window down a little, then lifts a scarf to her lips to keep out the cold and stop the dust from settling on her lipstick.

'Me neither,' I say, over-brightly. 'I do love Walter, but I simply don't believe in falling in love.' We are approaching our destination now and I find myself slowing the car down. 'But you know, you haven't told me much about your life before we met. One day we must sit down and have a good old chinwag about it.'

'I had such an ordinary life before I met you, Rose.' She dabs at her lips again with the scarf. 'There is not much to talk about.' I have no time to contest her remark because Canonbury is up ahead.

'It's quite something, isn't it?' I turn off the engine and we sit in the car for a moment, admiring the gothic-inspired mansion.

The Australian Jockey Club bought Canonbury at the end of the war from theatrical entrepreneur Harry Rickards, to accommodate returned sailors and soldiers who were permanently disabled, those who were unable to care for themselves and who did not have family who could care for them. It is not a charitable institution. It is a fully equipped, fully funded, fully staffed home with a mission to look after our most wounded men, who do not have to pay a penny for either the accommodation or the care. It sits on some of the most prime land in the country and in daylight hours, the view across the harbour is, in my experience, incomparable.

We are here to put on a little light entertainment for the residents. I have been training some local girls for our set at the Olympic Ball, and tonight is a dress rehearsal.

'The girls have come along, haven't they, Bell?'

'Yes,' she agrees. 'With a little bit more training, I think they will do you proud at the Ball. You are an expert teacher, Rose.'

'Thank you, but you know I think the secret of it is that dance is so much fun, don't you think? The ladies we have chosen simply love what they're doing and that gives them the enthusiasm to constantly improve their technique.'

'You're right,' she says.

We sit for a moment, taking in the grand scale of Canonbury, until a man on crutches comes to the gate. He leans against the gatepost to wave hello to us with one of his crutches and he reminds me of Eddie, although happily Eddie does not require crutches.

I get out of the car. Under my winter coat I am wearing Bell's willie wagtail-inspired dress. She cleverly altered an oyster-coloured silk tunic from my existing wardrobe, inserting black chiffon pleated sleeves that fan across my shoulders and down my arms. I watched her hand-pleat the chiffon and set it with vinegar myself. The sleeve on my left arm finishes just above the snake armband on my upper arm. As she comes to stand beside me, I put a hand on her arm. 'Thank you for my dress,' I say. 'You are a wonder, you know, Bell, and you are always so lovely to me.'

'Thank you.' She smiles. 'But you make it easy.'

17

Emma
Sydney, 2024

Lauren has exited the study by the time I head back inside, so I allow myself to read just one more letter before heading upstairs.

The Carrington Hotel,
Friday, 7th December 1923

Dear Birdy,

I have promised to tell you everything and so I must continue where I left off in my last letter. I'm sitting by a window at the Carrington, and I can see out across the lawn to the street. It is that time of day I love so much, when the sun has not yet fully set, and the sky is royal velvet blue. It reminds me of that evening we went to entertain the returned soldiers at Canonbury.

I know you won't remember, but when we pulled up outside the house, there was a puddle just ahead of us. I managed not to step in it and went to get the hampers we had made for the men from out of the boot while you went inside the house to find someone to help us carry them in. There were a lot of them, if you remember.

I had my back to the road, and I was so busy watching for your return that I didn't even notice another car coming along until it came to a roaring stop right in the puddle. Of course, it sent a spray of dirty water over my shoe and all the way up my right leg – I was wearing white lace stockings! I heard the car door open and Kitty Lonergan and the other dancers we'd recruited for the Ball poured out of the back seat, roaring with laughter.

I heard Kitty say something like, 'Ooh Griff, look what you've done,' and the next minute there he was standing beside me, helping me to balance on one leg. Don't laugh, I was furious. All right, laugh. I suppose it is funny in retrospect.

I gave him a piece of my mind. I was mad about my shoe and stocking, but I was also in a bit of a panic because someone had obviously recruited him to taxi our dancers to Canonbury and that person obviously wasn't either of us. What was he doing with our dancers? For all that Kitty Lonergan's laugh could peel paint, she's not just one of the local girls, she's one of the best dancers in Sydney and, as we later discussed, we wouldn't want him stealing her for his set.

What I didn't tell you then was . . . I will tell you now . . .

I think my panic was at least partly because I still found it unsettling that he looks so much like Alec. He wasn't wearing a hat and in the early evening light his hair looked almost the same colour. There was something else about him too that reminded me of Alec. Maybe it was the bow tie. Alec always wore odd bow ties, remember? Griff was wearing a red and white checked one that night. I remember fixating on it, thinking something like . . . I can't imagine my husband ever wearing a bow tie like that.

I don't want to talk about my husband. I never want to speak of him again. I must, though. Eventually. I owe you that much . . . Just . . . not now.

Anyway, so one minute I was standing there on one leg, leaning on Griff, and the next he was helping me to sit down on the tan leather seat of the Chevrolet. What a car! I know we've been in some beauties, Birdy, but that night, I was impressed. The front windscreen had been polished crystal clear, and it had a fine woodgrain dash with shining dials set into it, and a matching steering wheel. It looked brand new. It was so different from the Cadillac; lighter and somehow brighter.

But back to the point. When I inspected my right leg, I thought the damage was beyond repair. The shoe was wet through, and my stocking was covered in big, ugly splotches of mud. You'll never guess what he did about that – he stuck his head in the car and said, 'Want some help?' Can you believe it?

I just blurted out, 'With my shoes and stockings? No, thank you, sir!' But the devil took my shoe from my hands and wiped it clean with a kerchief from his pocket. Then – and this bit is even more shocking, or it was to me at the time – he leaned further into the car, lifted my foot off the floor and rubbed his thumb over the mud spots on my stocking – all the way up my leg!

I probably shouldn't tell you this, but what he said was, 'I can fix your shoe, but I suspect there's no hope of removing these tonight.' Then he gave me such a look, and added, 'The mud spots, I mean.'

He certainly wasn't talking about the mud spots, and I confess, for my sins, that for a hot minute I wanted him to remove my stockings. I also knew that one day, he would.

So, Birdy, that's the day it all began.

Perhaps I should have told you at the time . . . Even now, I have not told you everything. I am avoiding the difficult parts. I promise that I will tell all, as soon as I find my courage.

I love and miss you still, so much.

Me.

18

Rose
Sydney, 1923

We have been courting Bonnie Spark, the social reporter from *Life & Times*, trying to stem the vitriol that has been written up in *The Sydney Examiner*. She had honoured our invitation to join us at Canonbury the other night, and today, her column has dutifully appeared in the newspaper. I devour the write-up, which is very complimentary, breathing a sigh of relief. 'Job well done,' I say to Bell, who has spread the week's clippings out on Walter's desk.

'He won't mind?' Bell had asked when I suggested we convene in the library this morning.

'No,' I answer shortly. Walter is ever-present, ever-watchful, and yet I feel a distance. We are like ships that pass in the night. He is very annoyed, and perhaps also very concerned, that I won't even consider returning to the States yet, and it appears he feels honour-bound to stay.

I miss the easy camaraderie that existed before our marriage. I miss him. Every now and again the memory of our kiss seeps in under my skin, and I realise I also want more of him. The Walter who kissed me, the Walter who held me the long night of our wedding, seems to be slipping further and further away.

Of more pressing concern, Bell and I are nowhere near reaching our target of selling 150 tickets to the Ball.

'Do you think it is the . . . bad press—' I can't bear to mention Alec's death, '—that is holding people back?'

I sense her pause before answering. 'That's part of it,' she says slowly. 'And perhaps . . . Mr Griffin.'

I'm not given to anger, but Mr Griffin put me in an embarrassing position by ferrying our dancers to Canonbury and returning to take them all home. I'm still very cross about it. The only saving grace is that Bonnie did not pen a single word about it in her article, even though she must certainly have heard. Even unreported, however, there's no doubt the gossip would have been flowing thick and fast, and possibly still is. I sit down heavily in Walter's chair, wondering if it has reached his ears. 'We must distance ourselves from Mr Griffin,' I say. 'He's nothing but trouble.'

'I'm not sure that's possible,' Bell says. 'He's on the committee, and Miss Lewis is very fond of him.'

Miss Lewis . . . oh, she has such a weakness for the wrong kind of man. Her first husband died defending her honour in a drunken brawl and the second ran off with another woman. It's hard to imagine a lady having to face greater scandal, and yet somehow, Miss Lewis successfully behaves as though neither event ever happened. Perhaps she could be my role model.

'Well,' I say, with some resolve, 'we must do our very best to avoid him, in any case.' Then, for good measure, I add, 'April Lewis . . .' and shake my head.

Bell smiles, and for a moment I catch something whimsical

in her face. 'It's not hard to see why her head is turned, though, is it? He's . . .'

'Wicked,' I snap.

She laughs. 'Yes, wicked. But I'm still not sure we can avoid him. I've heard mention that he's offering joyrides on his plane as auction prizes.'

'*What?*'

She nods, watching me absorb this information.

'Joyrides? When I have offered a parasol, a glorified umbrella?' No matter that it is the very one I used in *Blue Skies under Heaven,* my most successful film to date. Mr Griffin is upstaging me. I feel all my annoyance return in a hot wave, and I begin to pace about the small room. 'We have to beat him at his game.' Then I stop my pacing. 'You know about aeroplanes,' I say suddenly.

'What? Why would you think such a thing? I know nothing about aeroplanes.'

'Yes, you do, you said so. When we went to the Tivoli storeroom, you said you went flying with George what's-his-name and his brother, Captain Penfold.'

'George Taylor,' she supplies. 'And I said no such thing. All I said was that George Taylor used to rent the building that is now the Tivoli store, and used it as an aeroplane factory.'

'I distinctly remember you telling me that you went down to Narrabeen Beach when he was doing test flights or something.'

'Yes,' she agrees. 'But I wasn't on one of the test flights. I value my life too much.'

'Did you see it happen at least?'

'Yes, but—'

'Good . . .' I'm trying to formulate a plan, a plan that will put Mr Griffin in his place and propel me back to centre stage with the committee. I can't risk being sidelined. I can't have my position in social and theatrical circles in Australia undermined, not with everything else that has happened. It would be very bad for me and therefore the company, at a time when we simply cannot afford it. 'We need to find out more about Mr Griffin and what his plans are. Can you arrange something?'

'Like what?'

'I don't know.' I go back to pacing. 'Perhaps a meeting.'

She gives me a long look.

'Why are you staring at me like that?'

'First you want to avoid him, now you want to meet with him? I don't know if that's wise, Rose.'

'I don't *want* to Bell, but I think it's the only solution.'

'It might start tongues wagging again, though. You've only been married five minutes, and nothing happens in this city without everyone knowing about it.'

'All right,' I say. 'I'll take you with me.'

'Dear God,' I mutter. I'm holding onto my hat, literally. We are walking across a field, and the breeze is capricious, picking at the brim. In the distance is J. J. Griffin's aeroplane. It is a biplane, and my guess is it is held together by little more than a few screws and a couple of wingnuts. I have never been faint-hearted – the very opposite, in fact. Throughout my career, I have been thrown into a crocodile-infested pool, I have ridden horses and walked tightropes, and I have always done all my own stunts – I was never doubled for a single scene in any of my films. Even before learning to high dive with Alec, I had no fear of heights, but this is a different kettle of fish altogether.

'He is expecting us to go up in that thing, is he?' I say to Bell, who matches my stride across the grass.

'I think that's the idea,' she says. 'It's the only meeting he would agree to.'

I shake my head. 'The nearer we get to it, the more I see an accident waiting to happen.' And heaven knows I've read of enough aeroplane accidents in the newspapers.

'People have been paying large sums of money for the briefest of joy flights,' she says.

'Some people have more money than sense,' I mutter.

'I really thought you'd be up for it,' Bell says. 'Remember that time you dressed up as a plane, for a benefit during the war?'

'That was a costume, Bell, and it was for a benefit, a good cause.'

'This is also a good cause,' she reminds me.

The memory of the benefit does make me smile. It had been to raise money for the supply of aeroplanes to the Allies. Bell and I had dreamed up the costume. We'd created a fitted dress from a fabric that had the most glorious silver sheen to it, and attached two beaded strips of black rhinestones to the bodice as straps for each shoulder. Bell had also hand-sewn rhinestones in the shape of aeroplanes onto the square neckline. But the headpiece had been the pièce de résistance – a close-fashioned cap onto which we'd fixed a wing-type structure, stiffened with cardboard, and covered in the same silver fabric, all of it also outlined in rhinestones.

It's a little ironic now, I think, that we had to hold benefits back in those days to raise money for aeroplanes for the Allied Forces – now they have too many and are giving them away to the colonies. But I am not sure the plane we are now approaching is one of them. As we near it, my heart sinks to my stomach, not just because it is nothing more than a glorified tin can, but because to the rear of it he has affixed a banner. For one stupid minute I pretend that it might be to publicise the Olympic Ball, to raise interest in our fundraising efforts. But I know it isn't. It will be something that benefits Mr Griffin in some way and, although I don't yet know what it is, I'm quite sure I don't want to be associated with it.

'An advertisement, Mr Griffin?'

He smiles, but only with one side of his face. 'Aeroplanes are expensive, Miss Carey. Every flight must be paid for in some way.'

And now I feel in his debt, left wondering if I should have offered to pay for the flight. Having been talked into it in the first place and not having money to waste in the second, it hadn't crossed my mind. For a moment I consider insisting on knowing more about the banner, or telling him I have changed my mind about the flight, but I feel trapped, as if I can do neither.

'I see,' I say lamely instead.

Under a black leather jacket, he is wearing what I know is a sidcot. The boilersuit is necessarily loose, fitted only at the waist, but nevertheless, he wears it well. I know it's called a sidcot because when Bell and I first saw it, a year or so after the benefit, we'd discussed whether we should have made something like it, rather than the dress. It would have better suited my personality.

'We invented them, you know,' I say, gesturing towards his clothes.

'Do you mean Gertie?' he asks, indicating the plane. 'You might want to check your facts with Orville and Wilbur.'

I don't like the way he talks. Not the words themselves – although there is plenty to take umbrage with in them – but his accent. It grates on my nerves. It is nothing like Walter's deep midwestern. 'No, Mr Griffin, I am not talking about Gertie. I'm well aware that the Wright brothers have claimed ownership for inventing planes. I'm talking about your suit. We invented it.'

'You and Miss Procter?' His eyebrows rise up into lines that crinkle his forehead. 'I take my hat off to you ladies. It's extremely practical – and as its creators, you would know it's now worn around the world.'

'Not us personally,' Bell says with a soft laugh. Is she falling under his spell as easily as April Lewis? 'She means an Australian invented it, Sidney Cotton.'

'Is that so? Well, hats off to him. Now ideally, ladies, you should be wearing one of these yourselves. However I don't have supplies. That's why I asked you to bring your dust jackets with you, as well as scarves and your warmest sweaters.'

He's painful, I decide as I take the items of clothing I have folded over my arm and put them on.

'And I hope you don't mind also losing your hats.' Without asking, he reaches for Bell's, then mine, and removes them from our heads, stowing them in the plane behind him. He hands us both leather caps and waits for us to fasten the chin straps. 'It's going to be noisy, dirty and cold,' he says. 'Mostly cold. You are going to need those scarves.' Then he inspects us, as if he were some sort of drill sergeant. He leans forward to fasten the top button of Bell's jacket and position her woollen scarf around her neck. 'I'll also need your purses.' He means our handbags. We pass them to him and he stows them.

'Now, some safety instructions. A plane is a vessel, much like any other.'

I eye the 'vessel' in question. It looks a long way from the reliable ocean liners I'm familiar with, but I decide not to raise my objections. 'She's equipped with the necessaries. A fire extinguisher,' he waves in the direction of one, near his seat in the cockpit, 'a first-aid kit,' he points to it, 'and a flare pistol. Don't worry about the pistol, I'll look after that.'

Every word he speaks makes the hairs rise higher on the back of my neck.

'There are also life vests, but I'm not intending to fly out over the water today. We'll just do a very quick circuit, ten minutes maximum. Do you have any questions?'

I have lots of questions. 'What is the point of the life vests? If we were flying over water and we did crash, wouldn't we die anyway?'

He laughs. 'Yes, probably. They just make it easier for people to recover our bodies.' Then he smiles, not at me but at Bell. He reaches into his pocket and passes us both small wads of cotton. 'We won't be able to hear each other speak up there. The noise of the engine is deafening, so it's better to plug your ears. The only way we'll be able to communicate is via hand signals, so here are a few.' He goes through the signals for 'okay', 'not okay', 'danger', 'fire' and 'go round', and then he climbs up into the plane. The next minute he is tossing us each a pair of goggles and fitting his own.

And then we are all onboard, Bell and I in the bench seat behind him, ears plugged, the hideous goggles strapped to our faces and my heart in my mouth. Two men come out from a shed to supervise take-off and spin the propeller. It takes more than one effort for the machine to roar into life.

The terrain is rough under the wheels, the slowly gathering speed terrifying, and into my head comes the sound of my mother's music, the piece that had been playing in my mind while in the crystal tank with Alec.

I will close my eyes, I will close my ears, I decide. Ten minutes, he said. Just ten minutes of my life and then I will be back on firm ground, I will be restored to my natural habitat.

Or, like Alec, I will be dead.

My eyes spring open again. If this is my last ten minutes on earth, I don't want to waste them. For interminable moments, there is just the ground under the wheels, and I wonder if we will really leave it or if we will crash into the trees at the far edge of the field. Then there is a bump and a jolt and a lift, and we are mere inches from the earth. I am now more afraid of crashing than I was when we were on the ground. We are higher now, and the air has turned bitter. It whips over the windscreen and slaps me in the face. I can't imagine what it is like for our pilot. The nose of the plane is pointed up, and as we rise higher and higher, my breath is ripped from my lungs.

I pull my scarf further up around my snap-frozen cheeks. We are in nothing but a silver bullet, hanging in the sky and our lives are literally in the hands of the man in front of us. I bite my lip, sink my teeth deep into it until I taste blood. I reach for Bell's leather-gloved hand, but when I look up, I see that she is looking out, not back at me. And so, for a change, I follow her lead.

Beneath us, the world is a carpet sown in green, buildings reduced to doll's houses. As we fly higher, the carpet becomes a patchwork of brown and green, trees shrink into stalks of broccoli, roads turn to string, and waterholes to puddles. The busy dance in my head slows to something more serene.

I am flying.

Although I am colder than I can remember being since a snowstorm in New York, a glow flows through me and a smile creeps across my face.

Griff turns back to briefly look at us, indicating that he wants to go higher, and we both nod enthusiastically. As he pushes up the nose of the plane, I feel a rush of adrenalin. It is the rush I am addicted to, I realise. I look over his shoulder, past the propeller, spinning in front of us, to the horizon. The blue sky is dotted with small, lofty white clouds. We fly on for moments that dissolve too quickly.

I have been so afraid since Alec died. I have not gone near The Dom and its diving tower. I have not even gone swimming in the bay. But Griff, for all his sins, has given something back to me.

Courage.

He indicates he is going to head for home. As he executes the turn, I have a perfect view of the banner flying proudly from behind us.

Mayfield & Co, Performers.

19

Emma
Sydney, 2024

I take myself and a pizza from Big Poppa's, the pizzeria across the road, out to the shed. I just can't be inside with Lauren at the moment. I'm not avoiding her. I'm just hungry, tired and feeling off, so I'm not up for any more arguments. And there have been plenty more arguments. Sighing, I put the pizza on the trestle table in the shed and sit down to eat it.

I should have talked to her about the job. She's right, what kind of relationship do we have if we can't talk things over? But I'd been convinced she would try to coerce me into throwing my hat into the ring, and I just don't want to. Hot Rain smacks of a three-ring circus to me, and I never want to do anything just for the money, the root of all evil.

No, I correct myself. That had been the topic of a debate at uni, and the correct quote is *'The love of money* is the root of all evil'; it's from the New Testament. I'd elected to speak to the negative, banking on my fellow students running with the hackneyed idea that all sins can be linked back to money, which I thought missed the point. Money is an inanimate object, which, I'd argued, few people could love. It is the power of money that is the root of all evil – the things it can buy and the things it can make happen. In our case though, a bit more of it might make the one thing Lauren wants happen.

The pizza is as delicious as it usually is, but I'm so despondent I can't finish it. I stow the half-empty box under the table. Maybe some time with Rose Carey will take my mind off my own troubles.

The letters are starting to make me feel as though I know the writer, I'm presuming it's Rose, very well. I find myself wondering about her as I go about my days. Who is she writing to? What is she constantly seeking forgiveness for? I want to rush ahead, read all the letters all the way through, because surely she must spell it out sooner or later? But at the same time, I know there is a finite number of letters and I don't want to come to the end of them. In any case, I've now stored them on a shelf in the study.

So, I decide to look at one of the reels of film. Like the first, it's not in the greatest condition, slightly sticky to the touch. I find a pair of cotton gardening gloves and put them on, then carefully unspool the strip of film and hold it up to the yellow overhead light. It's quite difficult to make out, especially the beginning of it, which has deteriorated the most. I hold it up with one hand and try to shine the torch on my phone through it with the other, but it's a no-go. I think I'm going to need a projector of some sort.

I sit there for a moment, thinking. Then I see a tack hammered partly into the shelf in front of me. If I can fit a sprocket to it at one end, I can stretch out the film and shine my light into it, and maybe get a clearer view. I give it a try and it works, in a fashion.

There are several frames of Rose Carey in a close-fitting bathing suit in some kind of aquarium. From the unseen surface, a light shines through the water down onto her. There are a few frames of the exact same shot, indicating that for a moment she is motionless, standing on one pointed foot, her hands linked overhead, her body as white and perfect and lifeless as the Venus de Milo. And then there is a quick succession of frames which tell me she is spinning in a pirouette, her arms moving in elegant arcs to her sides. Bubbles swirl about her as she travels upwards to the source of the light.

In the following frames, she is joined by a similarly clad male. I let the film unspool a bit more and follow the progress of the action via my phone torch. It looks like a beautiful underwater ballet sequence, perhaps an early form of artistic swimming. Rose has a neat figure, slim waist, strong legs; so does her partner. As she pirouettes and spins, another stream of bubbles travels upwards towards the surface.

But the film really isn't in great condition. There are what I can only describe as splodges on it, and the reel smells like old socks, or wet dog. I switch off the torch and sit back in my swivel chair.

I take the sprocket off the tack and wind the film back on its spool, wondering how to preserve it. I decide the best thing to do for now is just put it back in its canister. Then I wonder if air is getting to it, which might further deteriorate the film, so I find some gaffer tape and seal the can shut. I do this with each of the five reels, then I put them all back in the octagonal canister.

'I wish you had been honest from the very beginning,' she says.

We are lying in bed. I can't say we're lying there together, because Lauren is as stiff as a poker and keeping rigidly to her side. Her bedside lamp is off, but mine casts a yellow glow over my half of the bed.

'Well, I didn't see the point. I was never going to act on it, and if anyone,' I pause, not wanting to sound accusatory, 'thought it was a good fit, then they don't know me very well.' So much for not sounding accusatory.

'Obviously my sister thinks it's a good fit, and as she's regularly on Hot Rain, you'd think she'd know. But I wasn't talking about that.'

'Oh?'

It's her turn to pause. 'I wish you had said at the very beginning of our relationship that you don't want children.'

So, we're back to this. 'Lauren, I did tell you the truth. I did want children. But I don't think I do anymore, at least, not at any cost. Look what this process has cost us so far, and I'm not even talking about money. It's too much pressure on us and on our marriage. It's affecting every part of our lives. Our friendships, our relationship, our families – probably even our work. There's also the physical cost. The medical procedure makes me feel uncomfortable, it's difficult, and it's invasive.'

She considers that for a moment. 'So you wouldn't want to even try anymore? Even if we had the money?'

'I don't know, I honestly don't. The odds of success are so stacked against us, and we'd have to go through the whole hoopla again. I never thought I would say this, but I'm not sure I have the stamina for it.' I wave my hand about and notice the rash on the back of it has flared up. It seems to confirm that the baby issue is now taking a physical toll as well as an emotional one.

'Are you open to other ways of being a family?'

The short answer is no. I don't want to break her heart all over again, so I'm reluctant to explain my feelings, but given she's just accused me of being dishonest, I think I have to. So, I say it. 'No.'

She receives my reply in silence.

'Do you want to know why not?'

'Okay, why not?

'I think the children we might potentially be able to adopt would most likely come to us via foster care.'

She nods. 'So?'

'I don't know how to put this without sounding selfish.'

'Just spit it out.'

I make a half-hearted attempt at a laugh. 'All right.' I take a deep breath. 'I don't think I could bear the emotional heartbreak of taking a child into our care and then potentially having him or her taken away from us. It could happen over and over again. We would fall in love with those children, Lauren, you know we would, and I don't think I'm psychologically robust enough to deal with that.' To my surprise, my voice catches on the last sentence.

She rolls over and puts her arm around me, pulling me close.

'I could help you.'

I shake my head again.

She lets out a long, sad sigh and rests her forehead against mine. 'There is another solution, Em. Won't you please, please, please consider it . . . for me?'

She's biting her lip. She doesn't want to say what I know she will say next. She's afraid of my reaction. And seeing the look on her face, I realise I'm afraid of my reaction, too. I want to stop her from speaking, but she doesn't.

'Let's do it our own way.'

20

Emma
Sydney, 2024

I'm becoming addicted to reading Rose's letters, I know I am. Whenever there is a hint of discord in my own life – and sometimes even when there is not – I retreat to them. Like an addict, I tell myself that I can stop at any time. I check the bundle. There are still many letters left to read but one day I will have read them all and so I read this next one slowly.

The Carrington Hotel,
Friday, 14th December 1923

Dear Birdy,

What must you think of me, of us? Sometimes I wake in the night and my jaw is clenched tight. It seems that even in my sleep I worry you might think I betrayed you. You must have so many questions. I am going to answer some now, but I'm a coward and so I'm going to start with the easiest one . . .

Where did Griff find the canvas for that banner so quickly? He'd barely been in the country five minutes. I suppose I was already falling for him, but I also, honestly, didn't want us to play second fiddle to the likes of him.

The banner bothered me, perhaps more than the stunt itself. Canvas, such as planes were once made of. . . It worried me because it reminded me of something, though for a while, I couldn't recall what. When I did, the memory sent me back to the Tivoli store.

When I arrived at the store, Mr Randolph was, unsurprisingly, given the disappearance of our props, extremely eager to please. Of course, I knew that the store had been used as an aeroplane factory before, I also knew the names of the people who had used it thus, and I knew that they had gone off to America, so I asked him directly if they had left anything behind.

At first, he tried to skirt the question, then he admitted that they had, and that they had asked him to donate whatever they had not removed. When I pressed him on it, he said he'd sold some things to Griff. I knew I had him pinned then for the selling of the canvas and taking the profit, but I didn't call him on it because I needed to know what else he might have sold to Griff. He enumerated things like aeroplane stays, and wood fasteners and so forth, and then he told me about the silk. Yards and yards of it, intended for flying balloons.

I want you to know that's what I did, and that's the extent of it. I wanted to get to the bottom of the business with the canvas, and in the finding out, I also learned about the silk. What I did that day, I did for all of us, for the success of the Bull and the success of our company. I did it for our success, I promise you.

Love, Me.

Nausea grips me as I fold the letter up along its creases and put it back with the others. It has made me feel sick to my stomach.

Because it's a letter, from Rose Carey, I think, to another woman, begging forgiveness. For what? Unfaithfulness? Why does the thought of that bother me so much?

I step outside the study, walk out the sliding glass door to stand at the balcony rail. I take several deep breaths. My wife has not been unfaithful, I remind myself, and perhaps neither had Rose Carey. Besides, it could just as equally be a letter to Rose as from her. There's no way of knowing for certain without a proper salutation and a proper signature. 'Birdy' tells me nothing, 'Me' tells me even less.

Without warning, a conversation I had with my wife before we were so quickly married replays in my head. *You make me the best version of me,* I'd said. And she had answered, *You make me the best version of me too.* It had all seemed perfect then, except . . . if she'd said the words first, if she had been the utterer, not the echo . . . I'd never doubted her before. It had never occurred to me to question the sincerity of that echo. I'd just thought we were . . . on the same page.

But that was before . . . before we'd even thought of IVF, before I'd failed to give my wife a baby, before everything. 'Do it our own way . . .' she'd suggested last night, and then she'd gone on to explain that what she meant by that was we could get our own donation and try a turkey baster solution.

I had closed the conversation down. I hadn't wanted to discuss it. I try now to understand why I hadn't wanted to discuss it. Was I afraid she was angling to make good on the suggestion she'd put to Jax the night of the engagement party? Was I afraid she might suggest the easiest way to go about it was to simply jump into bed with him?

I mentally shake myself. This is ridiculous. Even if Rose Carey had actually slept with someone other than her spouse, that didn't mean my wife would. Lauren's thoughtless remark at the party had been just that, a thoughtless remark. She had been a little tipsy and so focused on having a baby, she hadn't considered how her words might be interpreted. I believe that in my soul, but my brain is having a hard time convincing my heart.

I pull myself together. There's no doubt I am sexually jealous of Jax, but it's not just that. I also feel threatened because he's Allie's fiancé. Hell would freeze over before I'd agree to him being 'our baby's daddy' but if in some strange parallel universe all parties did agree to such a thing, it would represent to me yet another thing gifted to us by Allie and that would gnaw away at me forever.

But it's time to face some facts. It's time to think seriously about what I want - not what Lauren wants, but what I want. Perhaps I would be happy enough if we never had children. If I'm honest, I haven't thought about what I want very deeply at all. My main concern has been centred around satisfying Lauren's maternal instincts - Lauren's, not mine - and how to pay for that.

So, what do I want? I want to make her happy. *Happy wife, happy life* - isn't that the way it goes?

No, I decide. I need more.

21

Rose
Sydney, 1923

Walter drops a large parcel wrapped in brown paper and string on the occasional table in the living room. It's the first time I've seen him, except in passing, for ten days, perhaps more.

'For me?' I have always had a childlike love of parcels, particularly unexpected ones. But a glance at his face tells me that it's not some wonderful, unexpected gift.

'In a manner of speaking,' he says, and there is not even a hint of a smile on his face. 'Unwrap it.'

The tone of his voice makes me now think I want nothing to do with it, but I reach forward anyway and begin picking at the string. The brown paper falls away. There, now sitting on the table in the middle of the living room, is a very much worse-for-wear Roman horse's head.

'They found our props?'

He nods. 'They washed up near the wharves in Woolloomooloo.'

I'm silent for a moment as I take it in. 'All of them?'

'I don't know. Probably.'

'How did you find them?'

He sits down opposite me on a chesterfield chair in the corner of the room. There is space beside me on the settee, but he ignores it.

'I didn't, Eddie did.'

'Eddie found our props? What, just like that?'

'No, apparently he had a message from Mr Randolph at the Tivoli store.'

'Mr Randolph talked to Eddie and not to us?'

'I understand Eddie has been making regular inquiries.'

I can't fault him on that. 'Where are the rest of them?'

'This was the only thing that was salvageable, Rose.'

I stare at it some more. 'This is not salvageable.' I poke at it with my forefinger and the papier-mâché sags inward under my touch. 'I don't know why you even bothered to bring it home.'

He crosses his legs and looks at me. His face is so stern, so unapproachable. I can't remember the last time I saw him smile.

'Are there any likely suspects?'

He smooths his moustache with one hand and when he takes it away, I notice the redness of his lips. I can't stop myself from staring at them. 'No.'

I stand up, feeling suddenly restless. 'So, our props disappear from locked premises in Surry Hills, and then mysteriously turn up in the harbour in Woolloomooloo.'

'That is about the extent of it,' he agrees.

'And we have no clue who took them, or who dumped them?'

'No.'

'Who on earth would do such a thing? Who would be so malicious?'

He seems to take a long time answering. 'What about your new friend?'

'What new friend?'

He doesn't answer, just goes on staring at me, waiting.

'Griff? You think Griff was behind this?'

It would make sense, I realise. He is . . . he is what, exactly? Unprincipled. He had no compunction about flying that banner behind us the other day, despite the fact that we are rivals, and, obviously, he knows I'm on the Olympic Ball committee. 'If you need any help with anything . . .' he had said after we landed, as I was in the rapid, angry process of removing all that paraphernalia we'd been required to wear for the flight. 'Please don't hesitate to ask.'

Did he know we'd been robbed of our props? If he did, then he would know we are struggling to put everything together, and I'm sure he would be quite prepared to take advantage of the fact.

'How well acquainted are you?' It's not an idle inquiry; Walter is suspicious of me.

I've never thought of Walter as being a jealous man. I didn't think being married would make any difference. 'We are not at all well-acquainted, and you do me a dishonour, Walter.'

He looks at me with one raised eyebrow. 'Do I indeed?'

He makes my heart race, I realise. Even when he's angry. This new realisation, this attraction . . . it was always there, and it never goes away.

'Yes,' I snap.

'All right,' he concedes. 'But I have my suspicions about him. And you must realise that he has the most to gain by any . . . misfortune . . . that might befall us.'

Of course he does. 'You think he's behind our money losses? How could he be?'

'I think he's behind our prop losses,' he corrects. 'That's all I think at the moment. It would be helpful if you could tell me what you know about him.'

I frown. 'I know very little.'

He gives me a lopsided smile. 'That's not the rumour.'

'You've never been one to listen to gossip. There's nothing going on.'

'All right.' He shifts on the chesterfield, and the leather squeaks at the movement. 'But I still need to know everything you know about him.'

I let out a long sigh. 'All right. He was an ace during the war, or so he told us.'

Walter lifts his head a little higher. 'Are you sure? An actual ace? Only a hundred or so Americans qualified for that title.'

I shrug my shoulders. 'That's what he said.'

'What else did he say?'

'About the war? He said he was some kind of volunteer pilot or something in the beginning and then he went to France . . .'

'Jesus Christ – he wasn't part of Lafayette Escadrille?'

'Maybe . . . I don't know. Why? Is it important?'

'Lafayette Escadrille was a French squadron made up mostly of Americans. The first squadron of American pilots ever . . .' He's deep in thought now, a series of changing expressions scampering over his face. 'Many of them were sons of very famous families, but there were plenty of ordinary men among them too – cowboys, mechanics, salesmen, taxi drivers, a black man who had been a boxer and played music halls . . .'

'I don't see how this is relevant to us . . .'

He looks at me, and it seems he's coming back from somewhere far away. 'You don't understand. This was a ragtag band of young men. They didn't expect to survive the war, and some of them didn't. Many of them were . . . wild. They flew hard and they played hard . . . they kept two lions as pets. But they were also exceptional . . . they led the way . . .'

'I still don't see why this is important to us.'

'But if memory serves me correctly, there was only one ace in that group, and it wasn't J. J. Griffin.'

'How do you know?'

'Because that ace was shot down and killed.'

'So, he's lying?' I don't know why, but that makes me feel better. I don't want him to be some kind of war hero.

He shakes his head. 'Not necessarily. Later in the war, Lafayette Escadrille was transferred into a newly established American squadron in France. It's possible he became an ace after the transfer. Or perhaps he was a member of the Lafayette Flying Corps . . .'

I raise an enquiring eyebrow.

'American volunteer pilots who flew with various French squadrons . . . a dozen or so of them became aces.'

I shake my head. I don't understand why Walter is fixated on what I see as the irrelevant past of an irrelevant person who just happens to have popped up in our lives.

'Who is he, Rose? And what the hell is he doing here?'

'What do we know about J. J. Griffin, Bell?'

Does she stiffen? I don't quite catch the look on her face because I'm watching the look on mine. We are downstairs and I am at the barre performing the exercises that are so important to maintaining health and fitness.

'Well, we know he's American.'

I throw her a glance before bending into a plié. 'Yes, we know he's American.' I repeat the plié. 'San Francisco, right?'

'Yes.'

I reach my arms up overhead and bring them back down to my sides in a graceful movement I call my swan arms. 'I wish more women knew there is no need to go bull-at-a-gate with exercise,' I say as an aside, ' it's just a matter of being consistent.'

'You said as much in your book,' she reminds me.

'So I did.' I repeat the exercise and then I continue, 'Do you think he has a college education?'

'No.'

'You seem very sure about that.' I move into another plié; I'm doing a total of ten.

'He doesn't strike me as a college-educated man, that's all.'

She is sitting at the little table in the ballroom, attending to my affairs. She has the diary open at today's page. A stack of cards, ready for responding to my fan mail, is set to the side. She's penned the word 'thank you' on the front of each in calligraphy, and inside I will later sign my name. Her penmanship is as beautiful as her design sketches; she really is very talented like that. 'You have several appointments today,' she says, 'and your self-defence class.' She rattles the appointments off. I have the oddest feeling that she's avoiding talking about Mr Griffin.

'What else do we know? What do you think convinced him to come to Australia? Surely *a flying ace* would have had other opportunities after the war?'

'Like what?'

'Well, he could have stayed on in the military, couldn't he?'

'I don't know anything about the military,' she says.

I wonder again about her own background. Bell never talks about her parents, or having any other family. It was almost a shock when we visited the Tivoli store and she said she'd lived across the road. I'd had no idea where she came from.

'No soldiers, sailors or pilots in your background then?' I go through my swan arm movement again.

'None that I'm aware of.'

Although she says the words pleasantly enough, I can tell she will not be supplying any more of her own personal information, so I persist with my questions about Griff.

'Has he ever mentioned his parents?'

'Not to me.'

'Why would a pilot come to Australia – of all places – to run a theatrical company?'

'Adventure?'

'Adventure . . .' I muse. I suppose it's possible that someone who might once have shared in the ownership of a couple of pet lions might think of coming to Australia as an adventure. But there is a lot more adventure to be had in Australia than here in Sydney, and more thrill-seeking occupations than theatrical manager. What even qualifies him for such a job? 'What theatrical experience do you suppose he has?'

'Didn't he say they'd employed him to do stunt work?'

'And fly banners off the back of his plane,' I say archly.

She laughs, but I add, 'It was a dirty trick.'

I finish my exercises and sit down at the desk with her. She has her hair pulled back into a ponytail with a simple red velvet band. It makes her look almost waif-like.

'Acting careers like mine . . . they really can't last forever, can they?' I muse. 'Which means we really must make sure to keep ownership of our patch here in Australia. We can't have someone like J. J. Griffin coming in and pumping up Mayfield's tyres, especially now.'

Walter has his head buried in the newspaper. When I sit down at the breakfast table opposite him, he looks at me from over the top of it. For a moment, I feel there are so many unsaid things between us. I feel tense and unhappy. I want him to hold me the way he held me on our wedding night. I want to lie with him the way he wouldn't lie with me then. 'Not in grief,' he'd said.

For a moment I consider getting up from the table to sit beside him. For a moment I imagine laying my head on his shoulder. I imagine another kiss, like the one we shared too long ago. We are staring at each other, and I hope beyond hope that he will see how much I want him. But he breaks the spell by saying 'More bad news,' and flicks the pages.

I don't know how much more bad news I can bear. 'What is it?' I push a strand of dark hair behind my ear. Even now that the weather is cold, it tends to have a mind of its own.

'The Longford-Lyell film.'

'Why is that bad news? It's the first time ever an American studio has released an Australian-made picture.' I have to admit to even being a little jealous about it.

'Yes,' he agrees, but the concerned look on his face doesn't change.

The sound of Bell at the piano again reaches us here.

'I believe it has been doing well at the box office, not just here but also in America. It's being sold to the British, too.'

He nods and folds his newspaper into a rectangle the size of a book before putting it down on the table.

'Australia is the problem,' he says. The winter sun is coming in through the window on the other side of the room. This kind of light highlights the gold in his hair. It is thick and glorious.

'What do you mean, Australia is the problem?' His face is the way it always is these days, sombre. 'The Americans clearly want our films. Americans clearly love our films. No doubt, so will Britain. How can our film industry do anything but grow off the back of all that?'

'Rose,' he says carefully, and I sense he is trying not to hurt me with his next words, 'who backed the Longford-Lyell production?'

I frown, trying to remember. 'I read they formed the company with four other directors and 50,000 pounds in capital?'

'Yes. Where do you think that money came from?'

'I would say the directors themselves, and perhaps a few other Australian backers.'

He nods. 'I'd hazard a guess that these backers are not happy with the return on their investment.'

I frown, shaking my head. 'But the film is doing so well.'

He sighs. 'You've had your head buried too deep in the Ball, Rose. I think you've forgotten that films are a business.'

'I've hardly forgotten,' I say. I would take greater umbrage at that remark if not for the grain of truth in it. 'So, you think they sold it too cheaply, or they did not strike a good enough deal?'

He shrugs.

'But things will improve, they're bound to. The Australian film industry will learn from this example and go on to do great things.'

He shakes his head. 'I think not.'

He's wrong. He has to be wrong. If he is not, then what does all this mean for us? We had staked our fortune on the fact that films in general are so very popular now, the world over. We'd also patted ourselves on the back for recognising that Americans were tiring of the types of films their studios are manufacturing. They crave something different, we told ourselves – exotic locations and exciting action. We learned that with our last studio film, *Daughter of the Sea*. Back then, along with playing the lead, I'd also taught dozens of extras to swim. Walter had been learning the production ropes that would ultimately lead to us forming our own company. We'd learned that movie-making is big business. Had we misstepped?

'How much did *Daughter of the Sea* cost to make, Rose?'

It's some time ago now, but with more than 10,000 extras, and the creation of a movie 'town', it was more than a million American dollars, I recall. He waits while I remember the maths, then he says, 'And what did it return for its investors?'

'It made more than a million at the box office,' I snap. I'm not across all the financials.

'My point is, Australia can't compete. I think we're beginning to see that Australian investors either do not have that kind of money or they do not have that kind of appetite, or both.'

I'm afraid that he is now also speaking for New Zealand investors, the people who invested in our film in the hope that it would raise interest in their country as a place for other citizens of the world to visit. Was it naïve of them? Had my love for my own hemisphere made me naïve, too? I believed everyone should experience the wonder of this part of the world and, as a businesswoman, I also believed it would deliver returns for our investors. Was I wrong?

'If Australian and New Zealand investors stop being interested in making Australian and New Zealand films – who will be interested?'

'Well, possibly Americans,' I counter.

He nods, but not in a convincing way. 'Let's suppose we, and others like us – Longford-Lyell, for example – could garner their interest in Australasian productions, which I think we already know is difficult, but let's just suppose. What kind of people will they want working on them?'

'What do you mean, what kind of people? They will just want the best talent.'

'They will want Americans,' he contradicts. 'They will want American actors, actresses, writers, directors, producers, mechanics. What good will that do Australia?'

'It's as we discussed. It will encourage more Americans to visit Australia and New Zealand and that in turn will benefit all concerned.'

I suddenly recognise the music Bell is playing in the ballroom. It is another piece my mother composed, and it's filled with a dreamy wistfulness. I have only ever heard her play my mother's music. It is, I realise, one of the many unspoken kindnesses she extends to me.

He shakes his head. 'No, I rather think it will not. Not in the short term. Forgive me, but I don't think a picture showcasing the underwater beauty of an island off the coast of New Zealand, or even Australia, is going to result in thousands of people queuing for boat tickets. They will not come, Rose, not even you will be able to entice them.'

'We will see about that.'

'We won't be able to beat block booking.'

Block booking . . . The major studios in America have been trying, for several years, to monopolise the movie business by forcing theatre owners to commit to screening whole blocks of their films, often sight unseen, and well in advance. It means independent filmmakers like us have our work well and truly cut out for us.

'We talked about this – our company is different. We are producing something the big studios aren't and can't. Films featuring—'

'It won't be enough, Rose,' he says, shaking his head. 'And I fear the Longford-Lyell experience is already proving that.'

22

Rose
Sydney, 1923

I am down in the ballroom with Bell, putting the finishing touches on the costumes for the Olympic Ball. From somewhere, Bell has magicked three mannequins, one of which she has set to my approximate measurements, one to Kitty Lonergan's, and the smallest to the measurements of one of the three children who will also be on the tableau with us. Bell has wound the first mannequin up by a crank handle, to match my height. Even on a headless mannequin, my gown, a close-fitting strapless silk shift overlaid in the palest sea-green tissue, looks like something out of a storybook.

'It's so lovely, Bell. You have outdone yourself.'

'I took inspiration from the plane gown,' she says. 'You reminded me of it.'

'It is more will-o'-the-wisp, more whimsical than that. I simply adore it.' I walk around it so that I can better appreciate it. So clever. I know it will fit my body like a glove, and yet the tissue gives the illusion of floating.

'And,' she says, lifting the skirt, 'here is another of our little secrets.'

'You fitted a pocket into it? Oh, you are such a whizz, darling!' I hug her and she laughs. Pockets are so useful, but are often left out by other costumiers I have had in Hollywood. 'We should bottle you.'

Centennial Hall, the main auditorium of the Town Hall, is to be made up like the Acropolis, complete with plaster Corinthian columns and white swathes of fabric featuring the gold key meander. It is an enormous space to fill. I encouraged the committee to think creatively about how to marry their individual tableaux with the overarching Greek theme, so there are a number of different motifs. I will be the central goddess on our own under-the-sea set.

'I am not in your league, Rose,' she says.

'You could have been a concert pianist,' I say, surprising even myself. 'And I would know, Bell, my mother was one.'

She is silent for long seconds, and I see something in her eyes then, a great sadness. What do I not know about her? Did she never know her own mother? I suddenly can't bear the thought that my words might have evoked sad memories, and so I rush in with, 'If I've never said so, I'm so very grateful for everything you do for me.'

She smiles, waves her hand at me and one of the pins on her pin-cushion bracelet drops to her bodice. 'You always say so,' she says briskly, picking up the pin and returning it to her wrist, and with those words we are back to the business at hand.

There will be six goddesses in total, including Kitty, and as we will be leading the parade, we must all be perfect. I move to the dress on the mannequin set to Kitty's measurements. It is a replica of mine, not yet adorned with tissue. I sigh again as I stroke the fabric. 'So clever the way we procured this silk.'

She sends me an odd look, but says nothing about it.

'We have everything organised, don't we?'

'I think so. Miss Lewis said at the last meeting that she has finished composing the song, and I think all the myrtle and laurel for the gallery have now been sourced.'

'Wonderful. How did we come by that? Or is that a secret?'

She pauses. 'I believe Mr Griffin sourced it,' she says, her eyes not leaving the mannequin.

J. J. Griffin sourced the decorations? How did I not know this? 'He seems determined to be quite involved, doesn't he?'

'He has made some useful contributions,' she agrees.

There's no negating that. 'I suppose so.' Although I remain a little put out by the banner and plane trick, I have to concede his contributions are very useful indeed.

'And he's coming to the Ball,' she says. It's a statement, not a question. As a member of the committee, his presence is required.

'It will be interesting to see what costume he will be wearing,' I muse. 'What is your prediction?'

'I'm sure I don't know,' she says, kneeling on a cushion on the floor so that she can attend to the hem of my gown where it sits on the mannequin.

'As his tableau is great Greeks, I think Homer,' I say.

She shakes her head.

'Why not?'

'Griff doesn't have a beard,' she says. 'Also, Homer was quite old.'

'Not always – and anyway, I think we are allowed a little poetic licence, especially for a poet. Perhaps he plans to wear a false beard.'

I find myself imagining him with a false beard until the fantasy morphs into the face of my husband.

'No, it doesn't suit him.'

I think some more. 'What about Alexander the Great? Do you think that's a better fit?'

She looks up at me, not even smiling. It's such a curious look. Does she think I'm indulging his inclusion on the committee – as if I had any say in it – or worse, is she suspicious of my idle questions?

'No, Rose,' she says, 'There was only one "Alexander the Great" and we lost him.'

'All I can say to this is, it's not me.'

Walter puts the photo down on the table between us. 'You think I wouldn't recognise my own wife naked?'

I want to interject, because the truth is he hasn't really seen me naked, at least not in the way I realise I want him to. But I can't seem to stop his tirade.

'The whole world would recognise you naked.'

Well, that's true, but it has never been a source of embarrassment to me. 'I repeat. This is not a photo of me.'

He puts his hands behind his back and paces up and down in front of me. He is back from the production studio. He has decided the film must be made. It can't wait any longer and so he is overseeing its edit here in Australia, at the studio used by Longford and Lyell. He worries his tie loose from around his neck. 'Do you realise it is not that you are naked in this picture that offends me? If that were the case, I would have been offended long ago.'

'Oh, I am so glad that my naked body does not offend you.'

'You understand my meaning.'

He says the words, but is his past coming up against his principles? Walter was born and raised in the Midwest. He rarely talks of it – I have no idea who his parents were, or if he has brothers and sisters. He calls himself a 'reinvented man'. I have formed my own conclusions – that he is not exactly ashamed, but is embarrassed by the fact that his upbringing was conservative with a capital C.

I have never been to Minnesota. It is too far north for my Southern Hemisphere blood; the winters are freezing. The only thing he has told me is that he started in show business after going to the Minnesota State Fair, held annually in Minneapolis.

'The human body is an art form and nothing to be ashamed of,' I say now.

'Oh yes, Rose, I know.' He stops pacing to stare at me and it is almost as if he is undressing me. 'You constantly remind me. As I said, it is not the photo that offends me. Although this example' – he gives it a scathing look – 'is less *artistic* than earlier representations.'

I can only agree with him. I have always been proud of my body, of the human body in general. And just as the lion and the dog and the fish are not ashamed to be naked, neither am I. Clothes might be a social and practical necessity, and if I'm honest, I very often enjoy them, but I also enjoy being naked, especially when swimming. But this photo . . . there is something naughty about it. Is it the turn of her calf, the slight shadow visible between her legs? Or is it that her hair does not quite cover her nipple? It seems an intimate portrait, as if the photographer knew his subject very well.

'You're right,' I say. 'It is artless.' I have always been particular about the way in which I'm photographed. I have been very careful to avoid just this kind of depiction. My image is not for the propagation of erotic photographs.

He turns and his eyes are like marbles. 'Who took this photo, Rose?'

I'm not going to let the fierceness of his inquiry shake me. I'm not easily cowed, especially by Walter. 'I don't know – as I said, the photo is not of me.'

He expels a long sigh. 'Turn it over.'

'I beg your pardon?'

'Turn the photo over.'

I walk to the table and do as he asks. There is only one word scrawled on the back of it. 'Tonight?' And then an abbreviated sign-off, just a scribbled letter: 'C'.

'Well, that's interesting. But I have no idea what it means.'

'Clearly the scribe, Mr "C", wanted to rendezvous with you. Who is he?'

'I have no idea. It arrived today?'

'Yes. I don't know on which night he wanted to rendezvous, so I'm sorry if you have missed an assignation.'

'Oh, for heaven's sake, Walter. For the final time, it's not me and there's no assignation.'

'It's not you?'

'No.'

'So why is she wearing your headdress?'

I look again. The woman's face is turned away from the camera but there is no doubt she is wearing a headpiece. It is a very particular headpiece, tall and cone-shaped with a veil. It is the headpiece that I wore for a Middles Ages set. We had discussed putting it up for auction but rejected the idea because it is made of cardboard and therefore of little intrinsic value. But it is pretty. If the photo had been coloured, it would look as beautiful here as it does in real life – covered in lilac sequins and festooned with pink and yellow silk strands down one side.

While it is worth very little, it is one of my favourites. It is also one of the props that went missing.

So now I also need to know . . . who is the woman in this photo, when was it taken, and by whom?

23

Emma
Sydney, 2024

My hand is giving me trouble. I think I might need to visit the doctor. Lauren is out at a super sewing day in Surry Hills. I'd watched her pack calico and fabric and the pattern she is currently working on into her sewing trolley.

'It's a six-hour class,' she'd said, with a perfunctory kiss goodbye. 'I won't be home until dinner.'

I'd intended to spend the morning in the shed, untape one of the reels and take a closer look at Rose Carey on film. But I'm beginning to suspect that contact with the film is what may have caused the rash on my hand, so I decide to read another letter instead. I settle into the swivel chair in the study and take one from the blue-ribboned bundle.

The Carrington Hotel,
Monday, 17th December 1923

Dear Birdy,

Now I'm going to tell you more about the silk. Mr Randolph had Griff's address and although I knew he didn't want to give it to me, he couldn't refuse. It would look bad for him.

As it turned out, Griff was also staying in Surry Hills, not far away from the Tivoli store, and although I wasn't sure I would find him there, I went straight away. It wasn't in the best part of town, but it wasn't terrible, and I was thankful that at least I hadn't had to seek him out in some hotel.

He was surprised to see me, but he invited me in. Even though it probably wasn't the thing to do, I entered the house behind him. When he went to close the door, I asked him to keep it ajar. Although I doubted there'd be reporters from The Sydney Examiner *lying in wait down in Surry Hills, I knew we could not afford any further gossip, so I was careful.*

I came straight to the point and told him I knew he had things that belonged to the owners of the aeroplane company in his possession. For my sins, I pretended that I was better acquainted with them than I was and that they were demanding their immediate return. But Griff is no fool, and he crossed his arms and raised his eyebrows at me. To be honest, I might have been disappointed if he had given in easily. He told me he had purchased the goods fair and square from Mr Randolph and he wasn't about to part with them. Well, I told him Mr Randolph was not at liberty to sell them and he said that in that case he would return them at once.

For a moment I felt checkmated, so I decided the only way was to fight my way out of it. Without even blinking, I told him I had been authorised to handle their safe storage, as the owners were concerned Mr Randolph could not be trusted. All right, that was a half-truth.

I think I had enough evidence to prove Mr Randolph could not be trusted – he had, after all, sold property not belonging to him. But as for being authorised to handle the safe storage of the items, well, that was a lie. In my defence, at that point I felt it to be a needs-must situation. We didn't have props, we didn't have money, and we were expected to furnish an extravagant set for the ball.

He actually laughed then, called me a clever little vixen, but in such a way that I felt oddly complimented, not offended. Then he said he'd make a deal. He'd keep the canvas and I could take the silk, and he'd even help me take the bolts back to Point Piper in his Chev – which he did.

Oh, let me tell you what it was like, riding in the car with Griff! It was such a beautiful day. He'd rolled the roof back and every scent of early spring seemed to float into the car and around us. It smelled of jasmine and golden wattle. When I looked over at him, he turned briefly to look at me and winked, and I felt as though he was saying something with that look, that we were partners in crime, as I suppose we were. But in a good cause, Birdy, you know that.

When the house came into sight, I got cold feet. I began to worry that if word leaked that I'd been in cahoots with him to acquire the silk – or worse, stolen it – it would reflect badly on all of us. So, when he offered to carry the bolts into the house, I told him no, that I'd ask my husband – even though he was the last person I wanted to ask for help. Nevertheless, Griff insisted on transporting the bolts to the back door and leaning them against the wall. He carried each one over his shoulder, fireman style, and all I can say is, the way his muscles flexed and bulged under the weight took me immediately back to that night in Canonbury when he ran his hands up and down my leg. In that moment, the late winter sun had never burned so hot.

When he was done, he came back to stand in front of me and said I should go flying with him again, without you, and I'll be honest . . . all I could say was, 'When?'

And I did fly with him, in every sense of the word. But I did not betray the company.

I know you have more questions. I know I need to supply more answers. I will write again.

Love, Me.

24

Emma
Sydney, 2024

I eye the queue in the doctor's surgery and briefly consider going home without a consultation. My appointment was for ten, it is already ten fifteen and I am told there are still three people ahead of me. But my hand isn't getting any better, so I stick with it.

I'm pulled out of my podcast by the noisy entrance of a mother and her toddler. She's trying to push the door open with the front wheels of the stroller, but the door is not cooperating. I stand up to let her in. The kid is screaming his head off.

'Thank you,' she says, her long dark ponytail falling over her shoulder.

I smile. 'No problem.' She checks in at reception and then comes to sit down in the chair located 1.5 metres to the right of me. As she fusses with her child, undoing the safety harness and pulling him out of the stroller and onto her knee, he stops screaming and reaches out a grubby finger towards me. Big brown eyes stare up at me from under dark brown ringlets, and I'm suddenly gripped by an unexpected and overwhelming longing.

I want a baby.

I'm so disconcerted by the sudden knowing that I tune back into my podcast, turning the volume up loud, until I'm called into the GP's room. She sits down behind her desk and smiles at me. 'How are you?'

This is the doctor who referred us to the IVF clinic. She is well-acquainted with our parenthood struggles and I'm afraid she'll want an update. I don't know how regularly or otherwise doctors look at their patient files, or how across the little details they are. All I know is that I feel too raw with the realisation that just overwhelmed me, that I don't want to rehash it yet, even though she would probably have some very intelligent insights for me.

'Well, I have this sore hand,' I say, presenting it to her.

She takes my cue, dons a pair of gloves and reaches for my hand, her face remaining neutral. One thing I've noticed about people in the medical profession is how schooled they are in not giving much away. I suppose they see and hear it all, and she has probably seen hands a lot worse than mine.

'When did you first notice it?'

'A few weeks ago. It started out as a mild rash.'

She takes a hand-held magnifying lamp from a charging dock on the wall, switches it on and holds it above my skin.

'It looks a bit like contact dermatitis,' she says, but softly, almost under her breath. 'You say you first noticed it a few weeks ago?'

'Yes.'

'When you first noticed it, did it hurt?'

'No, I don't think so.'

'Do you remember coming into contact with something and having to wash it off to relieve it?'

I pause to consider the question. I don't think the film came into direct contact with the skin on the back of my hand but should I mention it? 'I don't think so.'

That's a stupid answer. Why don't I tell her? Do I feel guilty for still having the film in my possession?

'Do you have the rash anywhere else on your body or is it localised?'

'It's only on this hand.'

'Hmm.' She flicks off the lamp and returns it to the charging station. 'It's not too bad, but it looks like something is irritating it.' She returns to her desk and starts tapping into her computer. 'Given that you've had it for some time, I'm concerned you may still be coming into contact with something that is continuing to irritate your skin. See if you can work out what it is. I'll write you a script for a steroid ointment but protect this hand as much as you can, and keep it very clean.'

'Okay.' I'll make sure I always wear gloves when I'm handling the film and that should solve the problem, I reason. *See?* I tell myself. *Not so stupid after all.* I can fix this without confessing anything.

'If you don't see any improvement in the next week or so, or it gets worse, come back and see me.'

'Okay.'

She looks up at me from her computer screen with a querying eyebrow. 'Anything else?'

Should I mention that I've been feeling a bit nauseous from time to time? Should I mention the cough? I hesitate, teetering on the brink of telling her. But I'm certain it's just stress. It's been a hell of a year so far, and it's still only September.

Come to think of it, maybe that's the problem – hay fever. I've never really suffered from it before, but it's always a possibility.

'No, thank you,' I say.

She emails me the script and I am on my way.

The day outside is lukewarm with a side of sunshine, so I pick up a roll at the banh mi place across the road and head for Pirrama Park. As I unwrap the roll, I make a decision. It's time to get my shit together. All this going around being mopey has to stop. I need to fix the things that are bothering me and get on with my life.

The thing that has been causing me the most angst is the baby situation. My encounter with the toddler in the doctor's surgery just now pulled at my maternal heartstrings in a way I hadn't expected. I realise that's a biological/emotional response, but my biological and emotional responses are as important as my intellectual responses. I don't think I've properly appreciated that before. So, given I now know I would like a baby, what am I personally prepared to do to make that happen, and what are my personal barriers?

If we had the money, I'd like to try again. I realise that is a truth I have been hiding from. While IVF treatment is becoming more affordable, I can't agree to paying for any part of it via credit cards or any other form of debt, and I refuse to accept a loan from family or friends. It's all well and good to borrow money from those who know and love you if some sort of devastating and unexpected crisis occurs, but I really don't want to lean on our loved ones to fund our life choices. That's the big one.

The next big one is the turkey baster solution that Lauren keeps suggesting. I realise, now that I am being brutally honest with myself, that she's not attracted to Jaxon. If my radar is right, she's not sexually interested in anyone but me.

This realisation actually makes me want to weep. I've been a bit of an idiot about this. The real reason I was so offended and defensive was because I can't afford to give her another shot at being a mum via the only way I find palatable. So, is the turkey baster solution now okay with me?

No. But not because of the men we might involve. The real reason I find the turkey baster so unacceptable is because I would have no biological connection to the child. It would be Lauren's baby. I really want that biological connection. The only other way would be for me to get pregnant. But I've already worked out that I don't want that.

I stand up to shake the last of the crusty breadcrumbs off my lap, then sigh. I now know what I want, and what I'm not prepared to do in order to get it, but the end result is still the same. We don't have the money to fund another round of IVF, I won't accept financial help, and time is ticking away.

There's another thing that's been bothering me – I'm not very happy in my job. I don't actively dislike it; Johnno and the crew are great, but I'd like to work on the gigs Hammer and Tongs has been doing for companies dealing with environmental concerns. When I started there a few years ago, we'd been a really tight little team, working together on everything that came our way. But that's not the case now that the company has expanded. Do I need to look for something else? If so, what?

Just because the Hot Rain opportunity has been handed to me doesn't mean I have to pursue it. If it doesn't feel like the right fit, then why would I override that feeling, even if it does make mathematical sense? So, that idea goes into the bin, even if it means Lauren and her sister will think I'm crazy.

The first thing I will do, I decide, is actively start looking for a new job. I'd always thought opportunities would come by word-of-mouth, and the Hot Rain opportunity is proof that they can, but I could be doing more than just sitting around and waiting for it to happen. I could look at Seek, I could brush up my LinkedIn profile, and I could even find out which recruitment agencies are working in my industry.

As I start walking back to our apartment, I wonder what I could do to earn that kind of money quickly. I could ask the crew if they know of any wedding work. Weddings are not my favourite gigs – so much emotion and so many people – but I know I do a reasonable job of them. I calculate how long it would take me to build the funds I want, based on my freelance rate – it would probably only take ten to fifteen gigs. *Ten to fifteen weddings,* I remind myself. But, all in a good cause.

What else could I do?

We could sublet the spare room, just temporarily. Rents are insane; maybe there's a student or backpacker looking for short-term accommodation at a reasonable rate. I do those calculations and realise it would take around twelve months. That's a long time when our fertility is only going in one direction, and a long time to share our personal space.

So, what else? As I turn into our street, I notice the sign over The Star. I could try the roulette wheel. I'm laughing at myself before the thought is even fully formed. There is no way a risk-averse person like me would even consider throwing money in that direction.

A car comes to a stop behind me and an older couple gets in. Uber driving. I could do it for just as long as it takes to earn the sum required. But how many hours a week would that take? Could I honestly work a full-time job and work outside those hours as well? I know other people do it, and I admire them for it, but I'd probably be a wreck.

I walk up the steps to my apartment block and wave my key fob over the security panel at the front door. As I wait in the lobby for the lift, I keep thinking. There must be a way to raise the cash. Maybe I could sell something. But what? We only have the one car, and I definitely need that to get me to and from work. There's stuff lying around the apartment that could go on Marketplace, but it's just rats and mice stuff.

The lift arrives and I step inside. We just don't have much else that's of any great value. As the lift chugs up to the top floor, I feel my mobile buzz in my pocket. I pull it out. It's a message from Simon. *Hey, have you seen this?* He's inserted a link. It has a shortened URL, so I have no idea what it will link to until I land on the page.

Hot Rain to launch dedicated climate change program

Fuck. Do I never see the wood for the fucking trees?

25

Emma
Sydney, 2024

I open the front door and head straight for the study. My heart is pounding in my chest. Why didn't I do more than glance at the Hot Rain stuff when Allie sent it through?

Because I'm so bloody pigheaded, that's why.

I push open the study door and sit down in the swivel chair, pull my laptop out of the desk drawer and turn it on. I wait interminable seconds for it to start up.

When is the closing date?

God, Allie had dropped enough hints . . . 'I'm under a non-disclosure agreement, so I can't say much . . .' she'd said. 'All I will add is, I think it'd be in your best interests to take a look at it.'

I start tapping my fingers on the desk. And how had I responded to that information? I'd taken offence. In my best interests indeed. Since when had I taken career advice from the likes of her? And an NDA? I'd thought she was just big-noting herself. Sure, a company like Hot Rain is really going to share their future programming plans with a fitness blogger, I'd thought.

Fuck, I'm an idiot.

Not only am I an idiot, I'm a disrespectful idiot. So what if Allie is a fitness blogger – which is what I privately call her, but is probably not what she actually is. But even if she is, what's wrong with being a fitness blogger? And how would I even know what her work entails? I've never taken the time to properly understand what she does. And why wouldn't Hot Rain want her opinion? She has a gazillion followers.

I'm embarrassed by how disrespectful I have been, and even more embarrassed because I've only understood the extent of my own disrespect because now that disrespect is, ironically, impacting me.

My head is beginning to throb. I rub my temples, and my hand itches in protest, reminding me that I haven't applied the ointment the doctor prescribed. I'll see to that when I'm done here.

Finally, the screen lights up. When I put my hands to the keyboard, they are shaking so much that it takes me two attempts to log in. I open the Messenger app, find the URL Simon sent me and click through. It takes me to the media release. Shit. That's not what I'm looking for. There's no link here to the expression of interest.

But Allie sent it to me. Please God, tell me I didn't delete it.

I go to my email account and sort the inbox alphabetically, but there's nothing from Allie.

Fuck, fuck, fuck.

I've engaged in reverse snobbery, I realise. Just because Hot Rain is a big news and entertainment network doesn't mean it can't be engaged in meaningful commentary on important issues. In fact, for all our cynicism, that's the point of a news and entertainment network, isn't it? Well, one of the points. I've let my reverse snobbery get in the way of pursuing something that could help raise awareness of issues that really matter to me.

No, I am not a reverse snob, I'm a snob, period. A social causes snob.

I rub at my brow, trying to massage away the awful feeling that I'm a bad person.

You are not a bad person, I counsel myself. *You were rude, but you were also going through a difficult time, and that made you less tolerant.*

No excuses, says my conscience. You were rude to Allie who is, above and beyond anything else, your wife's sister. That's unforgivable.

All right, I'm going to own my behaviour. I was rude and disrespectful, but my behaviour was not unforgivable or irredeemable.

I sit up a bit straighter in the chair. I will apologise to Allie, but right now, I have to find that bloody thing she sent me. I know it's useless scrolling the job sites. Hot Rain has probably engaged some super-specialist agency for the search, and it's possible it's not even listed.

I find the Hot Rain website and look for a 'work with us' tab. Of course they don't have one – if they did, they'd probably get a million applications from all over the country. Not from past-me of course, because past-me was a snob.

There's nothing else for it, I'm going to have to ask Allie to resend it to me.

Chances are, she won't even take my call, not after the email I sent in response to her.

Thanks for this. It's not currently of interest, but appreciate the thought.

At the time, I thought I'd been super polite. I'd certainly worded it carefully, because what I'd really wanted to say was, *If I wanted your help finding a new job, I would have asked for it.* The only thing that stopped me was the fact that she is Lauren's sister.

But wait. I know I deleted the email but had I deleted it from the deleted items folder? I go to the folder. It's there. I resurrect the email and open the attachment, skipping the over-the-top descriptions, searching frantically for a closing date. Five pm yesterday. I am so furious with myself, I immediately delete the email and its sodding attachments. For good measure, I go to the deleted folder, confirming, when prompted, that I want to 'permanently delete' the message.

Who needs a permanent reminder of their own stupidity?

I'm a firm believer in fate, but, conversely, I'm also a firm believer in making your own luck, so I'm having a hard time coming to terms with the fact that I've missed a golden opportunity.

The shower timer turns the water off automatically after the five minutes Lauren and I agreed on when I moved in. It's a minute longer than recommended by Sydney Water, but three minutes shorter than the average shower, saving around 30 litres per shower and reducing our carbon footprint. I stand in the cubicle for a little while afterwards, letting the excess water drip off my body.

I'm trying to be philosophical about the missed opportunity, and to understand that the experience taught me something important about myself. In future, I will explore opportunities properly, rather than being defensive and obstructive towards my own future success. I tell myself this, but it still cuts like a blade.

I reach for a towel and begin drying myself off.

'Aunty Julia needs us,' Lauren calls from the bedroom.

I wrap the towel around me and pull my shower cap off, running my fingers through my hair as I walk from the ensuite into the bedroom.

'What? Why does she need us?'

'She's torn a ligament in her knee carrying some old boxes or something down the stairs.'

'Ouch, that'll do it.'

We arrive at Julia's shortly before lunch. Her knee is strapped into some kind of brace, and she has a walking stick.

'Can you believe it?' she says as she opens the door to us. 'I'm not even close to sixty yet, and I'm hobbling around on a stick.'

'You're almost fifty-five, Aunty Julia,' Lauren reminds her gently.

Julia gives her a withering look. 'The doctor says there's no point operating, it's all rest, rest, rest – well, that and some nasty pills – until I can stand on it without screaming. Then it's walk, walk, walk, apparently.'

'I'm so sorry, Aunty Julia,' Lauren says, taking her arm and helping her to a seat on the couch. 'Probably best to do what the doctor says. We can help with whatever you need.'

'I have Maisie next door,' she nods towards the flat on the other side of the living room wall, 'so I won't need day-to-day help. What I do need, if you don't mind, is to move some more of those boxes from the upstairs room down here. I decided to do some tidying up,' she adds, tapping her braced knee with her walking stick.

'Very dangerous,' Lauren says solemnly. 'I always try to avoid it.'

We start bringing down the boxes and before long there's a neat stack of them beside the couch. Julia opens the lid of the one closest to us. 'Oh, look at that,' she says, pulling out a red painted wooden horse, 'a Dala horse.'

It's bright red and shiny. 'Lovely,' I say, as appears is expected of me.

Julia digs deeper into the box and pulls out a stuffed fabric bird and a complicated, patterned fabric star.

'Christmas decorations,' she says cheerfully. 'From Sweden.'

Lauren takes it from her and smiles. 'Aunty Julia is convinced our ancestors were Swedish.'

I smile, pointedly eyeing Lauren's blonde curls. 'Highly possible,' I agree.

~

'Well,' says Lauren in the car on the way home, 'that's helped me decide on one thing.'

The minor family emergency has somehow helped ease some of the tension between us.

'What's that?'

'Aunty Julia's birthday gift.' She pulls out her phone and starts tapping. 'She's always going on about being part Swedish, let's see if she really is.'

~

'Did Em tell you there's a Tarantino film festival on next month at the Ritz in Randwick?' says Simon.

'Sorry – no, I'd forgotten. Lauren, there's a Tarantino film festival on next month at the Ritz,' I say, and everyone laughs in response.

It's a glorious afternoon, even if the weather is still a bit nippy, and the four of us are sitting out on the downstairs balcony – Lauren, Simon, Tabitha and me.

'Oh, I'd love to go,' Lauren says, then laughs. 'That is, if you're inviting us.'

'I wouldn't have raised it if I wasn't,' Simon says with a smile. I pass him the charcuterie plate and he helps himself to a cheese-stuffed olive.

'Tarantino, Tarantino,' Tabitha muses. 'Didn't they say he's working on his final film?'

'That's right,' I say, quietly surprised. I didn't really think Tarantino would be her thing.

'Are they showing all his films?' I ask. I'm a diehard fan, particularly of *Pulp Fiction*.

'I think so – not all on the same night, obviously.'

I look up the details on my phone. 'It's kicking off with *Reservoir Dogs* on Friday the 25th, then every Friday night for eight weeks afterwards. The two volumes of *Kill Bill* will run over two consecutive nights – the Friday and the Saturday.'

'Shall we lock it in?' says Simon.

'What do you think, Lauren?' I ask.

She checks her diary on her phone. 'I'm not sure I can commit to every Friday night – it will be getting close to the end of the school year and reports. Definitely in for next Friday, though.'

'Oh, this is fabulous,' says Tabitha, 'a double date.' The new, improved me is not going to judge her for her enthusiasm. In fact, I try some reframing. Maybe the world could do with a bit more enthusiasm.

Simon turns to me. 'Speaking of films,' he says, 'have you looked at those old reels you found at the Carrington yet?'

'Well, I've tried to,' I say, 'but they're not in the greatest condition. Did you find anyone who might know something about them?'

'I did ask around, but nobody seems to know much about old films these days.'

I nod. 'I've had a quick look at two of the reels and I can make out a few scenes, but if I want to view it, I think I'll need a 35 mm projector.'

'Have you tried Marketplace?'

'Yeah, they all seem to be 8, Super 8, or 16.'

'I think those are amateur formats, aren't they?'

'It does look that way. I wonder if I could kind of hand feed it through something?'

'There are some on eBay,' Tabitha pipes up. She must have been searching, bless her. 'They're from the 1920s – is that what you're looking for?' She hands me her phone.

It's an actual motion-picture projector, from the 1920s. I can hardly believe it. 'Sold as is,' it says. 'Not tested but can be hand-turned.'

'Wow,' I say. 'That's amazing.' I scroll through the listing only to realise it's in America. The postage and import duties cost more than the projector itself. Damn.

'Thank you,' I say to Tabitha, handing back the phone. 'Unfortunately it's a bit out of my price range.' Especially given that I'm now determined to find the money to pursue another round of IVF. 'Simon, do you think I could potentially try to thread it through an old slide projector? I mean, it's basically just a light bulb projecting onto a screen, right?'

He frowns. 'I'm not sure, Em, to be honest. I mean, you said the film isn't in great shape – what if it ruins it? I really think your best bet is to contact the film and sound archive.'

'You're probably right.' He's certainly right, I know he is, but I just don't want to. I feel like this little piece of history belongs to me now, and I want to keep it all to myself for as long as possible.

'You never know, they might pay you for it. It could close an important cultural gap in our history.'

'I really don't think so.' It's possible that the National Film and Sound Archive would want the film, but I doubt it would pay for the privilege. Besides, I'd love to see the film in its entirety before surrendering it. Based on the little I've read about Rose Carey's films, I expect something similar to her earlier movies. Someone is in mortal danger, or has already died, as the result of a devilish act, perpetuated by someone Rose seeks out to avenge. All very early twentieth century in terms of plot, but to me that's not the point. I just want to view it.

26

Rose
Sydney, 1923

'Walter . . .'

I am standing at the entrance to the library and the light is shining on his hair. He looks up from the ledgers. His face is drawn and grey, and my heart plummets.

'Can we talk?'

He sighs, puts down his ballpoint pen, then rubs a distracted hand across his forehead.

'What do you want to talk about?'

I take this as an invitation to move further into the room, closing the door behind me. After a small silence, I say, 'I hate that we are so . . . distant.'

I can almost hear the clock ticking away on the mantelpiece as I wait for him to respond. 'Rose,' he begins, but somehow I know that the words he has put together will hurt me, so I hold out my hand to him, a peace offering.

'We used to once be . . . such good friends.' There is a catch in my voice.

He laughs, but there is a hollow sound to it as he ignores my outstretched hand and stands up. 'I was never your friend, Rose, you were mine.'

'You were never my friend?' I am not only hurt, I'm confused.

'No.' He moves closer to me. The words he is using are painful, but my body doesn't seem to care. 'I am your manager and your business partner, and now your protector.'

'And my husband.'

He laughs again, and again it has a hollow sound to it. 'For all that's worth.'

'You're still upset about the photos,' I say softly. I lay my hand on his chest, and I can feel his heart pick up its pace under my palm. He puts his own hand over mine, and for a moment I think he will remove it from his chest, but he simply holds it there. I look him directly in the eye. 'Walter, I promise you, those photos are not of me.'

He shakes his head; he doesn't believe me.

'I can prove it to you,' I say, and I step a little away from him. I am wearing a simple little day dress in lemon, crossed over my breasts and tied at my hip. I undo the tie and the dress falls open to reveal my white silk slip. I hear him take in a sharp breath.

'What are you doing?'

I let the dress fall to the floor. 'I am proving I'm not the woman in the photo.' The slip has thin lace straps and I slide one down my arm, exposing my right breast. 'My breast is bigger than those of the woman in the photo, Walter, see?'

He doesn't speak, but he can't take his eyes off me.

I slide the other strap down my arm and the slip falls to my waist. 'And my areolas are quite pink . . . they would have shown up much paler in a photograph.'

His eyes fixate on my naked breasts, and I can hear him breathing. I push my slip down over my waist, so that I'm standing only in my garter, short knickers, and white lace stockings. My fingers go to my waistband and he puts out his hand. 'I have seen enough,' he says, but the tone of his voice makes a liar of him. He's very close to me, so close I can see the pores of his skin.

I push at the silk of my underwear and slide the knickers down my thighs. They fall to the floor and I kick them to one side. 'You will see that I prefer to trim my pubic hair, it makes getting in and out of swimsuits so much easier. The woman in the photograph had not shaped her hair.'

He has averted his eyes and so I reach for his hand again. 'Will you please look at me, Walter?'

When he finally does, he emits a groan.

I put his hand on my breast, then take the other one and put it on one of my naked cheeks. He takes over now, pulling me into him. He is hard against me.

His lips begin razing a path from my ear to the hollow of my shoulder and when he lifts them from my skin to gaze into my eyes, he says, 'Dear God, I didn't want to rush our first time.'

'I don't care,' I answer back. 'I want you now.'

He groans again, looking for a suitable place to lay me down. I point to the armless, straight-backed wooden chair in the corner and lead him to it. I unbutton his pants. He takes over, pushing them down his legs before exposing himself from his underwear. He is ramrod straight, huge, and hard.

He sits down, taking me with him. I am in his naked lap, but he is not inside me. I position myself over him then pause, waiting until I feel the tip of him rise up to meet me, and then I am shuddering down, down, down on him, moaning into his mouth.

'I am not the woman in the photograph.'

27

Emma
Sydney, 2024

P.S. I am ashamed, because of course I am the woman in the photograph.

28

Emma
Sydney, 2024

I've decided that today's the day I'm going to see what I can do about viewing the film and I'm thinking about the postscript on the last letter I read as I step out onto the street. The weather is warm and almost balmy.

If the photos she is talking about are the ones I now have in my possession, why was she ashamed of them? My Google searches had led me to believe that Rose saw nothing wrong with the naked body, that she was even what you might call a naturalist, preferring to swim naked when and where she could. Why would she be ashamed to be photographed nude?

Because the photos are more erotic than artistic, I remind myself. Because they seem to be more about voyeurism than celebrating the human form. I had thought so from the moment I first saw them.

Why did she agree to be photographed in such poses then?

Probably for the oldest reason in time. She had been, if not exactly forced to, then perhaps compelled to.

I push the depressing thought aside. I've been on the phone with someone who seems to know a bit about old movies and projectors, and as Lauren's at a meeting for an upcoming production at the Genesian, I've decided to walk to the city to visit their store. I'm only fifteen minutes into the walk, crossing the Pyrmont pedestrian swing bridge over Cockle Bay, when I find myself wishing I'd worn a hat. A warm wind is buffeting display banners on either side of the bridge, encouraging pedestrians to visit the Sydney Modern. On a day like today, I wonder who could resist being out and about. I think it's going to be a long, hot summer.

When I arrive at the shop, I push open the door and ask the kid at the counter if I can speak to the owner.

'He's just gone to pick up a coffee,' the kid says. 'He won't be long.'

I'm happy to wait. From our brief chat this morning, I think he could be a good source of information.

I'm still not keen to reveal that I have what I'm beginning to think of as a lost film in my possession, although I'm not sure why I'm being so secretive about it. Perhaps it's because I feel as though I have a connection with Rose, a connection that goes deeper than just the film itself, and I don't want anyone to take it away from me.

For a moment I experience another sliver of guilt. The film isn't mine. It belongs to Rose Carey, or at least, her descendants. Who are they? Or is it actually the property of the production house that made it? Which would be the company that was named on the opening sequence. But does that company even exist today?

While I wait for the shop owner to return, I google 'lost films' again – even though I've done this search a dozen times before. A Library of Congress silent film project confirms that most American silent films created between 1912 and 1929 are indeed irretrievably lost. I've seen this before, but I've never fully explored it, mostly because it is so information-dense. There are eleven thousand films listed.

Would the film I have in my possession have been considered an American silent film, or an Australasian one? I search by Rose Carey, and five films immediately come up. The Library of Congress does not have a location for three of them, so they are presumably lost. It does indicate that two survive, and lists their locations. I note that one of them is held in New Zealand. But there's no mention of the one I have. It's almost as if it was shot and edited, but never screened. What is it, then? Because to me it looks as though it's a final product, something that would have been screened in picture houses, or whatever it is cinemas were called in those days.

The information from the Library of Congress is extensive, and I'm getting a crick in my neck trying to read it on my phone. I look up briefly to search the store. Has the owner returned without me noticing? It doesn't look like it. I rotate my neck to relieve the cramped muscles.

'He shouldn't be too long,' the kid behind the counter says.

I smile. 'Thanks.' There's a bookshelf in the corner stacked with second-hand tomes, so I wander over to it. There are plenty of books on photography and videography, and an industry paperback on Australians in film. I go straight to the index and check for Rose Carey. She's there, but there are only a few pages dedicated to her, and they don't tell me anything new. She was an Australian silent film actress and producer, who also directed and wrote her own scenarios. She was the first woman to appear naked in a major motion picture, she popularised a 'modern' version of the women's bathing suit, she performed her own theatrical stunts.

My phone pings. It's a message from Lauren.

Hey, are you able to pick up a script for Aunty Julia and run it over to her? She's just messaged me. I think she's in pain. Maisie's on hols.

I text back 'sure' and take the book to the counter to purchase it.

'I'm sorry, I gotta go,' I tell the kid. 'Can you apologise to Andrew for me?'

'Sure,' he says, with his best customer service smile.

I hand him the book, he scans it and presents the EFTPOS reader for me. I wave my phone over it.

'I would really like to have another chat with him, though, if he has a moment sometime,' I say as I take my purchase from him.

The kid has such an open face that I go one step further. 'Tell him I've found some old reels of what look to be a 1920s silent film. I don't have a projector to view them, so I'm wondering if he knows anyone who might. A collector or somebody like that.'

'Old movie, projector, got it,' the kid says with a smile. 'I'll ask him to let you know.'

I get Julia to email me the script and take it to the nearest chemist. There's a half-hour wait, the pharmacy assistant tells me, so I head for a nearby coffee shop, a favourite of the Hammer and Tongs crew when we're in the city. I take a seat to wait for my cappuccino, and start scrolling through my phone, still wondering how else I might be able to view the film if I can't find a movie projector.

What I need, I think, is a lamp that shines through a piece of film and projects it onto a screen. Does it really have to be a movie projector? Despite Simon's misgivings, I think I could use an old slide projector, if I went about it carefully. The only difference I can see between a slide projector and a movie projector is that a slide projector advances the film one slide at a time, at the user's pace, whereas a movie projector advances it at a pre-determined pace. Of course, there's also the fact that a slide projector can't handle sound, but that obviously doesn't apply to silent films. If I could somehow eliminate that stop/start thing from happening and manually feed the film strip I have through a projector, surely I'd at least be able to view it better than I can at the moment?

But in doing so, I could, as Simon also pointed out, only further damage the one-hundred-year-old film. It's already in a state of some disrepair.

I begin searching for vintage movie projectors on my phone. The one Tabitha found on eBay is still for sale, but the freight is still exorbitant. The ones available in Australia are either 8, Super 8 or 16 mm formats, not 35. That's the advantage of a slide projector. Slides are 35 mm.

I put the phone down and drum my fingers on the table. I haven't looked at all the reels yet; maybe one of the remaining three is in better repair than the first two.

The waiter delivers my coffee and as I look up, I spot Johnno standing at the takeaway counter. I quickly press the side button on my phone to lock it, before waving at him. I still feel guilty and even a bit silly for not telling him about rescuing the crate. He might even, as Simon suggested when I first told him about it, know something about early film. But given how long it's now been since the Blue Mountains gig, I think it's just too late for confessions.

Johnno makes his way towards me, takeaway coffee in hand.

'Fancy seeing you here,' I say with a laugh.

'Ditto.' He has his camera gear backpack on his back and what I recognise, from our conversations, as the newest, lightest professional drone currently on the market.

I tilt my head towards it and say, 'Working on a weekend?'

He sort of smiles. 'Always working,' he says noncommittally. 'Comes with the territory.' I find it refreshing that despite being the boss of what is a steadily growing business, he is still keenly interested in his craft.

I indicate the vacant seat beside me, and he sits down, settling his gear around him.

I sip my cappuccino. When I look up, he says, 'I'm glad I ran into you actually. Can we have a bit of a chat about something?'

Lauren came home briefly only to head out again with Simon and Tabitha to the Tarantino film festival. We saw volume one of *Kill Bill* last night. Tonight is volume two but I didn't join them this time, as I had committed to doing some work for Johnno after our conversation this afternoon.

I can't decide if I should tell Lauren about the conversation as soon as she gets home from the cinema, or if I should wait and see how things pan out. I get up from my desk, where I've been scrolling environmental topics on the internet, and go into the kitchen. I flick on the kettle, then pull a re-usable cotton teabag out of a drawer and fill it with tea leaves. Lauren won't be home until late. Volume two has a run time of over two hours. So, I should stay up and discuss it with her as soon as she gets home. That's what mature people in mature relationships do.

The kettle boils and automatically shuts off. I pop the tea bag into a mug and pour boiling water on top, jiggling the bag up and down until it's an acceptable golden colour. *No,* I think, as I top the mug up with a splash of milk. I shouldn't say a word yet; it's too soon.

When Johnno said he wanted to chat to me about something, I'd been worried he was going to comment on my attitude at work since returning from leave, which I have to admit has been somewhat lacklustre. As disengaged as I've been, the simple truth is, we cannot afford for me to be unemployed, so I was apprehensive. But if he's noticed my dour mood, he didn't mention it. That wasn't at all what he wanted to talk about. I am so relieved, so happy about what he told me that I feel as though a weight on my shoulders has been, if not entirely lifted yet, considerably lightened.

I take my tea back into the study and sit down at my desk. I really should concentrate on the work at hand. If I can get it done tonight, we'll have the rest of the weekend to ourselves.

I move the mouse and both screens light up. I go to the *allaboutcompanies* website, a forum where employees, customers, clients and service providers rate and review Australian companies. I plug in Hot Rain. There are hundreds of reviews, the company is rated an impressive 8.5 by its stakeholders and, even more impressive, the CEO, a woman, has a one hundred per cent approval ranking.

What Johnno had told me was . . . he'd submitted an expression of interest on behalf of Hammer and Tongs to Hot Rain and the submission has progressed to Stage II. Hammer and

Tongs has to pitch to the company within the next fortnight and he needs my help with the presentation.

I stared at him. 'How did you hear about the opportunity?'

'Hot Rain sent it around,' he said simply.

I put my head in my hands before telling him about Allie sending it to me. 'I thought she said something like she was under an NDA, that she couldn't discuss it.'

'She probably meant she couldn't discuss the new programming. I'd heard rumours there was something with an environmental focus in the wind over there, with the new producer on board. But the full info only came to me recently, when I was advised we'd made it to the second round.'

At about the same time that Simon sent me the media release, I realise. 'I feel like a prize idiot,' I said. 'I didn't pass it on to you because I didn't read it properly. I didn't even realise that the expression of interest was more directed at companies than individual contractors until just now. Allie probably thought I would forward it on to you. I'm so sorry.'

He laughed. 'In the first place, I'm glad you didn't apply for it yourself, you're one of our best and I'd hate to lose you. Secondly, there's not many opportunities I don't hear about, one way or another – it's a small world in this business. Don't beat yourself up.'

I was so taken aback by his rare praise and so glad to have been given a second chance to be a part of something I'm passionate about, that I actually cried.

'Hey, steady on mate,' he'd said, searching for a tissue box. 'Since when do you get all emotional over a potential new client? Pull yourself together. If we get this gig, I want you to take ownership of it.'

I smile to myself now and go to move my mug out of the way and onto the adjacent bookshelf, but I realise I haven't put Rose's letters away. They are sitting there on the shelf in their blue-ribboned bundle. And because it's Saturday night, and everything seems to be taking a turn for the better, I indulge myself. I'll just read one or two.

The Carrington Hotel
Thursday, 20th December 1923

Dear Birdy,

By now, I know you know . . . But I'll tell you again anyway, because I feel as though it's the only way I can explain what happened. You see, I fell in love with him. I didn't mean to – in fact, I fought hard against it . . . but . . . when I did, I realised I'd never really been in love before. Certainly not with my husband. That was a marriage of . . . necessity.

I can pinpoint the day, although I'm not sure I knew it at the time. I can remember every little thing that happened . . .

He said we'd picked a good day for flying. There was only the lightest dusting of cloud in the sky, little powder puffs, high up and out of the way, and no chance of rain. It felt almost warm . . . if I'd to guess, I'd have said we were heading for at least seventy degrees.

We walked towards the aeroplane, and he hurried me up, saying we wanted to be up and away since we had good weather, and that there was work to do. Honestly, I didn't know what he meant by work, not at that stage, but I did check there was no banner attached to the rear of the plane, I made sure of it.

He came to help me with goggles and cap, and as he adjusted the chin strap, his fingertips brushed against my lips. I think it was then, that moment. That's when I knew how much I wanted him. I wanted to turn my head and feel his palm against my cheek. But I didn't . . . I just stood there like a dummy until he finished what he was doing. He stepped back, as if to admire his handiwork, and we were looking into each other's eyes. I know I was the first to look away.

It wasn't until after he'd sat me into my seat that he shoved a cardboard box into my hands. Even then, I swear I didn't know what was in it.

When we reached a certain height, he gave me a signal, indicating that I should empty the box over the side of the plane and that's when I opened it. It was a box of flyers. The goggles made it difficult to read the type, but I recognised the stylised writing at the top: 'Mayfield & Co. Performers presents . . .' I stuffed one into my pocket, but I didn't read it, not until later.

And Birdy, I won't lie – I did it. I let those flyers loose, free to float down on the unsuspecting citizens of Sydney. Was it disloyal? I don't know. All I can tell you is I was amused by it, and I just thought, well . . . let him have his little stunts. He might have all kinds of magical flying tricks up his sleeve, but I thought it was a battle he couldn't possibly win because there was one thing Carey & Ryan had that he would never have . . . Rose Carey.

There's more to say about that day, but Griff is back now, and we are going for tea, and so this letter is short. I'll write more about it again soon.

I miss you.

Love, Me.

The Carrington Hotel
Sunday, 23rd December 1923

Dear Birdy,

I promised to explain my part in all that happened, and I feel I can only do that if you understand how things developed between Griff and me.

After the flight that day, he took me for a picnic. I could have turned him down, I suppose, but it seemed rude to, and he promised to drive me back to Point Piper. And besides, I wanted to go. A picnic . . . on the grass, where people could see us . . . it was risky – but you and me . . . we are cut of the same cloth, we have always faced risks the same way. Head on.

After we'd eaten and he was lounging on the picnic blanket, playing with a long stem of grass, I just blurted it out. I said, 'I am married.' And you know what? He didn't bat an eyelid, he didn't care. He seemed so, what's the word? Cavalier. After a bit, he said, 'Not happily.'

How did he know? And what should I have said? I tell you what I did say. Nothing. Eventually he started asking questions about the film, whether it had gone back to Hollywood, whether I thought it would be a success. I was immediately on my guard. He can't buy our trade secrets with a couple of sandwiches and a bottle of cider. Then he said the oddest thing. He said Australians would have a tough time making it when – and he stressed when – sound came to movies, because our accents would get in our way. Him, a San Franciscan, saying such a thing, the way he runs his words together. The cheek of him.

I openly challenged him on it. I reminded him how much people love the movies, insisting that sound would be no more than a fad. I told him if people wanted to hear actors and actresses speak, they'd go to the theatre. Then he straight out asked me if sound did come about, would we take the leap, would Carey & Ryan make talking movies.

I did not say another word about it. I did not give the slightest hint about whether we would or we wouldn't, and I was very cross that he would try to worm the information out of me like that. I stood up and demanded he take me home straight away, and that's the truth.

Later, I pulled the flyer from my pocket. As we now know, it was for the Mayfields production of Peter Pan. *I actually laughed to myself when I read it. I couldn't believe he thought he was going to transform Mayfields with a children's play. I didn't think for a moment that we had anything to fear.*

I will write again soon.

Love, Me.

29

Emma
Sydney, 2024

'Plans?' says Lauren, over toast and tea the next morning. She has discovered a low carb bread she finds palatable, and it is thick with butter and vegemite.

'I'm pretty much free today. What are your plans?'

She doesn't look at me; instead, she investigates her hands. 'I think I might start work on a Hanten jacket.'

'Great.'

'So . . .' she says slowly. 'Any more . . . thoughts?'

I consider telling her about Hammer and Tongs and Hot Rain, but decide against it. If it comes off, it will solve so many things, but if it doesn't . . . I don't want to set her up for more disappointment.

'About what?' I ask.

She lets out a frustrated sigh. 'About what? About the topic that has consumed our lives for the best part of a year. Doing our own thing with our own sperm donation.'

'Oh, that . . .

'Yes, that,' she spits. 'Do you think you could take some time out of your busy schedule to think about that?'

I am caught off guard by the sudden attack. Is she mad that I worked last night, instead of going to see the film? Or is she upset thinking I haven't even thought about her suggestion?

'I have thought about it,' I say, as calmly and quietly as I can.

'Well then, are you going to share your thoughts?'

'I'm not sure—' I begin, but she interrupts me before I can articulate what I want to say.

'What are you not sure about now?' she storms. 'Come to think of it, what have you done since our last negative pregnancy test to further the conversation about having children?'

'What have you done,' I counter, without really thinking about what I'm saying, 'to come to terms with the fact that we probably never will?'

The moment I see the way the words wound her, I want to take them back. But I'm too hurt and, suddenly, too angry.

'Right,' she says, standing up and pushing back her chair. 'Well, I guess that sorts one thing out.'

I'm terrified to ask what she means. She looks at me for long minutes as I refuse to ask. 'It has sorted out that I won't be having kids with *you*.'

I feel as though she's taken to me with a kitchen knife. 'Lauren . . .' I reach for her, but she pulls away and storms out of the apartment, knocking over her still half-full teacup on her way out. It falls to the tile floor and shatters. My usual response to her outbursts is to clean up the debris and wait for her to calm down, but I feel horribly misjudged. Worse than that, I feel silenced. She hadn't given me the opportunity to speak.

If she had, she might have heard what I do want, what I am prepared to do.

I leave the shattered remnants where they are. Let her clean up her own mess. I navigate around the broken teacup and go and sit out on the balcony for a bit. Pyrmont is busy; I watch families walking dogs and strollers down the road to Pirrama Park. The smell of freshly ground coffee wafts up to me from the street below.

I'm not sure what to do with my Sunday now, but I decide it's pathetic to just sit around and wait for her to come home. I put my shoulders back and straighten up. There are plenty of things I could do, including some I've been putting off.

Like phoning Allie and apologising for how rude you were.

'Hi Allie, it's Emma.'

'Oh, hi,' she says, although she must have known it was me calling, my name would have popped up on her screen. 'Everything okay? How's Lauren?'

'Sure, everything's okay. She's fine.' I clear my throat. 'Look,' I continue, then worry that I sound a bit officious, 'I'm just ringing to say . . . I'm sorry if I seemed ungrateful when you sent through the Hot Rain opportunity.'

'Oh,' she says, and I can hear how surprised she is.

'I think I jumped to some – wrong conclusions – not just about the opportunity, but about you, and I'm sorry.'

'Wow,' she says.

What does she mean by 'wow'?

'I was really rude to you, and I'm sorry.'

'Sure. Okay.'

Does she sound a bit frosty? That's unusual for her, she's usually so . . . upbeat, like her sister.

'No, there was just no excuse for it.'

Silence.

'So anyway,' I say lamely, 'I apologise.'

She's probably dying to get off the phone. She probably couldn't care less if I was rude to her. It is highly possible that I don't feature much in her thinking at all.

'Emma, I can't pull any strings, if that's what this call is about. I have no say in who they contract or who they don't. I was asked if I knew anyone, and I thought of you guys. But . . . after that, well, you're on your own I'm afraid.'

Oh my God. She thinks I'm asking her to put in a good word. She thinks I'm asking for special favours. 'I know that,' I retort. 'I'm not asking you to, that's not what this call is about.' All I want to do now is get off the phone myself. 'I wanted to apologise, that's all. Anyway, I've done that now, so I'll go. Hope you and Jaxon are well. Bye.'

I hang up, then sink my head into my hands. What the *fuck* have I just done?

I take a long walk, all the way along the Pirrama Park waterfront, and then all the way around Pirrama Park Wharf. I am almost oblivious to the grey gleam of the Harbour Bridge under an eye-smarting blue sky, and the sun bouncing off the silver scales of the Crown casino across the water. I walk on up the hill and onto the Pyrmont pedestrian bridge, across Cockle Bay and into the city.

I should call Johnno and explain how I've fucked up. But it's Sunday and I decide it can wait for tomorrow.

When I return to the apartment, Lauren is still missing in action. I'm not used to having to fill so much of my spare time without her. My identity, my life, is all tied up in her. I can't imagine – and don't want to experience – life without her.

I wander into our bedroom and sit down on the bed.

I need something to take my mind off myself and my mistakes. I pick up the book on my bedside table, the one I bought in town.

I'm not in the mood for reading. I'm not even very interested in the life and times of Rose Carey anymore, I think, as I flick through the pages. The info on her is nothing I don't already know anyway. Where she was born, the places she'd lived, some of her more daring stunts, her film and theatrical works.

After starring in numerous films, writing books, and touring the world with various shows, she became an avid promoter of women's health and fitness.

Okay, that's new information. But I'm not in the mood. I'm about to close the book when a single paragraph grabs my attention.

'Despite being long-term residents of USA, Miss Carey and her husband, Walter Ryan, spent a lot of time in Australia. In the early days, she was often accompanied by her constant companion, Bell Procter, and cinematographer Edward Quinn.'

The Carrington Hotel,
Monday, 31st December 1923

Dear Birdy,

The days are longer now, and even up here in the Mountains, it is hot. Sometimes there is not the slightest breath of breeze and it's then I think about our winters in America. Remember the time we went to Howelsen Hill in Colorado to ski? It was only supposed to be for people training for the Olympics, how did we get in?

Oh, now I remember.

Alec.

As I write his name, terror grips me by the throat, and I wonder how any of us will ever get over him. I am so upset I had to put the pen down for a moment while writing this letter. I can't bear it sometimes,

So let me talk of other things. Peter Pan. *Griff gave me a front row ticket to the matinee the day it opened. I didn't know he'd made the agreement with Kirby Flying. I'd no idea he'd use the patented flying apparatus so that Peter, Wendy and numerous Lost Boys would seem to fly across the stage. Sydney audiences would talk of nothing else for months. I know he had no obligation to tell me – quite the reverse, in fact. But I was still cross about the fact that he didn't pre-warn me.*

He suggested we take a drive. I was upset and annoyed and confused about my ever-entangling loyalties. Even so, I agreed. I agreed to every opportunity to be near him.

In the car, I confronted him over every trick he'd played on us. The plane with the banner, the flyers, and then Peter Pan. *I was so angry. I accused him of using me. I was convinced he'd been using me, and I was hurt and bitter. Do you know what he said to that? He said, 'Now as if that's not the pot calling the kettle black.'*

When I demanded to know what he meant by that, he said I'd tricked him into surrendering 'honestly purchased' silk. Tricked him indeed – he knew full well what he was doing that day when he drove me home with the silk. We'd struck a bargain – he would keep the canvas, I would keep the silk, and nobody would inform the original owners, Mr Randolph, the police, or anyone else about the transaction.

I told him that at least we were using the silk for a noble cause, and do you know what he had the nerve to say? That our involvement in the Ball was all about trying to repair our reputation, not about a noble cause at all.

I was so offended, Birdy. Of course we needed to repair our reputation, but we also cared more deeply about the Ball's success than anyone else. We not only wanted to help our athletes, we wanted to honour Alec's memory. I told him so, and then he said something almost unforgivable. He said, 'A noble cause would be fashioning clothes from that silk for those who need it. Charity would be giving it to the mothers and children of Surry Hills.'

He cut me to the quick with those words. I spat back at him, I said something like, 'You'd have the mothers and children of Surry Hills running around in silk, would you?'

Then I made him take me home, back to Point Piper, miles and miles away from Surry Hills, far, far away from deserted parents and bastard children.

I'm tired now. Surry Hills is not something I want to talk about, and I think you know why. I'll write again soon.

Love, Me.

30

Rose
Sydney, 1923

When I had thought about it, and I can now admit that I had, I always imagined Walter would be a sensitive lover, and he is. But that doesn't mean, as I had thought it might, that he is not exciting or passionate.

One long rainy afternoon, as we lie together naked in his bed, he says, 'We are well-matched in this too, Rose.'

I roll over onto my side, rest my head on his arm and stroke the other with the tips of my fingers. He has strong biceps, beautiful skin.

'Yes,' I agree. 'I enjoy having sex with you.'

'I noticed.' He smiles, but shakes his head a little. 'And you are not afraid to use the word.'

'Why would I be?'

There is something just behind his blue eyes, something I don't quite understand. 'You believe that sex is as natural as breathing, don't you, Rose?'

'Of course. You do too, don't you?'

He traces the line of my nose to my lips. 'I believe lovemaking is an art.'

I prop myself up on my elbow, intrigued. 'An art?'

'There are at least sixty-four lovemaking positions, Rose.'

'Sixty-four!' We have had sex in several positions; we have pleasured each other with our hands and our mouths, the way lovers do. I cannot imagine how anyone could know sixty-four positions.

He chuckles. 'Can I show you some?'

My nipples are already hardening at the thought. 'Yes.'

He leans forward. 'The first part of this position, and every position, is kissing.'

'We have already kissed.' I am impatient for the new act, not the kiss.

'We are going to kiss some more,' he insists. 'There are more nerves and muscles in the tongue, Rose, than in almost any other part of the body.' He comes closer and explores my upper lip with his tongue. I sigh and close my eyes.

'Keep your eyes open,' he breathes against my mouth.

I do as he asks, and I feel somehow mesmerised, out of my depth. His mouth is focused entirely on my upper lip. He draws it into his mouth and out of instinct, I begin to suck on his bottom lip. His tongue somehow finds the small piece of skin connecting my upper lip to my gum and the way he teases it sends an unexpected shock wave of pleasure directly between my legs. I find myself writhing beside him, wrapping my leg over his hip. The kiss goes on and on, and just when I think I can bear no more of it, he pulls back again.

'Are you ready?'

I am panting, I am more than ready. 'Yes.'

He stands up and I see that he is, as he has always been in bed, hard and straight. He leans forward and spins me around so that I am lying crossways on the bed, then he pulls me to the edge, so that my legs fall to the floor.

He leaves me momentarily, then returns with one of my chiffon scarves. He lifts my left leg and rests it on his shoulder, ties the scarf loosely to my ankle. Then he lifts my right leg and binds it to my left. He pushes my bound legs slightly back towards me, and I strain them towards my head. I'm desperate for him to enter me, but he doesn't. Instead, he leans forward to kiss my bound ankles, then each toe and between them, the balls of my feet. His mouth travels up the backs of my legs and his tongue focuses on the tender skin behind my knees. I hear myself as I wait for him to reach my thighs. 'Walter,' I beg.

'Kissing is very important, isn't it, Rose?' he says, his voice husky and close. His mouth is now between my legs, and I bend my knees to encourage the entry of his tongue. But he seems to be waiting for something. I don't understand.

He repeats the question. 'Isn't it, Rose?'

I realise he wants an answer.

'Yes,' I agree. I am quivering, waiting for him. I almost can't bear it.

'If I put my mouth on you, will you come?'

'Yes!' I am almost shouting, I am desperate for release.

'So how important is kissing?'

'Not as important as fucking,' I cry out, using a profanity that has never before crossed my lips.

He stands up and for a moment I think I have lost him. But before I can even form the words to complain, he is ramming into me with such unexpected force that I explode.

'I want Eddie to take the film back to the States,' Walter says a few days later.

I look up at his reflection in the mirror on his dressing table. It is fair to say that I have all but moved into his room. His face is solemn again, he worries so – about me, about the film, about our accounts, about everything.

I put my hairbrush down on the table and stare at it. Then I wave my hand at him. 'Alone?' One of us is usually always with Eddie. It's a kindness to him, really. His leg troubles him and he needs help.

Walter takes his time answering me. I have much to do for the Ball, it is now only a month away, and Walter is still here with me. I take great comfort in that, but despite the beautiful sex, I had a terrible night's sleep and now I have a headache to match. I had the oddest of dreams. Bell, wearing the tall, cone-shaped headdress we had discussed putting up for auction, the one that appeared in the photo sent to Walter, and the two of us in J. J. Griffin's car, but with Alec at the wheel, taking that terrible road in New Zealand. It's all mixed up, memories and dreams. I realise I haven't told Bell yet about the photos sent to Walter.

'Yes, alone,' he confirms. 'I can't leave you, and I know you won't agree to go until after the Ball,' he says. 'It means too much to you.'

'It is very important to me,' I agree.

'For Alec.'

I nod. 'Alec is one reason.' I have many reasons for needing to stay for the Ball, and one of them is so I can help athletes like Alec realise the same kinds of dreams that he did. His death, however accidental, happened on our watch, and I feel a deep sense of obligation to honour his memory in this way.

'You were in love with him.'

I'm shocked. 'Walter . . .' I stand and walk over to him. 'Alec loved men. You know that.'

He shakes his head. 'That doesn't mean you weren't in love with him. Love is not sex, love can't discriminate. Love only knows love.'

He is telling me something, but I can't quite grasp it. 'You have no need to be sexually jealous of Alec, Walter.'

He shakes his head, as if that is not what he means at all. 'Love is inconvenient,' he continues, and there is something reflective in his eyes now. If I had to name that look what would I call it?

Sadness?

'I was not in love with him and, if it is important to you, I did not have a relationship with him. I loved him, yes, but as a friend. I have not had sex with anyone except you since we left America. We have only been married such a short time, but I am faithful to you. Please believe me.'

'Rose.' Is his sigh defeat or exasperation? 'There is no need to lie to me. I know you are not.' And with that, he passes me an envelope.

His name is written in copperplate on the face of it, and it is addressed to his private Sydney post office box. I already know what will be inside; it's not hard to guess. I let out a sigh to match his, and turn it over. Then I unwind the string around the washer.

More photographs, just as I suspected, and once again, Walter thinks they are of me. I take them back to the dressing table and sit down to inspect them more closely. I wonder why he would mistake them. He has seen me naked, he has made love to me many times now.

The photos that have been taken of me nude are tasteful; these are not. In the first, the woman's naked breasts spill out between the folds of a length of pale fabric. She hides nothing but her face, which is turned away from the camera. On purpose, I suspect, to hide the fact that she is not me. I shuffle the photos, but they only become less tasteful. Here she is wearing a dress, but it is pulled up to her waist to reveal her nakedness. Another is taken from behind.

I put them back down on the dressing table. There is no sense being angry about them; my anger would only convince him I had something to do with them. 'Just as before, these are not photos of me.'

Walter walks up behind me and picks one up. He points to her arm. She is wearing a silver snake armband.

I feel my heart pounding. First my headdress and now my armband. But still, I keep my response measured. 'They are very popular, Walter, I believe even April Lewis has one. Someone is trying to make trouble between us – help me discover who it is.' My words are as close to a plea for his understanding as I have ever allowed myself. I have never had to beg for it before.

He stares down at me and for a moment I see him warring with himself. In the end he says nothing.

Eddie.

His name comes to me without warning. I remember that it was Eddie who saved me that day in New Zealand.

Of course, I'd known that all along ... what I hadn't remembered was ... When we started up our film production company, Walter and I each took out a life insurance policy on the other. As I was, at the time, a big movie star, my life was valued at substantially more than his, because the loss of my life would have caused the greatest damage to the company. I'm insured for a great deal of money, and Walter is the sole beneficiary.

I look up at my husband and for the first time in my life, I'm afraid.

He is at the bedroom door, but my next words halt him.

'Where were you that day in New Zealand, the day of the accident? You said you would be in the car right behind me.'

A slight pause. He turns back to look at me. 'And I was.'

'No, you weren't.' I remember checking the rear-vision mirror; nobody had been right behind me.

'Yes, I was, Rose. You drive so fast, nobody could keep up with you. But Bell and I were in one of the cars right behind you, and Eddie was in the car just ahead of us. Together, we were the first on the scene. You simply don't remember. The doctors said you might not.'

He's trying to make me believe it. I don't think I do. My heart begins to trip. I draw in a deep breath.

What do I believe?

I'm always so impatient, that's true. We had been delayed all morning and I wasn't prepared to delay any longer. Usually, Walter and I travelled in the same car; if Walter was not with me, then it was Bell. But that day, I just jumped in the car and told them to follow when they were ready. I remember this clearly now . . . Knowing me as he does, and how much I loved driving, Walter had called, 'We won't be far behind you.'

'But you weren't there,' I insist. 'Why weren't you there?' I am not asking him anymore, I am asking myself.

He starts to walk towards me, but I hold up my hand to fend him off. I don't want the flood of memories interrupted again.

It was Eddie who had opened the back passenger door. It was Eddie who'd pulled me clear, only moments before the car crashed through the barricade and tumbled into the water thirty feet below. Why wasn't it Walter? It should have been Walter.

And now I am remembering something else. Dusty boots and bolts and the tyre . . . what is that memory at the back of my head? What does it have to do with anything?

'It definitely wasn't an accident,' I say, the words falling out of my mouth even as the thought forms. I see some sort of shadow move across his face. 'Oh my god . . .'

'No, Rose,' he says, as if he can read the conclusion I am quickly coming to. 'Don't even think it.'

As another memory assaults me, the tables turn. I'm not under his scrutiny now, he is under mine. 'The crystal tank . . . that really wasn't an accident either, was it?' I had tried so hard to pretend that it was.

His face pales and turns a shade of grey. 'Rose, don't do this.'

My mother's music is dancing in my head, I hear it as clearly as if Bell were playing it on the piano downstairs. Bell . . . She's been behaving so oddly lately. Disappearing at strange times and when I need her most. I haven't had a moment to tell her about the earlier photo. Where is she now, for example? I struggle to remember. She'd said she was going to stay with a sick aunt for a couple of days. What aunt? It's the first I've heard of her having an aunt. Why hadn't I questioned her more about it?

I've been too busy with committee meetings and last minute things for the Ball. I've been too preoccupied. But these are things she usually helps me with . . . Where was she yesterday? Where was Walter?

A terrible realisation occurs to me. 'You and Bell,' I say. 'You want me out of your way . . . you've always wanted me out of your way . . .'

My husband has been having an affair with Bell all this time. Bedding me was just about making sure I didn't suspect . . .

Oh no.

Would he have bedded me at all if I hadn't literally thrown myself at him? The memory of stripping naked in front of him, and the way that scenario had ultimately played out, sends a cold rush through my body.

But he had wanted you, as much as you had wanted him.

Yes, but that doesn't mean he isn't also having an affair with Bell.

Why hadn't I seen it before? Why hadn't I realised?

Because I am in lust with my husband. I refuse to call it love. I have never been in love. Love is a figment of a wishful imagination. The nausea is rising to my throat. My husband and my best friend . . . It is the oldest of old deceits.

'You're wrong. Whatever it is you're thinking, you're wrong.'

Bell . . . she is beautiful and still young, and lately she has been . . . What? Different, as if her life has been retouched by a new palette.

My breathing is ragged, and I feel faint. But if I faint, am I placing myself in more danger?

Something doesn't make sense – what is it?

I inhale a deep breath. As dangerous as it might be to ask my husband about it, I must know. 'Tell me everything then, from the day of the car accident.'

He comes to stand next to me, then he crouches down beside me so that we are eye to eye.

'I was as annoyed by the delay as you were that day,' he says.

'What does that have to do with anything? Tell me what happened when you arrived at the scene.'

'Your car was hanging over the railing.' He swallows. Is that troubled look on his face genuine? 'Eddie was already there.

Bell and I were further delayed because, despite him looking over the cars, mine was running low on gas.'

How could that be? Eddie is so meticulous about car maintenance, even more so now, since the accident.

'We had to refuel, but I'd hurried him on after you because I didn't want you travelling alone.'

I want to believe him, oh how I want to believe him.

'When we arrived, he had already jumped out of his car, but the shock of it all must have rooted him to the spot. I went running towards you and he jumped into action.'

Now he's trying to put himself into the position of hero.

'He reached you moments before I could. You would have died if not for him, but everybody worked together to save you that day, Rose. I have come to believe it is as you said. It *was* an accident.'

As I stare at him I know for certain that it was not. Icy fingers of fear grip the back of my neck.

'And the crystal tank?' The fear makes my voice harsh and snappy.

'The tank was an unfortunate error in judgement.'

Why has he changed his tune? I am silent for so long I can hear us both breathing. 'Someone is trying to kill me, Walter, and you know it.'

There is another long, hideous pause, this time from him. 'It is not me,' he says finally. He looks at the photos on my dressing table. 'I will get to the bottom of whatever is going on, Rose. I promise you.'

Can I trust him? I never expected to have to ask myself that question, but now I find myself questioning his every motive. Does my husband want me dead? If so, why? His life and his livelihood are both so intricately wound into mine, why would he?

Because, as we have no children, he would inherit my fortune – and while that might currently appear to have a cloud hanging over it, there is also a sizeable insurance policy on my life, and he has always been the beneficiary, since the moment we formed the company.

He was very annoyed about me using my father's money for the Ball, and he has been so worried about finances. The payout would make all those worries go away.

But do I honestly believe my husband, the man who before any of this was a most trusted friend, would kill me for money? He has never displayed any form of physical violence, not towards me nor anyone else. He has sometimes been angry, and we have sometimes exchanged heated words . . . however, I've been as vocal as he . . .

Is he in love with Bell, as I fear, and does he want me out of the way so that he can be with her? Would my husband kill me for love?

It doesn't make sense. If the two accidents were in fact attempts on my life, they happened before we were married. He didn't have to kill me in order to marry Bell – he was a free man.

Maybe he felt he was going to come under suspicion for the accidents sooner or later, so he married me in order to allay any future suspicions.

But that doesn't make sense either because both incidents had already been ruled accidents and besides, he wasn't the one who proposed marriage in the first instance, I was. He only married me when he felt I – and the company's reputation – needed protecting.

If he truly wanted me dead, why would he go to those lengths to protect me? Why would he take so long about killing me, and wouldn't he have tried more than twice?

There are more questions than these to answer. Who is sending him the photos, and why? Perhaps nobody. Perhaps he has sent them to himself. He's bought the pictures from someone, somewhere, and tried to convince me they are photos of me. Where do men procure such things? But these are not entirely anonymous photos. Whoever is in them wears my props. Why would he go to so much trouble to make me look like an errant wife?

To give him reasonable grounds for divorcing me, and ensure the only shame associated with it falls on me? Then why marry me in the first place? Nothing adds up, nothing makes sense.

I am surprised how much even the thought of him wanting to divorce me affects me. I have always been my own person. I have prided myself on my great courage. I know I would survive his betrayal, if that's what this is, but oh, how I pray it is not. I don't want to live my life without him, although I know I can if I must.

He's said he will stay with me until after the Ball. He has said he will even attend it himself, if I wish.

He's said he will get to the bottom of whatever is going on. Am I a fool to hope that he will, that there will be some plausible explanation for whatever it is? Or will the tenuous trust I have decided to place in him for now prove unfounded? And if so, have I just signed my own death warrant?

31

Rose
Sydney, 1923

If there is one mantra that has guided me through every trauma of my life, it is this: *The show must go on.* With or without Walter. With or without Bell.

I have insisted on separate rooms. I will not sleep with my husband until his innocence is proven to me beyond reasonable doubt. I believe he thinks the same of me. He is still suspicious about the photos. I can't shake the feeling that the accidents were no such things, and I worry about his hand in them. We are civil to each other, but at night, I lock my door.

There is no denying that I miss him and the intimacy we had just begun to share, and there is no denying that my body craves him.

I try my best to act as if nothing is wrong, but I think Bell is also keeping a secret from me, perhaps more than one, and I am keeping secrets from her. We have never been this way before, and it burdens me.

But today is the day. The Olympic Ball.

Bell and I are in the ballroom at Point Piper with the ladies and girls that make up our set. We are all dressed in the silk gowns Bell made for us, overlaid with tissue. She is wearing a version of the same garment, although she will not be in the set with us. I run my hand down the length of my dress. She is a costumier like no other. Will she always be there for me?

Our eyes meet, and for a moment it feels as if we are the only two in the room. 'You are so beautiful, Rose.'

I smile, but I can sense that it does not meet my eyes. 'Because of you,' I say.

She shakes her head. 'You have always been beautiful and more than that, you have always been so kind to me,' she responds. The comment is unexpected, and I think for a moment that she will go on, tell me something I really need to know, but then she appears to think better of it. I wonder if, after this evening, anything will be the same.

Before we enter the Town Hall, our set is to lead the parade, circling all four sides of our city's most impressive building, before proceeding into Centennial Hall via a fabricated Athenian Temple. Behind us will follow all the other sets. I stand now at the head of my own contingent. This is a performance like any other, I remind myself. I blank all else but this from my mind.

'Ladies,' I say, raising my long-gloved hand. Immediately they stop chattering. 'Please remember, we are the leaders of this pageant,' I straighten my back to encourage them to do the same, 'so we must serve as wonderful examples to those who follow us, as I know we all will.' They mimic my posture and assemble into position.

We haven't rehearsed this part of our set on site, but I have every confidence in them. We had approximated the walk around in Mr and Mrs D's ballroom and they are now as well-trained as any dancers and any extras I have ever worked with.

'Thank you. Now, as we rehearsed, first we are going to parade around the outside of the Town Hall,' I indicate the route with my hand, 'before returning here and entering the building via this entrance.'

As well-rehearsed as they are, it was impossible in that ballroom to replicate the throngs of people now lining the street to witness the parade, or even to convey to my ladies how big the crowd of 1500 people will be once we are inside the hall.

'When we return here, please remember to fall in behind me and wait for my signal.' It is, as with all performances, a matter of great timing.

I bend down to the two children dressed as sea urchins who will precede me, like flower girls at a wedding. 'Jean, Dorothy, are you ready, my best girls?'

Jean looks up at me and flicks the rope of pearls that attach her to me. 'Ready, Miss Rose,' she lisps. 'Ready, Miss Rose,' Dorothy mimics.

'Good girls.'

Bell has further improved on my exquisite silk gown, attaching a tissue train that fits neatly about my waist. As I walk, it parts to expose the silk beneath, and spills into a sea of green behind me. I am effectively a creature of the sea. My shoulders are swathed in the same tissue embroidered with giant pearls, which falls about each arm to form gossamer, mermaid sleeves. On my head is another wonderful Bell creation, a seahorse crown in green and silver. The ladies who follow me are dressed as sea anemones, their silks swathed in tissue in every soft colour of the rainbow.

Where is Bell now? I look around me. She was supposed to be coming with Walter and Eddie in a follow-up car, but I can't see her. Not that it's imperative. It's just that I expected her to be here by now. She's always beside me before any performance, for encouragement and also to adjust my wardrobe as necessary. I can't see Walter either.

I don't have time to worry any more about their absence. It is time. I nod at my flower girls. As we circle the building, the crowds roar.

But the thunder in their applause awakens that wanton beast named grief. It comes at me without warning, rearing up behind me. It cares nothing for me, nothing at all, and it will devour me.

I so want to do Alec proud, I so want to honour him. I can't go down without a fight, I can't surrender. But the beast is in a rage, causing a red sea mist to form before my eyes.

Why was it Alec who died in the tank that day? Answer me that! Why did he have to die? Tell me at once! And while you're about it, tell me the truth – was it really supposed to be me, not him?

I feel paralysed, frozen to the spot until Dorothy, whose little hand I have been holding, begins to cry. Somebody needs me. Instantly, the red mist monster evaporates. What a fickle beast.

I bend down beside her. 'Are you frightened?' I whisper close to her ear, so that I might be heard above the noise of the crowd.

She nods, her finger in her mouth. 'Me too,' I say. 'Let's do this together, shall we?'

When she nods again, I lift her up and we wave to the crowds. My ladies follow suit.

Then we are back at the rear entrance, and Dorothy has found her courage again. I set her down and she joins hands with little Jean. Together, they lead us along the north corridor to the backstage entry and up onto the stage. We form a line near the top of the choir steps that stretch across the stage. We are standing in front of the grey pipes of the magnificent grand organ. Almost three storeys tall and set in ornate cream casing, embellished with gold, it is the biggest and best pipe organ in the world.

I stand at the centre of my ladies, and the band, comprised of ex-servicemen, starts up. They are playing Miss Lewis's wonderful march specially composed for the ball, and this crowd also breaks into spontaneous applause. The sound of it crescendos through the great hall. We work as a choreographed team, proceeding down the choir steps and onto the stage itself. As I walk, I feel the slight tug on the tissue train of my dress as the hem catches momentarily on the stage-to-floor steps that have been put in place for us. They lead down to the hall itself. Bell fashioned the train precisely to achieve this effect, to snag briefly so that it will fan out behind me, briefly catching the rush of breeze we cause with our movement and creating the illusion of waves. The ladies who follow me create a similar effect. The frilled hemlines of their gowns float about their ankles, faithfully mimicking the colourful sweep and sway of sea anemones. We are all exactly as Bell had envisaged. She is a genius.

All the painstaking work of the decorations committee has also paid off. White and gold friezes run the length of the balcony railings, decorated with long strands of myrtle and caught at intervals with laurel wreaths. Pillars have been transformed into Greek columns, and the brilliant electric-lit chandeliers overhead are swathed in green and gold gauze.

Amber light streams down from them, illuminating our pathway through the glorious hall. It is as enchanting as any set I have ever worked on, perhaps more so. When I turn at the furthest end of this magnificent room, I look up to see a banner stretched between the columns, bearing the words *Bring back the laurel wreath of victory.* Oh, I do hope we do.

Our performance is over. I wave to the crowds, they applaud and I find myself searching the sea of faces, looking for J. J. Griffin – no doubt the banner, being of canvas, is his contribution. But it is a wasted effort, I can't locate him. I still can't see Walter either, or Bell . . .

Now that we are done, the ladies and little girls in my set gather about me under the magnificent crystal chandelier in the vestibule, their faces flushed with the thrill of the opening, and my attention is momentarily diverted. When the remaining sets have paraded through in my wake and the children's mothers have collected them I tear myself away, heading back into the body of the hall in search of my own people. It is crowded with players and partygoers. I run straight into Eddie.

'Oh, Eddie,' I say loudly, in order to be heard above the noise of 1500 excited folk. 'You're here. Did the others come with you as planned? I can't find them.'

'Um,' he says and he seems edgy, uncertain. 'Walter is over there.' I look in the direction of his pointed finger and see Walter standing to one side of the hall, in conversation with Miss Lewis.

I nod. 'What about Bell?'

He pauses before saying, 'I don't know where she is.' I scan the room, but it's impossible to spot her; she's so much shorter than Walter.

'Photographs?' he asks finally. 'I've set up the tripod and camera in the vestibule.'

'Oh have you?' I hadn't noticed in all the excitement. 'But yes, of course.'

We head back out to the vestibule. Several members of the committee join me for group photographs and he takes numerous shots of me, but it is an arduous task and the evening is frantic and warm. When I recognise Bonnie Spark waiting to speak to me, I make my excuses to Eddie. 'Let's do more photos later,' I say, laying my hand on his arm.

He looks down at my hand and I instantly remove it, but he gives me a warm half-smile. 'Sure.'

I go to move away and then I stop. 'Eddie,' I say quietly, 'can I please ask you to let me know if you see anything . . . unusual.'

The most curious look comes over his face. 'Unusual?' he repeats.

'Yes.' But how can I ask him to look out for me? It would alert him to the fact that I don't trust my husband to do that for me.

'Yes . . . if you see anyone acting . . . oddly.' When he continues to stare at me, I add lamely, 'You know . . . wearing anything that reminds you of our stolen props.'

'Of course,' he says.

'Ladies and Gentlemen, the Viennese waltz,' announces the Master of Ceremonies.

I predict they will play Mr Strauss's *Blue Danube*. I lift my head but Walter is already walking towards me. This is the music we had used to choreograph our own interpretation of the waltz. I realise only now that I have always thought of *The Blue Danube* as belonging to us.

'Mrs Ryan,' he says. It is the first time he has called me by the name that marriage has bestowed on me. 'May I have this dance?'

For all that I'm afraid I can't trust him, I cannot refuse. Convention demands that I accept and . . . more than that, I want to dance with him. I extend my white gloved hand to him. As he takes it in his, a lock of his thick hair falls across his forehead. I want to reach up and stroke it back from his face.

Under his carefully groomed moustache, his lips are forming a polite smile. All I can think about, as the orchestra begins to play a short interlude, is the whispers he breathed on my skin as we lay in bed that long, rainy afternoon. It has been too many days ago . . .

We walk hand-in-hand to the dance floor and the crowd makes way for us, forming a circle around us as we reach the centre of the room. The shimmering opening bars of the waltz sound in my ears.

He stands a foot or so away from me and bows. I gather my tissue train, loop it over my arm and curtsey. We promenade around one another before standing side by side. He extends his left hand to me, I take it.

We move together and apart in time to the music, our free hands meeting briefly, touching at every turn. Then with a brief spin, he draws me to him, and my hand is on his shoulder, his arm is about my waist. He holds me there, a fraction too close for convention, a fraction too long, and yet not nearly close enough, not nearly long enough.

He steers me around the dance floor. I am vaguely aware that our fellow dancers have not yet joined the waltz, they have paused to watch us. We fall into the familiar steps of our routine: one, two, three, spin; one, two, three, spin.

Beneath the light touch of my palm, his shoulder is as strong as it was all those nights ago, his hold around my waist as tender and familiar. I step back with my right foot as he moves forward with his left and I feel as though I am feather-light, gliding above the ballroom floor on the breeze created by our movement. I am being carried by him on a wave of longing that seems embedded into the music.

We go through our routine again, and when the music swells and quickens, he turns me in a dizzying series of spins, before catching me at the waist and lifting me off the floor. I raise my arms above my head in the classic fifth position and I hear the crowd around us draw in a hushed, collective breath.

He continues to spin me in a circle but this time, he does something we have never rehearsed. As he moves to set me on my feet again, he slides me all the way down the length of his body. My breasts flatten against his chest, my arms reach to wind themselves around his neck and he pulls me closer. I am staring into the sea blue of his eyes, and I want nothing as much as I want his kiss. He obliges.

I expect the crowd to be scandalised, or at least to feign it, but long before the kiss ends, I hear the sound of gentle laughter, followed by applause.

I realise with an intense wave of gratitude that they have forgiven me for Alec's death, and more than that, they have accepted me. Our ruse, if that's what it was, has worked. Marrying has wiped our slate clean. Sydney society has been seduced by the fairy tale of us.

But as Mr Strauss's music finishes in a dramatic flourish, I realise a terrible truth. I have done what I said I would never do and, in the doing of it, I may have put myself in terrible danger.

I have fallen in love with him.

I am outside the Town Hall staring up into the night sky. It had been difficult to find a quieter spot, but there is no doubt I needed one.

The knowledge that I am in love with Walter has made me feel skittish, uncertain. I don't think I have ever before felt so . . . upended . . . by my feelings for a lover. I don't like it; I don't like the vulnerability that goes hand in hand with it.

I draw in a deep breath, trying to calm myself. I must not panic. I must try to think rationally. Walter does not wish me harm. Walter loves me, I'm almost certain of it. Looking back, I think he has always loved me – and, subconsciously, I always knew it. I probably even used the knowledge to my own advantage, if I'm honest. I don't want to consider whether or not that was wrong, all I know now is that being in love, that phenomenon I had summarily dismissed as frivolous nonsense, is anything but. It is fierce, insistent, uncontainable . . .

When the dance ended, I'd given him a brilliant smile, curtseyed and left him, informing him that I had other duties. After that, I kept myself busy, made sure my dance card was full. My feet in their silver slippers are now throbbing.

'Rose.'

I turn to see him standing at the rear entrance, the yellow lights overhead bringing out the highlights in his hair. He walks down the stairs to stand beside me. I move slightly away. After a long moment he says, 'Are you happy with the results?'

'Oh yes,' I say and my voice sounds as skittish as I feel. 'But this is not all my own doing, as you know. The committee and subcommittees worked so very hard. For our part though, I think Bell and I created something spectacular on a very limited budget, and I was very careful how we spent my money.'

He sighs. I had removed my headdress for the dancing and he is close enough to me that his breath sends a little wave through my hair. 'Oh, Rose . . . you are too generous. Not just with your money, but with your time.'

'Would you have me any other way?'

'No,' he admits. 'But—' He clears his throat and I realise he is trying to find the words to tell me something. 'Rose, I promised to get to the bottom of things, and—' he pauses again, 'I think I have.'

My heart starts to pound. I'm not sure whether I should move closer to the hall or step into the shadows again.

'I have some difficult news.'

Do I want to hear it, here, with the lights of the Town Hall blazing inside, with the sound of the band playing another waltz? Do I want to hear it in these grounds, underneath the midnight blue blanket of Sydney? Whatever it is, I find I now want it to wait for another day. I don't want my world to shatter, as I know it will. I don't want the shards to pierce through the evening, the way the glass sharded through Alec.

'Can it not wait?'

'No.'

I breathe out a long, deep sigh. 'All right,' I say with the greatest reluctance. 'Let me hear it.'

I see that he wants to take me in his arms. Now I find myself remembering the way he comforted me in bed during those long nights after the tank accident. How he had taken both my hands and wrapped them around him before wrapping his own around me. We were bound together in sorrow then. But I can't allow myself to be bound up with him now, not while the shadow of doubt still hangs over him. I watch him carefully construct his next sentences.

'Rose . . .'

'If you must tell me, tell me quickly.' Perversely, I now want him to be succinct with his words.

'It's Bell.'

'Bell? Has something happened to her? Where is she?'

I still haven't seen her. Walter had organised cars and drivers for me to go ahead to the Town Hall in the early afternoon with my ladies, and little Dorothy and Jean. We couldn't be late. Bell wasn't in the set, so she was to leave a little later, with Walter and Eddie, in the Cadillac.

'She's not here, Rose,' he says quietly.

'How do you know? Why is she not here? Where is she?'

He lets out another long sigh. 'I don't know where she is.' It is exactly what Eddie had said.

'Walter.' I use my sternest voice. 'Tell me what you do know.'

I want his arms around my waist now, but still I can't allow it and so I hug myself, as if I am cold. We were so very close once, and I had taken our closeness for granted. I thought I could never lose it. I hadn't acknowledged the magic of him, the strength in him. I hadn't recognised that when I breathe, I breathe him in. I have always been too busy to notice, too busy to understand how much I seek his shelter in our storms, how long I have done so – long before we had a sexual life together.

'Bell . . . is not who she seems.'

'What are you talking about? Of course she is who she seems.'

'No, she is not.'

I have known Bell half my life. Surely there is no secret she could have kept from me, not until recently, no confidence she would not have shared, and vice versa? She is like a sister to me.

You haven't told her about the photographs Walter has been receiving . . . why not?

'You are wrong, Walter,' I say, but my bravado now feels false. 'You do not understand the nature of women's friendships. You do not understand Bell. She is my dearest friend, my confidante, my helpmate. Nothing you say about her would take me by surprise.' But I am lying, lying because these past six months . . . everything has somehow been different between us and . . . what has she ever told me about her past, her parentage, her life before me? *Nothing.*

He looks at me for long moments, and there is such deep sadness in his eyes. 'If only that were true . . .'

'It is true,' I insist.

He shakes his head.

'Well then, what is it about her? Please stop talking in riddles. Tell me straight or don't tell me at all.'

He draws in a deep breath. 'It is Bell who arranged the theft of our props, it is Bell who has been stealing our funds. I believe, although I cannot prove it, that it is Bell who was responsible for the crystal tank incident and the car accident. It is Bell who has, all these years, been carefully and meticulously plotting to bring you down.'

I am winded, wounded. 'That,' I finally gasp, 'is a lie.'

He dares to reach for my hand and I'm powerless to stop him. He holds it very tightly. 'When have I ever lied to you?'

I thought *never*, and then I thought *always*. Now I'm more uncertain than I have ever been. I hear my breath coming to me as it might on a snow-covered mountain. It burns as it enters my lungs, and as it shudders out of me I fear I will be physically ill.

'How do you know this? Why would you think this? Not Bell, she would never do anything to hurt me, to hurt us. You're wrong, you have to be wrong. You must be.'

The worst I had thought she could do was sleep with my husband.

He is holding me up, I realise, he is taking my weight. 'She has access to our chequebook. She has been using it. They showed me the evidence at the bank. I have arranged an appointment for you with the bank manager next week so that he can also show it to you.'

In fact, the bank has already called me to confirm the appointment. I had been so busy I hadn't bothered to ask what it was about, I'd just taken the details. Walter is telling the truth, I realise. 'But . . . of course she has been using it, she has authority to use it.'

He shakes his head. 'That's why it took so long to uncover the nature of the theft. For many, many years, she has been taking small sums, a little here, a little there.'

'There has to be some explanation, Bell is scrupulously honest.'

'No, Rose, she is not.'

'You said she is responsible for the theft of our props.'

He nods. 'She organised the theft and arranged for them to be disposed of in the harbour.'

'This simply cannot be true.'

He waits as I digest it.

'It was Eddie who found the Roman horse's head.'

'That's what he told me in the beginning, but . . . it was bothering me. Something didn't add up. I tackled him on it after you left for the Ball this afternoon and it turns out, he was covering for her. He also said the horse's head was part of a larger containment.'

'What are you talking about? What containment?'

'She had a box of other things. He gave me what remains of them today. It contained the evidence.'

'What evidence, Walter?'

'There were some . . . things in it that belonged to you. She had stolen them over a period of time and for whatever reason, she wanted to get rid of them. When she organised the disposal of the props, she also organised for the disposal of other . . . things.'

'What things?' I haven't noticed anything missing.

He clears his throat. This he doesn't want to tell me. I can see he believes it will hurt me beyond repair. 'Some things . . . of your mother's.'

'Not the sheet music? Oh, please tell me she did not destroy my mother's sheet music. Dear God, Walter, no.'

He nods and I let him take me in his arms. Apart from on the dance floor tonight, it is the first time I have allowed him close to me since he showed me the photos with the snake armband. He strokes my hair, runs his hands down my back.

'Did any of it survive?' I sob into his chest.

'It was . . . unsalvageable.'

'Why? *Why* would she do such a thing? Did you confront her with it?'

He nods. 'I did . . .'

I take a step backwards. That is why he and Eddie were late to the Ball.

'Why didn't you wait for me? I should have been the one . . . There must be a reasonable explanation. She must have had a reason. She wouldn't have done this without cause . . . she's my best friend.'

'That's the very reason I didn't involve you. How terribly awkward it would have been for you to say these things to her, and on such a night. How awful it would have been for you to see the look on her face when I confronted her . . . you would have known in a heartbeat, as I knew immediately, that she is guilty. I wanted to spare you that.'

'What did she say?'

'Very little. What could she say?'

'She didn't deny it, or try to explain?'

'No.'

'She didn't protest her innocence?'

'No, Rose, the evidence was overwhelming.'

I put my hand to my mouth. 'Where is she?'

'I don't know.'

'She left, and you don't know where she went?'

'That's right.'

'Did she take anything with her?'

'She took a bag of her personal belongings. I asked her to allow me to check it before she left.'

How humiliating for her, to have Walter inspect her personals like that.

'I know you love her,' he continues gently. 'I will do whatever you want to do about it. But I think . . . '

'You think what? Don't stop there, tell me.'

'I think she thought . . .'

It is clear he is finding it difficult to say the words. He clears his throat and starts again. 'Bell might have assumed she would somehow share in your . . . inheritance.'

The words send a cold chill down my spine. Bell knows the contents of my will, she was a witness to it. She knows she is a small beneficiary. But is my life really worth so little?

Walter moves instinctively towards me. 'I'm sorry, Rose,' he says, and when I'm close in his arms again, he says, 'She's gone now.'

But I am having such difficulty believing that Bell could ever do me harm. I lift my head from his shoulder, trying to think clearly. 'Can we . . . leave aside the . . . accidents for now . . .' The truth is nothing he has told me so far has implicated her hand in those occurrences . . . 'You are saying that all our money worries . . . stem back to her?'

'Eddie says he suspected she was behind our problems some time ago, but he didn't want to make things bad for her when he had no proof.'

'Oh, why couldn't he have said something? Anything? Doesn't he owe us a little loyalty? Don't they both?'

'To be very fair, we did not confide the extent of our financial difficulties to Eddie.'

'But Bell knew. I never thought for a moment that she couldn't be trusted.'

'In a way it was honourable of him not to say anything, don't you think?'

'I suppose so,' I agree. 'It didn't honour us, though, did it? Will our money be returned to us, Walter?' I find I hardly even care about the money. I know that the thing that is most important to me, my mother's music, is irrevocably lost.

'I'm not sure. I am in consultation with the bank. I do have a question for you, though.'

I sense he is finding it difficult to put it to me.

'We can't prove the accidents weren't accidents, we can't prove that she was involved, no matter what we personally believe, but . . . the extent of the theft is quite large.' He pauses. 'I am wondering if . . . you want me to take it to the police?'

Oh, how my heart plummets. What would happen to her if I said yes? Would she ultimately go to prison? I don't think I could bear that. Even now I still think of her as my friend. I could not stand to see her reduced in that way, it is too difficult to even imagine.

But she is not my friend, I remind myself, she is a traitor.

'What would happen if you took it to the police?'

'She could be arrested.'

Only recently I had read in the newspaper of a youth sent to prison for four years with hard labour, for defrauding a bank. I had also read of a woman sent down for three years for stealing from dwellings. I think of my Bell, how like me she is now that we have been together so long. Where would they send her, if she were convicted?

'Have you finished tallying up all the sums?' I ask.

'I can only estimate, but I believe it is grim, Rose.' The number he tells me makes me clap my hand over my mouth. It is a fortune. 'How did we not notice until now?'

'As I said, it was very gradual. A little here, a little there. It is only that she made such a large withdrawal, at a time when we were struggling to get other funds into the Australian account, that it came to the bank's attention. It was a silly error on her part, given how she had gotten away with it. For someone we thought we knew so well, we actually know very little about her. She seems to have come from nowhere.'

'So all our money troubles stem from her?'

He shakes his head. 'No, there are certain truths that still prevail. For example . . . you are as beautiful to me now as you were the day I met you, but you are not growing any younger. And . . .' he pauses again, 'as enchanting as I find your Australian accent, I don't think it will work when motion pictures include sound, and I believe that day is coming. It pains me to say it, but I think your days as a movie star are indeed coming to an end, if they have not already.'

I already know this and I am not so vain as to mourn the fact, but I do feel a great sadness that a part of my life that brought me to this point is now over. 'Yes,' I agree.

'The industry itself is changing, as we both know, it is being manipulated by the big studios. We have spent a lot of our time producing things that have cost a lot of money, and we are yet to see a return.'

He's talking about the film that we made in New Zealand, the film we would have taken back to America already if not for me. I've been foolish, I realise. We should have gone to organise its distribution, just as he said, months ago.

'I was a nostalgic, sentimental fool to insist on us staying here,' I say, 'I'm so sorry for making it difficult to leave.'

'Rose, please don't be too upset with yourself. I understand why you are reluctant to leave your homeland. It has been a very difficult time for you.'

I make a face. I don't want to be reminded, I don't want to feel even more sadness.

'All is not lost,' he continues. 'The film is edited now. I've had a chat with Eddie and he is willing to take it back to the States as early as next week. We can follow him as soon as you are ready.'

I nod. 'It's a smart idea. Thank you.'

He doesn't want to say whatever it is he feels he must say next. 'But the extravaganza . . . we cannot afford to do what you want to do, at least . . . not yet.'

He is right. All I can do is nod in agreement.

'You astound me with your courage, Rose,' he continues softly. 'You have achieved so many things, things I thought if not impossible, then improbable. I want to believe in everything you want to do, it's just that this time . . .' His words fade out, as if he doesn't want to say them.

I manage a half-laugh. 'It's all right, I know it. This time, I am wrong.'

32

Emma
Sydney, 2024

I have never heard of a cinematographer called Edward Quinn. But why would I? He belongs to the twentieth century and most of my life has been spent in the twenty-first. Could he have been related to my family? If so, wouldn't someone in my family have mentioned it along the way?

Maybe, maybe not.

I reach for the bundle of letters. I have read all but three now and I want to savour them.

The Carrington Hotel
Friday 11th January 1924

Dear Birdy,

Did we fool anyone? And if so, for how long? I don't know. Did we fool you? He sent me an invitation on a postcard, to meet at the California Chocolate Shop in Pitt Street, to make up for the tricks he had played on me, I think. I went to meet him because . . . oh, I could give lots of good reasons, but they are all excuses. I went because I wanted to.

That first day, he bought me a box of chocolates and handed them to me with such great ceremony that I laughed and then he said that if I would laugh like that again, we should meet every week.

Every week? After that we met all the time. Whenever I could get away from the busy diary, whenever I could escape my husband. On Sundays, when I was under much less scrutiny, I would meet him at the top of the street, and he would drive us places that I had not yet discovered. We took short trips to outer suburbs and a little way down the coast. We parked on a clifftop once, then sat in the long grass, looking out to sea. We talked all the time.

Another time we drove to the country and ate chocolates in a rotunda. He put the box in the sun until they melted and then he dipped his forefinger into them, leaned forward and painted my lips. It was the moment before our first kiss.

And after that kiss, I started to see myself as I think he sees me. I started to forgive myself for the things I unwittingly did. I will never forget Alec, nobody should, but I forgive myself for him.

I didn't go over it with Griff, but the stories he told me on our drives, stories of war and flying and fortunes lost and found, made me realise I had laid all the blame for the crystal tank at my own feet. But it wasn't my fault. It really wasn't. It was Eddie who had been responsible for estimating the thickness of the glass that would be required, not me. It was Eddie who told me what to order and from where. I didn't know anything about glass manufacture or aquariums. I was your right-hand woman, not your tank man. I didn't know much about construction at all.

If you don't already know, the wrong thickness of glass had been used for the tank. That's why it shattered, that's why a shard of it pierced Alec's heart and killed him. But when the authorities called for our order book, the page had been torn out. There was no trace of who had ordered what, or when.

Later, Eddie spoke to me privately. He blamed me for it. I had misunderstood his specifications, he said. He told me we must keep very quiet about it. He knew my secrets, he said, more than just that one, and he would hate for them to come out. It could all play out very badly for me.

I could not bear for any of us to suffer any more and, if I'm honest, I wasn't ready for Eddie to tell all. So I did as he said. I kept quiet, and every day since, I have carried that burden of guilt and regret.

'I told you the specifications,' he insisted, 'but you said we should get the thinner glass because costs were blowing out, and it was cheaper.'

It's true, costs had been blowing out. But I would never have risked the lives of the people I loved most of all, not knowingly. I couldn't have known such a choice would prove fatal. If I made the wrong choices for reasons I thought right at the time, then am I to blame? Since that time . . . I have tried to stand back from decisions like that. I have focused instead on the things that I do well.

Griff has taught me that I must forgive myself for my mistakes in the same way that he has forgiven himself for accidents he took responsibility for during the war. 'Life is not really about lessons, that's not the right word,' he says. 'Life is about . . . experience. We live, laugh, love, hate, grow, forgive . . . it is all an adventure.'

'And misadventure,' I'd added.

The early evening is upon us, and Griff wants to walk, now that the day is cooling down, so I must go. I'll write more soon.

Love, Me.

33

Rose
Sydney, 1923

I leave Walter on the pretext that I have formal duties to attend to, and I do, but I run through them like an automaton. For the first time in more than a dozen years Bell is not at my side, and it is Walter who removed her from me.

I am sick, thinking about her betrayal. I had thought there was something . . . sacrosanct about our friendship. She had been my partner in so many enterprises. She was my mainstay, my confidante.

The Town Hall is emptying. The last of the partygoers are exiting the building. It has been a wonderful evening but even Miss Lewis, after gushing about our success and congratulating us all, is on her way out. Walter, it seems, has been pressed into escorting her to her car. He looks over her head to smile back at me.

'I will be back,' he mouths.

For some reason, I can't leave yet. I feel this was my last

theatrical hurrah and I am bowing under the weight of the realisation.

More than that, I am troubled. Would Bell really steal from me, not just money, but my mother's music? I don't want to believe it.

I'm not a person who weeps, but as I head for the exit, the tears come. Bell has been with me throughout every joy I have experienced in my adult life, every heartache. She laughed and played with me, she sympathised and soothed. I can't remember a time when we spent more than a week or two apart.

I love Bell and I will miss her, as dreadfully as I miss Alec. In some ways the cruel ending of our relationship is a thousand times worse. Alec loved me and did not choose to leave. The knowledge that Bell might have had some hand in his death, in an 'accident' meant for me, doesn't bear thinking about. But if what Walter says is true, I must come to terms with the fact that Bell never loved me, nor, perhaps, did she love Alec.

Why, *why* would she betray me? She could not have been jealous of my success – she was a contributor to it. She walked beside me every step of the way. She helped me create the swimsuit that changed the world for women. Every creation I ever wore, she made. I tried to always let her know how much I valued her contribution, and I always rewarded her for them, always. She was more than well remunerated for her devotion to us and her role in our success. She didn't have the same financial rewards that we had, but that was only fair; she took none of the risk. But she understood that . . . didn't she? Except she wasn't devoted, I remind myself, and rather than playing a role in our success, she actively sought to undermine it.

The staff have removed the decorations; I am the only one left here.

Walter had suggested that if I were dead, Bell might somehow share more of my inheritance. I can't believe it. It just doesn't make sense. Does it?

I thought I knew her as well as I know myself, but I probably didn't even scratch the surface. She cannot be who I thought she was. So, who was she? I try to remember what I knew of her when I first met her. She had been working in an office in London, as a typewriter girl. She'd liked her job, but not the environment because . . . because why? I'm struggling to remember. It was where, I think, she learned shorthand and perhaps some bookkeeping skills. Skills, is that the right word? If what Walter has told me is true, she'd been cooking our books from the moment she joined us.

I wander towards the vestibule, and my feet in their little silver slippers with their tiny heels echo over the glorious floors.

We'd shared so many ideas, explored topics close to both our hearts. Bell would talk about how long some countries were taking to allow women to vote, and to work outside the home. I became passionate about helping women to devote time and care for themselves.

But she never talked about her past, I realise now. She never mentioned her mother or father or whether she had siblings. Where did she come from? For me, it was almost as if Bell's life began in England, when I met her. Did I ask her about her life in Australia? Probably not. It was always all about me.

When we visited the Tivoli store in Surry Hills, and she'd said she lived across the road, in an unremarkable street, in an unremarkable part of town, I hadn't asked her many questions about herself. I'd been so interested in what she'd told me about aeroplane factories and balloonists that I hadn't bothered to question her much. I hadn't asked about her family. I hadn't asked who she'd lived with. I hadn't asked her much at all.

When I'd first invited her to join us, it was as my secretary. Then she'd morphed into a kind of personal assistant . . . and finally, she had become my costumier and, I thought, my friend. She hadn't been just one thing to me, she had been many things.

I look down at the dress she'd made for me tonight. When I'd put it on, I'd felt beautiful. It was the perfect gown for an evening that had started magically. How quickly life can change.

34

Emma
Sydney, 2024

I check the time. Lauren's not home yet, but surely she will be sooner or later. I could be doing something more constructive than sitting around reading old letters . . .

One more. I'll read just one more.

The Carrington Hotel
Thursday, 17th January 1924

Dear Birdy,

Our honeymoon is coming to an end. We must return briefly to Sydney, Griff has work to do. But we will be back at the Carrington and very soon. The owner is quite the entrepreneur and also has two theatres to his name, right here in the Mountains. And, as you no doubt already know, he is a newspaper man. He and Griff have been 'in discussions' as they say. I can't spill too many beans yet, but it is very exciting and we will have a home base here. Oh, I am so in love, Birdy.

I want to tell you now, how it is with us.

The first time we came right here, to the Carrington. It is the sweet memory of that time that brought us here for our honeymoon. Well, it is the honeymoon capital of the country.

Of course, this is not a real honeymoon – being married already, I can't marry him . . . I hope to one day, though.

I told you I had a sick aunt, and even though it was a lie, probably the first direct lie I have ever told you, I wasn't sorry. You were so preoccupied at the time, and there was so much fuss about the film and who would and who wouldn't be going back to America with it, remember? My husband had said he would go alone; then there was the idea that we all would go. But that was never going to happen, you were too busy with the Ball, and promises had been made that would not be broken. It was stalemate and I didn't think it would hurt for me to be out of the picture for a few days.

'I won't be missed,' I'd said to Griff, although I knew it wasn't true. I knew I would be missed, for practical reasons. At that time, there seemed still so much to do. But my conscience was clear . . . our dresses for the pageant had been completed and were hanging on a rack downstairs in the ballroom. We'd rehearsed the routines until I'm sure we could have performed them in our sleep.

Did I mean to fall in love with him? I hadn't thought about it. But is that the truth? Or am I making excuses for myself? Because a faithless wife might be forgiven some indiscretion, especially in my circumstances, if I were in love with him.

I won't ever allow myself to be dishonest, not with myself at least, and so I have confronted the truth. I was always attracted to him, and I knew it, despite all his outrageous antics, or perhaps because of them. I love how he loves life, how he is making good on all the promises he made himself during the war, when he truly expected to never make it home again. Yes, I was always attracted to him . . . but that is not as forgivable as love.

Did I love him on that first meeting, or was that just . . . lust? Remember how many conversations you and I had on this very topic?

All I knew at that time was, if in the beginning it was only lust, it wasn't anymore. It was something finer and more . . . breakable.

I wish I could have met him in America, before I was married . . . I have to close my eyes tightly, because the alternative life that plays out in my head is so brightly coloured and beautiful it starts to sting.

'We have today,' he's fond of saying, 'and all the days that come afterwards.'

Of course we do.

That's all I can write for the moment. But I will write again, I promise.

Love, Me.

35

Rose
Sydney, 1923

'Rose,' a voice says.

I look up and brighten. 'Oh, Eddie, I thought you must have gone.'

'No,' he says and then he hesitates, as if he is reluctant to ask. 'I am so terribly sorry, but I realise I have left some of my equipment in the clock tower and . . . everyone has gone,' he looks about him to confirm the fact, 'so there is nobody else to ask. Can you help me bring it down?'

'Oh . . .' I'm hardly dressed for it but as I look about us I realise the room is indeed all but empty.

'It's just that I'm worried my equipment might be a bit exposed to the elements up there, so I would like to retrieve it as soon as possible.' He seems edgy again.

'In the clock tower?' How odd. Why would he have put equipment in the clock tower?

'Yes,' he says and on seeing my puzzled look, explains, 'I took some photos from up there before the Ball. There is a wonderful panoramic view of our city from the top.'

'Oh, yes, of course there is.' I look down at my shoes and the little train on the back of my dress. They are not suitable for climbing a spiral staircase. I have a very strong feeling we should wait for Walter. But why? The equipment is not too heavy and I am always willing to lend a hand when asked. 'Just a moment.' I carefully unpick the train from the waistband of my dress and remove my slippers. 'Let's get on with it, then.'

The bird-cage elevator could take us part of the way, but there is no attendant to drive it for us and so we head for the stairs. Eddie is quiet. It's his way. I fill the silence, as I always feel compelled to do. 'Walter mentioned you're leaving for the States ahead of us, that you'll set up the meetings for the film's distribution. All I can say, dear Eddie, is thank you. There is so much to tidy up here. But I believe Walter has booked us on the boat next week, so we will be there not long afterwards.'

'Yes,' is all he says as we head further up the stairs. He is right behind me.

'Walter has told me all you know about . . . Bell,' I continue. Then I pause. We are at the first curve of the staircase. 'Is it true, Eddie? Is it true what you told Walter about her?'

'It's true,' he confirms.

I shake my head and continue the journey upwards. 'I don't understand what made her so resentful that she would . . . steal from me.'

'Some folk can't help themselves,' he says gruffly.

'I thought we were friends,' I say, with a little catch in my voice. 'I think back on all those photographs you took of us.' He had been trying out that new camera he'd imported from Germany, and I'd seen the results. Photos of us at the tennis, at the Cavalier, in the garden at Point Piper. 'I always thought we both looked so happy in each other's company. I never guessed how . . . resentful she must have been.'

The spiral staircase is narrowing now. I look over the railing and down to the ground, so many floors below. Almost all the lights have been turned off, there is just one lone lamp to light the way.

I begin to feel uneasy. Eddie could not have left his equipment up in the clock tower, I realise, if he was ever even up there. He arrived too late to photograph anything from the top before the Ball and he had used the camera later in the evening to photograph me in the vestibule.

My heart begins to race. He is very close behind me, and the stairway and the building itself is empty. Nobody will know I'm here. I suddenly know, with absolute certainty, that my life depends on me keeping up a false front.

We reach a spot where the beautiful staircase with its wrought-iron balustrade and ornate, polished handrail transforms into more utilitarian stairs. Further ahead, I see steeper, metal, ladder-like steps. I worry that soon I will be stranded alone in the dark with him. I feign tiredness. 'Oh, let us stop for a moment, Eddie,' I say. 'I'm exhausted, it's been quite a day.'

What now, I wonder. How will I safely navigate my passage back down the staircase, past Eddie? I sit on the narrow landing.

'It's getting late,' he mumbles.

'Did you think of her as your friend too?'

'*Friend?*' he spits. 'No, she was not my friend. She is my wife.'

His wife?

'Bell? Bell is *your wife*?'

'Yes,' he says.

'When . . . how . . .? Why did you never say? Why did she never say?'

He laughs. It's a hideous sound that echoes up and down the spiral staircase. My brain is rattling like a train about to derail.

'Bigger fish to fry,' he says.

Bell is his wife . . .? I don't understand why they needed to keep their marriage a secret. I don't understand why I didn't know. And if they are man and wife, why don't they live a proper life together? Why is she always with me?

Talk to him calmly, I tell myself. *Don't let him see you're afraid.* 'What do you mean, Eddie?' I ask quietly.

He's shaking his head. 'Stupid woman,' he says. 'Stupid, stupid woman. You don't even recognise your own kith and kin.'

'I have always recognised Bell as my kith,' I say, equally quietly. If I get angry, my anger might feed his.

'She's not your kith,' he shouts. 'She's your kin.'

'What?' He's gone mad.

His only answer is to laugh.

Why does it come to me now? Those haunting opening bars of my mother's *Pour ma petite Bellbird*? Her simple little composition, the one she had me learn when I was very young, the only thing I ever really learned to properly play. I can still remember Bell's face the first time I played it, in the house in Point Piper, from memory. 'It's called *Pour le petit bellbird,*' I had said gaily. 'She named it for one of our Australian birds. *For the little bellbird.*'

'*Pour* ma *petite Bellbird,*' she had corrected me. '*For* my *little Bellbird.*'

I'd laughed. 'All right, *Pour ma petite Bellbird,*' I echoed. She named me for a bird, too, did you know that? Rosella.'

Dear God. I'd thought nothing of it. Nothing at all. 'She's . . . my mother's daughter?'

He laughs again. 'She's your parents' daughter.'

I have to sit down. I find I can't breathe. Why did I never see it before? How could I never have known?

'My full sister?' How is that possible?

'Your mother fell pregnant to your father before they were married. She didn't tell him; she didn't want him to marry her just because of it. So, she hid herself away and then she gave Bell to a couple. When your father found out, later, after they were married, they tried to take her back. But the couple wouldn't have it, and in the end your mother decided it would be unkind to remove her. She had never known any other parents.'

I have kin. When my parents died, I thought I was alone in the world, the last living Carey in this line. Now I know I was never alone. I have a sister.

'Does she know?'

'Of course she knows. Don't you see? We set it up, her and me.'

I feel ill. 'You set what up?'

'It wasn't right, was it? That you inherited all that money when your parents died, when you could earn whatever you wanted, while she got nothing. Might have been all right if you had let me go.'

'What are you talking about Eddie?'

'You wouldn't let me go and register my patent, would you? You know, a couple of friends of mine, they did and, well, they're millionaires now, thanks to what they did with their cameras.'

I don't know much about patents or cameras. What I do know is that Eddie had not created his 'invention' himself. It had been a joint effort, with a number of other people, including Walter and two other cameramen. It may have been worth registering, it may not. But Walter had insisted that Eddie did not own it and therefore he would not endorse the patent application. I didn't think it had bothered Eddie that much, but it clearly had. I didn't know he would harbour such a grudge.

'We are going to get our share of the spoils, you can count on that.' The yellow light shadows his face, darkening the ugly frown between his brows. He makes a move towards me.

'Perhaps,' I say, quickly, trying to halt his progress, 'you could tell me – what is it the two of you want?' He is all but standing over me. I know I must stay calm, but I can hear my voice beginning to shake.

'The lot,' he sneers. 'We want the lot.'

How could my friend, *my own sister*, be so duplicitous?

I stand up and, careful to keep my voice neutral, I say, 'You are never going to get that.'

36

Rose
Sydney, 1923

'She really did want me dead . . .' I muse.

'We both wanted you dead.'

'I still don't understand why.'

'You don't understand why?' His laugh is awful, raucous, like a magpie squawking when you get too close to her nest. 'Because everything you own would have passed to her.'

He knows the details of my will. It says something like, 'There being no living relatives, I bequeath . . .' but that, I realise, opened the way for Bell to make a claim, because she is in fact a living relative . . . Of course he knows what's in the will because Bell witnessed it. But he couldn't know about the life insurance policy, which was always going to Walter. Or perhaps he does. Perhaps he . . . perhaps they were happy to have everything else.

Now though, following my marriage to Walter, everything will go to my husband, except the small allowance I made for Bell, and Eddie, I realise, is furious about that.

He lunges for me and suddenly he's pushing me against the railing, his hands around my throat. I will fall, and I will certainly plummet over the handrail to my death. I can't speak but I can struggle, and I do, violently. He's heavy on top of me, but he won't take me out by force. I am fit and well and strong. Nobody will ever destroy me by force.

Alec.

I see his face swimming before my eyes. This goes back to Alec. Eddie was the person responsible for the crystal tank. I designed and wrote up the specifications, but not alone. Alec and Walter and Bell were also involved. But Eddie . . . he was the one charged with supplying the specifications to the manufacturer, not me. That's why he wasn't there that day. His leg hadn't been bothering him at all. He'd wanted to stay as far away as possible from an exploding tank of water. Does he even have an injured leg? He'd wanted to kill me, but he hadn't factored in Alec, and so it was Alec who died, not me.

He has his hands about my throat now and despite my agility and strength, the world about me is narrowing, darkening. But I can hold my breath; I can hold it for three minutes and twenty seconds – how long has it been now? I can feel the oxygen trapped in my lungs, burning to escape. I must be close to my best time.

The car accident in New Zealand . . . that was Eddie too. That odd memory that kept escaping me . . . that had been of Eddie standing to the side of the dirt road just before I took off, dust on his boots. He'd been rattling long bolts in his hand . . . he'd driven one into the front tyre. I'm as certain of it as if I'd seen him do it myself.

And Bell was in on it.

Rage consumes me at the realisation, and it is a terrible pounding in my blood. I use every ounce of it to break free, using a technique Alec taught me. 'Every lady should learn the basics of self-defence,' he'd said. *Oh Alec, you've saved my life twice.*

I tear away from Eddie. He lunges towards me, but his feet slip on the floor and he slides into me instead. I slam into the wrought iron of the balustrade, but reel immediately forwards, out of his way. His head hits the floor with a satisfying crack, and I jump on him, my hands moving to his throat.

'Rose!' Walter's voice echoes all the way up the spiral staircase, but it's almost as if I don't hear him at all. The blood is pounding in my ears now, filling my face. I want to tighten my hands around Eddie's neck. I can hear my own breath. I am almost salivating with rage.

'*Rose!*' I hear the sound of his racing footsteps across the floor. I hear him clambering up the stairs.

I won't be stopped. I won't save this man's life when I can take it, not after what he has done.

'Get off him Rose!' Walter shouts, now on the landing below us.

'No!' Nothing will stop me from ending Eddie now. He has stolen my money, he has tried to destroy my livelihood, he murdered my childhood friend, and he has attempted to murder me, not once, but three times. He must also die.

'It's him, Walter,' I shout back. 'He is the one who has been defrauding us, he is the one who has tried to kill me, he and Bell. She is his wife, Walter, and she is *my sister*.'

I choke on the words, but he doesn't react the way I expect him to; it's almost as if nothing can shock him anymore. 'You won't solve anything by killing him, Rose. Get off.'

I will not. My fingers tighten, and Eddie gags. 'I will kill him,' I scream.

I see spittle appear at the corners of Eddie's mouth. 'He is a murderer. He killed Alec.'

'Rose.' Walter's voice is closer now. He is moving carefully up the stairs towards me. He is the cool voice in my ear, the steady hand on my wheel. I am the sea, and he is the breeze.

But I must level the score. I must avenge the death of the man who died because of me.

I don't realise I have spoken the words aloud until Walter says, 'My darling Rose, it was not your fault. None of it was your fault.'

I feel my arms begin to tremble and my resolve begin to falter. I look down at the gagging man beneath me and all the adrenalin rushes out of me. I release my stranglehold on his neck.

Walter is behind me. He lifts me off him. Eddie moves into the foetal position on the floor.

Walter throws off his jacket and waistcoat, unbuttons his suspenders. He laces the suspenders around Eddie's hands and ties him to the balustrade. 'You'll stay,' he says to him calmly, taking me into his arms as he does, 'until the police come. I am going to call them now, and you will stay until they come for you.'

We walk all the way down the spiral staircase and I drop into his arms. 'I thought you'd gone,' I say into his chest.

'No. Miss Lewis wanted to take some of the floral arrangements home with her. It took time to load them into her car.'

'I'm in love with you,' I say.

He lets out a long, jagged breath, as if he has been holding it in for too long. I've put him through hell, I realise.

He rests his forehead against mine, then I find the space on his shoulder, the one that was made for me. For a moment, it's almost as though he can't speak. 'I thought you didn't believe in falling in love,' he says finally, into my hair.

'You shouldn't believe everything I say and do,' I counter. I'm trying to sound my normal self, but my voice shakes. 'I have been known to be wrong.'

'I will miss my country,' I say. 'It is still my home.' We are packed and ready to go. We have had to organise a driver; we have had to organise many things. 'I relied on Eddie and Bell too much. I caused resentment because of it.'

'No,' says Walter, 'We gave them both a good life, but they chose something different.'

'Bell . . .' I say wistfully.

'She's in love with him,' he answers.

He's not talking about Eddie now. There were more surprises in store for me that night. After the police had arrested Eddie, after we arrived home, after Walter had helped me change, tended my bruises and abrasions, wiped away my tears, and told me he has been in love with me since possibly the moment we first met, he sat down beside me and talked some more.

'I don't know how or when Bell discovered she was part of your family, but I suspect her adopted parents told her. It seems . . .' and now he hesitates, as if he doesn't want to further hurt me. 'It seems as if the moment they did, she decided to join your family, you, in any way she could.'

In the strangest way, that warms my heart. She wanted to be near me. Even if I never knew, which I might never have, if not for Eddie.

'Do you honestly believe . . .' I begin, and I am alarmed by the way my voice trembles. 'Do you really think she helped Eddie to . . . plan . . . things . . .'

He shakes his head, taking both my hands in his. 'Knowing what we now know about Eddie, I do not,' he says. 'I think he probably bullied and harassed her into giving him information about our private affairs . . . and things that allowed him to steal from us. A chequebook, for example. It is Bell's signature on the cheques, but I think we might discover it was his handwriting on the face of them.'

'She was at the warehouse when the tank exploded,' I muse. 'If she'd known about it, surely she, like Eddie, wouldn't have been anywhere near it that day.'

He nods.

'And . . . the car accident?' I remember Bell's face when I'd emerged from the wreck unscathed, I remember the way she'd hugged me hard for long moments. She hadn't faked that, I am certain.

He shakes his head. 'I now believe all the attempts on your life were arranged by Eddie, without her involvement.'

'But Eddie rescued me from the wreck.'

'I have been thinking about that, too. He only went to help you after he saw me running towards the car. He must have realised he'd come under suspicion if he didn't make an attempt to save you.'

'The photos . . .' I say, the thought of them suddenly rushing into my head. 'It was Bell in the photos that were sent to you, wasn't it?' Why hadn't I realised? Why hadn't he? Clearly, Eddie had taken them. Perhaps he forced her to sit for them; perhaps she wasn't a willing participant.

'I suspect you are right,' he says, a wry smile on his lips. 'I'm sorry, I allowed my sexual jealousy to cloud my reasoning.'

I laugh. 'I forgive you. Where is she now?'

'I believe she's run away with the circus.'

'What are you talking about?'

'Bell has left Eddie for Mr J. J. Griffin,' he says.

37

Emma
Sydney, 2024

The woman sitting opposite me is my mother's age, but unlike my mother, this woman is wearing glasses. The frames are a rather wonderful iridescent blue. The lenses must be strong, as her eyes behind them dominate her face. She seems very excited by the information she is about to share with me.

'Have you discovered a connection?' I ask. I've been brought here by pure curiosity. Call me crazy, but the minute I saw the name 'Edward Quinn' beside the name 'Rose Carey', I just had to find out if there was any connection.

The historian shifts in her seat in the library's private study room. 'Let's start with your family tree,' she says, with the same intensity as a *Who Do You Think You Are?* genealogist.

'All right,' I say, reluctantly. Patience is not one of my virtues, and I really wish she'd just skip ahead to the good bits.

'So I don't do this usually, but I've chosen to have your tree printed out.' She unfurls a long roll of paper which displays my family tree and lays it out on the table, fixing paperweights at each corner. It is populated with many, many more people than I have ever heard of.

'This is you.' She circles my name in red. I hope she has another copy that I can take home with me, unmarked. I'd like to look at this in greater detail later. 'For the reasons you explained to me,' she says, 'I have not included your mother's family.'

'Okay,' I say.

'And of course, this is your wife.' She taps Lauren's name with the tip of the biro, and then, oddly, she circles it too.

'Now, here is your father, Michael,' she circles his name, 'and this is his father, Richard.' More red circles.

Both my father and his father bear the surname 'Quinn'; so far, everything I already knew has simply been confirmed. The details of everything she is providing me with today, she has explained, have, as far as possible, been verified, so we know they are reliable.

'Great,' I say, my eyes skipping ahead to my great-grandfather. Was his name Edward?

'Now, here is where things became a little interesting,' she says, standing up to get a closer look at the chart. She makes an odd clicking noise with her tongue, before going on. 'Your great-grandmother's name was Sarah Jane Nicholson.'

'Okay.'

'Nicholson was her married name.' She says it with a kind of 'ta-dah!' tone, but I am none the wiser.

'Okay . . .' I struggle to put two and two together.

'She married this fellow, Francis Nicholson,' she taps his name with the pen, 'quite soon after her first husband died. She was pregnant with her first husband's child, and he was a Quinn.' She moves the red pen to the left of Sarah Jane and taps a name: Charles James Quinn. I bend over the name. This isn't the

Quinn I read about the other day. This isn't Rose's cameraman, who I think must be the owner of the Leica camera I now have in my possession.

'Would you like to hear my theory?'

'Sure. Okay.' But I'm starting to feel very disconcerted.

'I think your grandfather was born just before or just after his father died.' She taps his date of birth and then taps his father's date of death. 'It is the same year, 1924. I think Sarah remarried very quickly, possibly because she had no other means of support. It was not unusual in those days.'

'Oh,' I say.

She tells me some more about Sarah and her second husband before informing me that somewhere along the line, my grandfather, Richard, must have discovered his real parentage and reverted to the name Richard Quinn.

'Now,' she says when she is done, 'I just want to divert for a little while, because the next thing I have to tell you may be difficult.'

I raise my eyes from the paper scroll on the table. There are no windows in this room, just a painting by an unknown artist of the Three Sisters, the iconic Blue Mountains tourist attraction that Lauren and I had walked to that day in Echo Point. The people she is talking about died so long ago, they are as distant as strangers to me. I don't imagine I will find anything she has to say particularly difficult.

She rolls the page up. Then she pulls out another scroll and lays it across the table in front of me. It is headed 'Rose Carey Family Tree'. I am suddenly on high alert again.

'For this tree, I started with the names you gave me: Rose Carey, Walter Ryan, Bell Procter and Edward Quinn.' The only name she circles on this chart is, unexpectedly, Bell Procter.

'Yes?' I push a strand of my hair behind my ear.

'It is a known fact that Rose Carey was married to Walter Ryan.'

Why are we starting with known facts? 'Yes.'

'What is not well known is that Rose actually had a full sister.' She looks at me over the top of the iridescent blue frames.

'What?' In spite of myself, I am quite shocked now. As far as I was aware, Rose had no siblings, and no children of her own.

'So . . .' I pause. 'Her father had an affair?'

'No . . . Her mother had a child out of wedlock, before she was married.'

I am even more surprised now. While that would hardly be scandalous today, it almost certainly was back then. 'The child was adopted out. I'm not sure if her mother ever saw her again.'

'Did this child know?'

'Well, we can't say for sure. But at some stage, possibly . . .'

What a period in time it must have been, when there was so much need for secrecy.

'The name of this child . . .' and now I can hear another drumroll in her voice, 'was Bellbird Alouette Procter.' She pauses, perhaps waiting for me to connect the dots. 'Bell Procter,' I murmur. The woman mentioned in the book I bought. She nods and continues. 'Bell was married to this fellow,' she's using her pen as a pointer again, 'Edward Quinn.'

She moves her hand from the section of the chart she had been hiding. There is more, I can tell – a lot more. She has a kind of Cheshire cat look on her face.

'I'm related to him, aren't I?' I say quickly. 'I knew it, I knew I was connected to Rose.' My enthusiasm is, however, short-lived.

'No,' she says, 'you are not. There are in fact no connections between you and this Mr Quinn.'

'Oh.' The disappointment is so keen I feel it like a body blow.

'You can be quite pleased about that, actually. He was a grifter and a conman. Passed himself off as a war hero, but he was no such thing. He was a deserter. From what we know of him, and it's hard to sort fact from fiction, he claimed he learned all he knew about photography from Australia's First World War photographer Captain Frank Hurley, but that seems unlikely. He was shot dead escaping custody in 1924, allegedly for the attempted murder of Rose Carey.'

'Attempted murder?' I'm quite shocked. 'Why hasn't that come up in my Google searches?'

'Well, it's a long time ago and it looks like he was shot dead before he was convicted. I discovered this information via Trove.' When I give her a puzzled look, she continues, 'Trove provides free digital access to Australian records, for example newspaper articles, held in places like libraries, archives, museums and so forth, from the early 1800s until quite recent times. It's a fabulous resource, provided by the National Library.'

'Okay . . . '

'The other interesting thing I discovered was that from about 1924, Rose stopped using the name Carey, preferring her married name. As Rose Ryan, along with her husband, she founded the Aviary Club for Women.'

'Aviary Women? The American fitness company?'

'The very same,' she confirms. 'She was very passionate about health, fitness and beauty and believed that women should learn to love, celebrate, look after and protect their own bodies.'

Today, Aviary is an international, publicly listed company, and a household name. It has a single-word slogan: *Fly.*

Which would be a whole lot more interesting to me if I were related to Rose, but it appears I am not, not even remotely.

What all this means is that I am not entitled to keep Rose's letters, or the film, or any of the other memorabilia in that box. I should do what I should have done all along – contact someone much more expert than me about what to do with it.

'It's just a coincidence, Emma,' she says, quite gently. 'Your Mr Quinn, the one you in fact, are descended from, is someone much less complicated. Someone who was loved and respected in the Blue Mountains community.'

'Oh.' I want to cry. Someone to be proud of? Irrationally, I briefly wish he were not.

'Your Mr Quinn met with an accident.'

She passes me more papers. I read a tragic tale of a man, a local bank clerk, and his pregnant wife, out for a walk on a sunny autumn day in Katoomba in 1924. I read how he came to slip and fall. A simple accident, one of many in the mountains back then, I suppose.

Subsequent stories tell of a collection by his workmates to have a memorial stone placed where he died. His wife, my great grandmother, Sarah Jane Nicholson, had an inscription chiselled into it: 'Our Quinnie'. These are my people. My feeling of connection to the memorial stone was correct – but it had nothing to do with Rose Carey or her cameraman.

'It happens sometimes,' the genealogist continues. 'Quite often, in fact. We draw these links, but they are tenuous at best. However . . .' She draws a breath and seems quite excited, but I am deflated, and losing interest.

'Did they have children? Rose's sister and . . .' I debate saying 'the murderer', then settle for, 'Edward Quinn?'

'No issue,' she says.

I absorb this for a moment, then stand up again. 'Right, well, thank you. Very interesting.'

She smiles, and there it is again, that Cheshire cat look. What is that about? 'Not so fast.'

She's hiding something on the paper with her hand again. 'Bell had another partner, and from that union, there was a child.'

'But that child was not a Quinn, right?' I ask.

I'm trying not to sound bored, but I am. I can see how and why people get sucked into genealogy rabbit holes, but for me the whole point of the exercise was to – vainly, I know – link myself to Rose. Now that I know that no such link exists, I just want to leave and get on with the rest of my boring life.

'No, the child was not a Quinn.'

I swear, if this room was larger, she'd be dancing.

I smile. 'Well, as I think I explained . . .'

'The child was a Griffin.'

It's Friday night, I realise. Tarantino night. There's a curt note on the table from Lauren. 'Gone to see *Inglourious Basterds* with Simon and Tabby. Later.' And her usual sign-off, a big X. There's no 'Darling', or even 'Emmie', because she's cross about me not being home to go with her. I check the time on my phone and notice a string of messages from her.

5.07 pm: *Coming?*

5.48 pm: *Okay, so I guess not coming?*

6.17 pm: *We've gotta go now. I'm calling the uber.*

6.39 pm: *Leaving now. Meet us there?*

7.07 pm: *Feature's about to start. See you when I get home.*

Again, no 'Darling', no 'Emmie', no kisses in the sign-off.

I keep fucking this relationship up.

I go to the kitchen to grab a drink. There are wine glasses on the bench, a half-eaten plate of brie and crackers. I pull out the bin drawer and tip them into it. Then I rinse the plate and the glasses and put them in the dishwasher.

'You really, *really* don't have to pick up after me,' she is always saying. Yes, I do. I don't think she realises just how often I do it. If I didn't . . .

But maybe I'm wrong. How would I know how she lives when I'm not living with her? I go back into the living room and sit down.

I can't assess how I feel. I'm still numb with the shock – is that the right word? The genealogist had drawn connections with her red pen, from Bell Procter and Rose Carey, all the way down to their direct descendants. Today, there appears to be only three . . . Lauren, Allie and Aunty Julia.

One of the things that made it a bit easier for the genealogist to find those connections was that Lauren and I had given her aunt a DNA kit for her birthday. Julia didn't have her own family tree account, and, 'not being all that computer literate', had asked us to set one up. I had set my own up some time ago, so Lauren had deferred the task to me. Together, the three of us had populated it with the names and relationships we knew, shared our two trees and given each other manager permissions. When the DNA results arrived, Julia had shared them with me and, with her formal consent, I'd shared everything with the genealogist who'd pieced things together.

I have the paper scrolls the genealogist gave me in my satchel, red-inked and all. I'd asked for clean copies, and she said she'd arrange them, but in the meantime, she'd provided me with a neat A4 folder containing the information she'd told me. She'd also shown me how to view the trees online.

'You're obsessed with Rose Carey,' Lauren had observed the other night. 'I think you spend more time reading her letters and poring over her nude photos than you spend naked in bed with me.' I think she was only half joking.

I didn't understand why I'd been so consumed by it, but now I do.

I had felt an affinity to the memorial because, as the genealogist had pointed out today, he actually was my great-grandfather. It doesn't explain the phenomenon itself, but I don't need that explained to me. I've often felt weirdly connected to places and later discovered there is some family connection. I wish Lauren would come home, so that I can share with her all that I've found out today.

I'm playing with the family tree online, investigating all the little tree links, when something occurs to me. I plug the brand name and model of the camera I have in the shed and the year 1923 into my phone and google it. The results make me sit up in shock.

I'm still sitting in the study, still feeling stupefied. I have no plans of my own tonight. I'm itching to tell all to Lauren but I have potentially hours to get through until I can. What am I going to do all night that doesn't involve more trawling for information about old films and cameras and Rose Carey, or reading some of her letters? I pull open the desk drawer and stare at the blue satin-ribboned bundle. There's only one letter left to read now and I'm saving it.

I pick up my phone. Nothing from Lauren since that last message at 7.07 pm. I check my other messages. Looks like I have a few missed calls from Johnno. I really need to stop turning my phone to silent. He's also sent a text.

Oi. Where the bloody hell are you? Things to discuss.

Is that code? Does he have good news?

I check the time. It's 9.17 pm. Too late to call? Maybe, but not too late to message. He doesn't have to answer if he doesn't want to.

I can talk now? Fine if prefer morning. It's a shorthand he'll understand.

The phone starts ringing almost the instant I press 'send'.

'That was quick,' I say.

'Where've you been, Em?' he asks, but before I can answer, he goes on in a rush, 'We got it.'

'Oh my god . . . we got the Hot Rain gig?'

'Yes! Yee-ha!'

He's laughing now, and I can almost see him running around the room, punching the air. 'Can you fucking believe it? Hammer and Tongs picked up Hot Rain.'

'Of course I believe it. You've worked really hard on building the company, Johnno. You deserve it.'

'Thanks,' he says. 'But team effort.'

'Yeah, especially that bit where I made my sister-in-law think I was trying to call in special favours.' I eye roll myself. 'Which I wasn't,' I add hastily.

He laughs again, in the same way he'd laughed when I'd confessed the conversation to him. 'You worry too much, mate.'

'Probably,' I agree.

He sobers for a moment. 'Em . . .'

My heart starts to pound. What is he going to say next?

'I really mean it. This wouldn't have happened if not for you. I'd like you to come into the business with me. As a partner.'

'Johnno, you built the company from the ground up.'

'Yes, but we can't grow if we don't continue to seriously invest in ourselves. I want you to come on board, not just to manage the Hot Rain contract, but as General Manager – with the corresponding pay rise, of course.'

Would I have jumped at this chance at the start of the year? Yes. It would likely have paid for another round of IVF – and straight away. We wouldn't have wasted all that time. But now? Having discovered all that I have discovered today our future might be taking a very different turn.

'Honestly, Johnno, that's the nicest thing you've ever said to me, and I really appreciate the offer, but—'

'Oh yeah, yeah, of course, silly me – talk it over with that wife of yours, then let me know, okay? If you like, you can still be an employee. I'm not asking for capital – well, only intellectual capital.'

I hang up. If I hadn't been before, I am absolutely burning to talk to Lauren now. What's the run time of *Inglourious Basterds*? I google it. Two hours, thirty-three minutes. I'm sad to have missed it. It's probably my favourite Tarantino movie, after *Pulp Fiction*, and it's about old films.

I pause to admire the poster that pops up. It features three male leads, including a young Brad Pitt, dressed in heavy boots and leather jackets against a red-washed backdrop of the two female leads and the Nazi villain. The red is to hint at the fire that features in the film's climax, no doubt.

I stare at it as a feeling of impending doom suddenly washes over me.

Fuck . . . The fire in the movie . . . it was the result of nitrate. Cellulose nitrate – the stuff old films are made of.

I try to calm down. *Inglourious Basterds* is just a movie, I remind myself. A fictional movie . . . But I already know the answer to the question I'm putting into Google.

Is cellulose nitrate film dangerous?

'Cellulose nitrate film, later referred to as "celluloid", is extremely dangerous. It catches fire very easily, is almost inextinguishable and, when not stored correctly, and/or when in stages of decomposition, may spontaneously combust.'

I quickly google the era cellulose nitrate films were made . . . about 1895 to about 1950.

Oh my god, oh my god, oh my god. The film in my shed is fucking cellulose nitrate. Of course it is, it was made in 1923. What the hell else would it be?

Fuck. I stand up, wiping my hand over my face. Sweat begins to form on my upper lip. Stored correctly? How the fuck is it supposed to be stored? Possibly not in a crate in a shed on a balcony.

I inhale a deep breath. It survived god knows how many years in the storeroom of a Blue Mountains hotel, I remind myself, without spontaneously combusting. It's probably fine.

But the Blue Mountains climate is, on average, at least five degrees cooler than Sydney, isn't it?

I stride out onto the balcony, go to walk into the shed, then stop myself. It's a very warm night. I slide down the wall and sit on the pavers. *Think!*

I google *What should I do if I find a cellulose nitrate film?*, then click on the first result.

'If the film shows any signs of deterioration, do not store it. Contact your fire and rescue authority immediately. While awaiting your fire and rescue authority, keep the film away from occupied buildings. Do not attempt to seal the cans in which the film is stored.'

Fuck. I had taped them closed.

The more I read, the worse it gets. Deteriorating film can give off toxic fumes. Skin contact can cause serious irritation and inflammation. I look at the rash on my hand.

I can't wait any longer. I stop scrolling and call 000.

38

Emma
Sydney, 2024

The fire and rescue team has come and gone. Lauren arrives in the middle of all the drama and I reel off what I'm sure is an incoherent library of information now compiled on my phone. The worst part is explaining how I had put myself, her, and apparently the whole neighbourhood at risk. Although the film is not technically a bomb, fire and rescue had called the bomb squad to dispose of it. We, and neighbours from every floor of our building, are standing outside on the street while the squad is upstairs, dressed in what I think of as astronaut suits, 'dealing with it'. When they come back downstairs, an older member of the team tells us we will all now be 'safe as houses', because the crate is being walked out of the building and out of my life by the leader. Despite everything I now know, I can't let go of the crate without a fight.

'Excuse me,' I say, hurrying after him.

'Stand back,' he orders.

I stop, but I shout to him from where I stand. 'Why do you need to take the whole box? Isn't it just the film reels that are the problem?'

He shakes his head as if I am unbelievable. 'We are disposing of it,' he says.

'There's a very valuable vintage camera in it, you can't dispose of the camera,' I protest. 'It belongs to my wife's family.'

'Lady, you want the camera, or you want us all to stay alive?' He nods at the contents of the box and then continues. 'The reels are taped up – bad idea, by the way,' as if he knows I'm responsible for doing that. When I don't respond, he turns and marches off. I watch him load the box into the vehicle and the squad drive away, then sink down onto the pavement, unsure if I will ever get up.

When I finally do, I see that our fellow tenants are milling around Lauren, buzzing with curiosity. Later, I suppose, they will be pissed off at being thrown out of their homes in the middle of the night, even though we have now been given the all clear to return. I suppose I should be grateful for that. But I'm not. I'm devastated. I try to pull myself together, then go back to the group.

Lauren is breathless as she retells the story.

'Em rescued this box of stuff that was headed for the tip in the Blue Mountains a few months ago,' she tells them, and her eyes are all but popping out of her head. 'Thinking about it, it was probably an excellent thing that she did – we've just found out it could have gone up in flames at any time, and god knows what that would have meant for the people of the Blue Mountains.'

I expel a long sigh. All I feel in her retelling is that I'm a prize idiot. Why, in all the time I'd had that box of stuff, had

I never remembered that old silent movies are almost always cellulose nitrate?

She's checking her phone now, finding proof for our gobsmacked neighbours. 'It is so hazardous, it's not supposed to be transported anywhere without, like, specialists,' she says. 'Thank god the firefighters were able to get the bomb squad onto it right away.'

She goes on reading for a moment and then grabs my hand, holding it up as 'Exhibit A'.

'Listen to this, Em – it deteriorates over time, exuding toxic gases, and when it comes into contact with the skin it can cause serious problems. You should check back in with the doctor.'

I nod, removing my hand from her grip. Everyone now seems sympathetic, except one ageing neighbour who says, 'And you didn't figure all this out before . . .?'

All very well for you to roll your eyes, I think. You were probably alive in the 1920s. Then I mentally smack myself. That was uncharitable, and besides, he has a point. I have a sudden urge to cry. Why didn't I figure this out before?

But that hadn't been the focus of the searches I had done. My focus had been on Rose's letters and trying to discover why, when Rose Carey had spent the best part of two years in this hemisphere, the film was never screened in cinemas.

'Well, no, I guess she – we – didn't put two and two together,' Lauren says, and I can hear in her tone that she is about to launch into a defence of me. 'I guess neither of us is a *silent film expert*.' No doubt the emphasis on the last three words is to point out that perhaps he is not one either.

'I only remembered when Lauren went to see *Inglourious Basterds* tonight,' I say. Lauren shouldn't have to come to my defence.

A couple of people look at me blankly. 'The Tarantino movie?' I offer. More blank looks. 'The narrator tells the audience about how flammable nitrate film is and then, at the end of the movie, the protagonist's lover lights a stash of it, which sets off explosions and the cinema burns to the ground.'

'So, wait – you had a bomb in the shed?' one of the neighbours asks.

'No,' I say, 'we had a film in the shed. But cellulose nitrate films can combust if they're not stored properly.'

'So, you weren't storing it properly, is that right?'

I look away. I would rather be anywhere else at this moment. Maybe at the bottom of one of Rose's oceans.

'No, we weren't – but that's because we didn't realise,' Lauren huffs.

'Isn't she a videographer?' the neighbour presses belligerently. 'Shouldn't she know about that kind of stuff?'

I feel myself shrink. Should I have known? Maybe somewhere in the deep recesses of my mind, I had. I could easily have found out, if I'd been prepared to ask more questions. But I'd been so secretive about that box, so protective. Probably because I'd felt guilty for taking it in the first place . . . as if I'd stolen it. Which, I hastily correct myself, I had not. If I hadn't taken it, it would now be buried in landfill, a ticking time bomb, threatening to set the Blue Mountains alight.

'She's in digital,' Lauren snaps. 'It's much more sophisticated technology. There's no need for her to know about film from the 1920s, or how to store it.'

She is perfectly correct, but this fact brings me no joy whatsoever.

'Well, then, she had no business storing it at all, did she?'

And he's also right, but we are never going to win this argument, if it's even about winning.

I hold up a hand and say, 'All I can do is apologise for the inconvenience, and say good night.'

~

'Well,' Lauren says, bouncing in the middle of our bed. 'That was a bit of excitement.' Excitement that seems to have thawed some of the frostiness that had existed between us.

But I'm not sure I have the words to respond. I think I've lost the ability to speak.

She gets up off the bed, moves to stand behind me and puts her arms around me. 'Come on, Em, it's all good,' she says softly. 'Nobody died.'

I shake my head, and she lays her face against my back. 'Of course, a few more days and it might have been a different story.'

I can't even laugh at her valiant attempt at a joke. I let out a long sigh. 'Lauren, I have some things to tell you.'

'Some things?' she says. 'Plural?'

'Yes.'

She drops her arms and comes around to face me. 'Uh, oh – looks serious.'

I stare at her for a few moments, then I lead her back to the bed. We both sit down on it, and I take her hands in mine. 'It is serious.'

'Come on then, out with.'

I pause some more. She has always been a band-aid-ripping-off kind of person. 'Good news, or bad?' I ask.

'Oh god – bad news.'

'Okay . . . the good news.' I look up at her with a wry smile. 'We scored a new client at work, and . . . Johnno wants to make me a partner in the business.'

'Ooh. That's wonderful, Em. But . . . will that mean you have to buy in or something?'

'No, it means he's going to give me shares in it, and . . . I'll be General Manager. It's an immediate pay increase.' I tell her the deal Johnno has offered and how much it would mean, in dollars, if I accepted. Then I tell her how much it would mean to me, to be part of something that is bigger than myself. Last of all, I tell her who the new client is.

She laughs out loud. 'Oh, darling,' she says, 'look at that. All roads have led to Rome. Of course you should take up the offer . . . if you want to,' she hastens to add.

'Thank you.' I clear my throat. 'We wouldn't see the money for a little while yet, but as soon as we do, I want us to try again for a baby, Lauren.'

She is deadly quiet. I can almost hear my heart pounding. After the things we'd yelled at each other over the past few months, the accusations we'd thrown . . . would she even want to try again?

She moves in closer to me. 'You're a sweetheart for saying that,' she says, laying a hand on my chest.

I stroke her hair. She must have washed it tonight, it is smooth and light. 'I do mean it,' I say.

She is silent, and almost still. 'I think you're saying it just for me.'

'No.' I don't want to protest too much because it would only make her doubt me more. 'I'm saying it because it's true.'

She turns her head to bury her face in my blouse.

'But there is a caveat.'

She looks up at me and her eyes are so expectant, so hopeful. I feel as if she would say or do anything in order to have just one more shot at this.

'I'm only prepared to do the egg retrieval process one more time. I know that makes me incredibly selfish, I know that you'll go through a lot more than me, both physically and emotionally, but I just wouldn't want to do it three times.'

'Okay,' she says.

'And I'm sorry, but nothing else will sit right with me. I don't want a turkey baster, and I don't want your eggs fertilised by our donor, and I don't want to adopt. I just want what we always said we wanted. If that can't be, well then, I would rather be the world's best aunty to our siblings' children.'

She takes a deep breath and expels it slowly. 'All right. Thank you for being so honest with me, and for the record, I don't think you're being selfish. I think you're telling me how your needs can be met, and that's as it should be.'

'Yes, but it impacts you, so now I need to hear what you want.'

'I want our baby,' she says. 'Just like you. If you were willing to explore other options, I would, but you're not. You're the most important person in my life, so I respect that. I would rather we do only what we agreed to do at the beginning than do anything that would hurt you or, not sit well with you.'

We hug for a long time, my head on her shoulder and hers resting on mine.

'We will probably have to wait a little while to save up the money for the next round, even with your raise,' she says finally. 'Which means we'll be even older, so it probably won't work. But I'm . . . surprisingly okay with that. We'll have given it our very best shot and we've already been through so much.'

She's reminded me of the thing I still haven't told her, the thing that was supposed to be the magic solution to our problems. The thing that would have been the solution, if not for Rose Carey's lost film.

'I have something else to tell you.'

She looks at me through watery green eyes. 'That sounds serious.'

'I went to see a genealogist.'

She frowns, confused. 'Okay . . .'

For a moment, I just play with a long strand of her hair. 'This sounds – absurd – now . . . but I was utterly convinced there was some connection between Rose and me.'

She laughs, but not unkindly. 'Yes, I realise that. Is that the bad news? You've discovered you're not, after all?'

'Well, yes, I discovered I'm not, but that's not the bad news.'

'Okay,' she says. 'So spill it. What's the bad news?'

'The bad news is,' I say, and the words are now falling from my lips in slow motion, 'you are . . .'

'I am what?'

I give her a few seconds to compute what I've just said.

'Wait a minute . . . *I* am related to Rose Carey?'

'Yes.'

She sits bolt upright. 'How do you know?'

I go to answer, but she interrupts.

'I'm related to Rose Carey . . . the film icon? The one you're obsessed with? The one they named a ferry after? *I'm* related to *that* Rose Carey?'

'Yes.'

She stands up and starts walking around the room. She walks all the way around the bed, then comes back to sit beside me on it.

'How am I related to her? Why didn't I know this already? And how do you know and I don't? And why is this bad news?'

I clear my throat. 'Which question do you want answered first?'

'All right,' I can see a pulse ticking in her neck. 'Tell me how I'm related to her.'

'You are her sister's descendant.'

'She had a sister?'

'Yes.'

She considers this information. 'What was her sister's name?'

'The name she was given was Bellbird Procter.'

'Okay . . . was that her real name?'

'Well, she was adopted, but she was the child of both Rose's parents, born out of wedlock.'

'So, this Bellbird Procter, what was she, my great-aunt?'

'No, she was your great-grandmother.'

'Oh . . . so, I'm really, *really* related to Rose.'

'Yes, you are closely related to Rose, and so are your aunt and your sister.'

'They'll enjoy hearing this.'

I try to smile.

'Okay, so who did she marry? How did she end up with our name?'

'She didn't marry him exactly . . . she couldn't, she was already married.'

She blinks. 'Why, we are perfectly scandalous!' she says.

'Her husband was a fellow called Quinn. No relation,' I add quickly.

She falls backwards on the bed and then immediately sits up again. 'Well, thank fuck for that. We'd be kissing cousins or something, wouldn't we? If he had been?'

'I don't know.'

'Okay, now please tell me how you know all this, and why you are so certain I'm related to these people. Is it something to do with the genealogist?'

'Yes. Remember how we shared family trees when we gave Aunty Julia a DNA kit for her birthday?'

She nods.

'The genealogist saw some connections, investigated them and that's what she discovered.'

'Wow, this is amazing, Emmie.' She gets up again and starts parading around the room like a queen. 'I'm related to a movie star – always thought so. Have you told Aunty Julia yet?'

I shake my head.

'Oh, she is going to love this.' She claps her hands.

I laugh, momentarily forgetting the final things I have to tell her.

'So . . . do you want to know who your great-grandfather was?'

'Was he also a movie star?'

'No.' I shake my head. 'His name was John James Griffin. He was an American flying ace in World War I.'

'Oh my god – seriously?'

I nod.

'Did he die in the war?'

'No. He survived the war and came out here to work for a theatrical company that was quite famous in its day, for stunt work.'

'Which is how he met Rose . . . and Bellbird.'

'Which is how he met Rose and Bell,' I confirm.

'Wow . . . so much information!'

I pause, letting her enjoy it. 'But I don't understand,' she says finally. 'Why is any of this bad news? Did he die tragically . . . or something?' She sits down beside me.

'Yes,' I say, stroking her shoulder. 'He died tragically, not all that long after they met. He was killed while performing a stunt in Sydney. Bell was pregnant with his child.'

'Oh, that is sad.' A small frown appears between her brows. 'Maybe that's why our family didn't know anything about him. Maybe Dad did . . .'

'. . . but he died without telling you,' I finish.

She looks so sad about this, so I hug her.

'I'm still wondering why this is bad news, Em.'

'The thing is, Lauren . . . Bell's lover died and her husband was arrested . . . For the attempted murder of Rose Carey.'

'Oh my God . . .'

'He was later shot dead trying to escape custody . . . Bell was still officially married to him.'

'I hope she wasn't still in love with him.'

'No . . . I mean, I don't know, I don't think so. I think she was a single mum, in the 1920s, all alone in the world . . . We think she must have been at the Carrington Hotel in the Blue Mountains at some stage because, as you know, that's where I found the crate in our shed. We think it actually belonged to Bell, not Rose. The crate that *was* in our shed,' I hastily correct. 'The genealogist thinks it's possible that Bell never actually took possession of it because she was in Sydney when her lover died. Maybe she knew about it and didn't want anything to do with it, maybe she wasn't even aware of its existence. I guess we'll never know.'

'What about her sister? What about Rose?'

'Rose spent the rest of her life in America. I think she might have thought Bell had something to do with her husband's crimes.

'Oh no. How horrible. I bet she didn't.'

I brace myself now, to tell her the bit I don't want to say. 'When her husband died, Bell inherited all his worldly goods . . . that would include all the things that were in that crate.' I pause. 'The film they took from us tonight. The lost film of Rose Carey. We think he stole it from them. It was certainly never shown in theatres. Ever. It was lost, as in, really lost.'

She gasps.

'The photographs and newspaper clippings and so on . . . ' I clear my throat. I'm stalling for time, but I have to say it sooner or later. 'And his camera – a Leica 0-Series.'

'Okay . . .' Comprehension is dawning in her eyes. 'Are these things . . . theoretically . . . mine then?'

'Yours and your Aunt Julia's and Allie's . . . I think so. I think for the genealogist to make some of the connections, someone else on your tree must have done a test, so maybe you'd be sharing with them. But probably not, because it looks like the three of you are the only direct descendants.'

More silence, more wheels turning. 'Are they worth something, Emmie?'

I sigh. 'The film? I honestly don't know. The camera . . .'

'Yes?'

'There was one that sold at auction that was extraordinary, because it belonged to a photographer who had something to do with its invention. These cameras were pre-production prototypes . . . only a few were made. I don't think the one I had, the one that belongs to you, had the same . . .' I struggle to find the right word, 'provenance, I think they call it.'

'How much do you think it's worth, Emmie?'

I clear my throat again. 'I think it's worth . . . about five million dollars. And it's just been disposed of by the bomb squad.'

All I have left are her letters, the ones I'd scooped up on being told to evacuate the apartment without delay. I had believed my home was going to catch fire, and the things I'd saved were the lost letters of Rose Carey.

39

Emma
Sydney, 2024

I've tried to contact the squad that removed the crate from our apartment but I seem to be going around in circles. I explain what happened to a perfectly patient professional on the phone, who tells me not to worry, 'The crate and its contents will be safely disposed of.'

I clear my throat. 'You don't understand,' I say. 'Along with the films, there was a very expensive antique camera and some private family photographs.'

'Oh, I see,' she says. 'Well, I think they have probably all been safely disposed of.'

'But the camera and the photos aren't dangerous. Why would they be disposed of? And what does that mean, anyway. When you say disposed of?'

'I'll have someone call you back,' she says and I give her my number. I hold out no hope that anyone will do any such thing and hang up despondently.

I am having a great deal of difficulty reconciling the fact that memorabilia that was in my care, worth more than five million dollars, has potentially been destroyed. Memorabilia that belongs to my wife's family. I feel hugely responsible for it.

Lauren, however, is philosophical. 'Don't worry so much, darling,' she says. 'If we never had it, we can't miss it, right?'

No, not right, I think. If I hadn't been so intent on keeping the find largely to myself, I might have discovered a lot more about it and she would be several million dollars richer.

'It's kind of you not to blame me,' I say. 'But I do blame myself.'

'Well, don't. I don't think being rich is all it's cracked up to be.'

But being rich, or even just a little richer, would have helped us move more quickly towards a goal that is now slipping further and further away. I know that Lauren is beginning to be at peace with the fact that we might never have a baby, and I know that one day I will be too. It's just that I wish it were different.

Still, there is still some sliver of hope. Johnno has made good on his promise, I have been promoted and I do have a pay rise. All is not lost, yet.

And so I've come to this; the very last letter. I have a suspicion about these letters now, more than a suspicion. I take the letter out from under the ribbon with something like reverence. I don't want to be at the end of them . . . Through these letters I have come to know not just the writer and those around her, but also 1923. The world is very different now . . . but in some ways, not so different at all. We all still live, die, love, hate, laugh, cry. Just like 'Birdy' and 'Me'.

I want to take my time with this one, and so I sit down at the desk to read. It's a long one.

Sydney
Tuesday, 12th February 1924

Dear Birdy,

We are back in Sydney but only for a brief time, and I know you have already gone. I so wanted to see you before you departed, but I left it too long. My only excuse is that I was afraid – that you wouldn't receive me, that you wouldn't acknowledge me, that you wouldn't love me.

I didn't go back to our old haunts, I went back to where we began. I took a tram, walked, took another tram until I found myself standing outside the house in Surry Hills. It is the house opposite the Tivoli store that I knew as a child, just down the road from the pub, where there was, back then, work to be had.

You know, you visited once. I'm going to tell you the story, exactly as I remember it. I have replayed it so many times in my head, I can recall the smallest of details.

You arrived in the morning, in a horse and carriage. I saw it from the window in the front room and it was such a rare thing for a carriage to pass down the street and to stop – a cart, yes; a carriage, no. I ran to the door and opened it. And all of a sudden, the two of you were standing on the stoop. She had you by one hand and her hat in the other. I remember there was lace under the brim and small fabric flowers and ribbons. She had closely curled hair pulled back from her face, which was the most beautiful thing about her.

You were wearing a white frock and a blue satin ribbon in your hair. You were not very much younger than me, and you had the same dark hair as the woman, but it fell in ringlets to your shoulders.

'Come away from the door,' Mum called from the room behind me. When I didn't, she clattered to where I was standing, and I hid behind her skirts.

'I'm Alouette,' I heard the woman say to her. She had an accent I knew later was French, but there was a melody in her voice that reminded me of the call of a bird I once found lost in the backyard. When I remembered it later, I recognised it as the currawong.

'I can see that,' Mum said, and I could tell, from knowing her well, that she was in a dither what to do about it. 'We don't have visitors.'

Alouette stood her ground, 'We won't stay long,' she said, and I knew at once that she couldn't be waved away just because Mum wasn't keen to share biscuits and tea.

'I'm really here . . . just to see the child . . .'

I put my nose out from behind Mum's skirts, at the same time you poked your head out from behind Alouette. You were both dressed so very fine, in a fabric with a sheen to it. I remember how much I loved that dress, how much I wanted one just like it. Alouette's dress was the same colour blue as the ribbon in your hair, and your dress had lace frills. I put one of my bare feet on top of the other, as if hiding one might conceal the fact that I was shoeless.

'He wouldn't like it,' Mum said.

'But . . . he's not here, is he?'

Mum shook her head. 'The child will tell.'

They were talking about me. 'No, I won't,' I protested. I could keep secrets, even then. I reached out my hand to you. You tilted your head to one side and your ringlets danced on your shoulders. You took my hand, and I pulled you into the room behind me.

Alouette looked for a place to sit. It was difficult; we didn't have much, and what we did was put to use. But Mum cleared a space on the tea chest that served as a stool, and added an old cushion for Alouette's comfort. She sat down and to her great credit, she didn't wince or make a face about it, even though I knew from experience how uncomfortable it was, with or without the cushion.

'I named them both for birds, you see, because I was named for the lark,' she said, and I fancied that she stared at me for longer than she looked at you. 'Sweet little Bellbird,' she said softly, and then she paused. 'This is Rosella . . .'

You went to sit down on the floor, and I was instantly worried about your dress. 'Come outside,' I said, and you toddled beside me to the back door.

I heard Alouette stand up immediately behind us. 'Be careful . . .' But Mum interrupted her. 'Let them play for a bit,' she said. 'They likely won't ever get the chance again, will they?'

'It's just . . . she's still a baby, really.'

'I'll take care of her,' I said, and I made a promise to myself to do that, for as long as I could. We sat together on the back stoop. I pointed out the willie wagtail sitting on the broken paling of the back fence. 'Birdy,' you said, and ever since then, that's what I've called you, at least in my heart.

Then you pointed to the overgrown grass and the hole in the fence and finally the path to the clothesline, where our brown and grey clothes were hanging. The path was lined with spring flowers, tiny things with sunshine hearts and miniature white petals.

'Shall we make a daisy chain?' I said, and you looked at me with your big eyes and put your finger in your mouth and nodded.

I took you by the hand and walked you into the yard. I sat you down and picked you a lapful of flowers.

And now, just for a moment, as I gaze at the house, I think I see you . . . and there we are again, sitting in the long grass threading daisy chains . . . Someone is standing at the fence, someone calls from inside the house, 'Rose, come back here this instant.'

I freeze for a moment, but of course, it's not you. It's just someone who has stolen your name.

So, my darling little sister . . .

Please know that I never meant to hurt you, that I never actively or knowingly worked against you. All I ever wanted was to be close to you and perhaps, in that way, come to know our mother.

I promise you I didn't know the extent of what Eddie was doing. No, that's not entirely true. I did know some things.

I knew he'd stolen the company chequebook, the one with the cheques I'd pre-signed. I didn't know he'd stolen the props and drowned them in the harbour, I didn't know it was Eddie who'd taken our mother's music in a fit of rage and thrown it in the harbour with them. But I did suspect.

I had to stop writing then, for a moment. The memory of all that happened is causing such a pain in my chest, I have had to sit down. I have to wait for it to subside. It's not good for my baby.

Yes, there's a baby, Rose. I am so blessed to have a new life growing within me. It feels like . . . redemption.

But I'm not finished telling you all yet. I didn't know Eddie was behind the attempts on your life. Please believe me when I say I had nothing to do with them. Nothing, I promise you. And I had nothing to do with Alec's death, either.

This is what happened. While we were still in the States, Eddie discovered we were sisters . . . Alec always knew. Remember, he was my childhood friend too. I asked him to never tell you and the darling never did. But he let it slip once, in front of Eddie. Not overtly, but Alec was always such a one for jokes – 'birds of a feather' and so on. Eddie knew your name was Rosella and he found out mine was Bellbird, and he put two and two together, then presented the facts to me as if he knew. I didn't deny it, I couldn't. I begged him not to tell you . . . and he didn't. But he held the knowledge over my head like the sword of Damocles.

I tried to shrug it off. So what if, one day, you discovered the truth?

Then with those pre-signed cheques, he started stealing from the company. Nothing was the same from that moment on. He forced me to marry him, threatening to expose me as a thief if I did not. He said he would tell you my motive was that I was your jealous, unknown, unloved sister, and in doing so, he would expose me twice.

What could I do? I had pre-signed the cheques. I did know about the thefts. I am your unknown sister. Not jealous, though, and, I think, not unloved. Not then, anyway. In my own defence, I didn't realise that marrying him would be only the beginning . . .

I've asked myself a million times why he wanted to, why he thought he deserved any part of your money, and I realise it stemmed from not being able to register the patents he believed would make him a millionaire.

Which brings me to the most difficult part of this confession. The things I am about to tell you I only realised later, much later, after I had run away with Griff. Griff opened my eyes to so many things.

I realised that Eddie, knowing I was your sister, believed that if you died, all that you owned would go to me, there being at the time no other living kin. As my husband, that meant, in his mind, your riches would go to him – and so he tried to kill you. Once by driving a bolt into your tyre in New Zealand and again when he ordered the inferior glass for the crystal tank. But I didn't know all this before I ran away. I swear on our mother's grave I did not. If I had, I promise I would have warned you.

Oh, but I must be honest. I was suspicious. I challenged him on the tank, I threatened to tell you and Walter that he had ordered the inferior glass and he said he would turn it around, tell you I was responsible. And so I said nothing. How I hate him. How I hate myself.

When Walter confronted me about the thefts the night of the Ball . . . I didn't know what to say, how to explain anything, how to defend myself. I thought it would just be better for everyone if I disappeared. I found Griff and he thought it best too, at least for a while. He was already planning a trip to the Mountains, to investigate the business opportunity he has now secured. He made it possible for me to go with him.

The third attempt on your life, which I learned happened that very same night . . . I think Eddie must have become unhinged, more unhinged. He realised your marriage made Walter your next of kin. That was why he had me sit for those awful naked photos. I know he scribbled on the back of one of them, implying you had an assignation with a mythical Mr 'C' and sent it to Walter. He was trying to upset the marriage before it had a chance to really begin. Divorced, Walter might get nothing after your death except the money from your life insurance policy and once again, Eddie thought I might inherit. But it would take time, this new game plan of his, and in the end his fury at perceived injustices made him simply more determined to kill you, with or without financial gain.

But . . . all this . . . it's too late now, isn't it? I must face the terrible truth that if you had wanted to hear my side of the story you would have confronted me, not left it to Walter. You would have heard me out.

Whatever my sins, I know, and God knows, I never meant to hurt you. I never would. It is the only way I can forgive myself.

My baby is three months in my belly. When I head back up the street to the tram, I will walk slowly. I am overcautious, I know, but I don't want anything to happen to our child.

It is getting late now, and I want to meet Griff at the airfield.

The streetlights are coming on and little pools of gold are starting to fall on the pavement. I think of happy thoughts, the way you always told us we should. I think of Griff and our baby, and it lightens my mood. I am creating a brand-new family now.

When I think of it, a great weight seems to lift from my shoulders and for the first time in my life, the road ahead seems suddenly clear, my future bright. The only cloud on the horizon is that you have gone back to America, without me.

I know I will look for you everywhere, always . . . in the faces of strangers I pass on the street. One day, I will sit in cinemas and watch your movies and I will always, always lift my head to check, just in case, when I hear someone call your name.

And I will always be
Your loving sister,
Bell.

I stand with the letter in my hand for long moments. I have to swallow the lump in my throat.

As I suspected, these are not letters written by Rose Carey, they are letters written to her. Everything in that crate, even the letters, had indeed belonged to her sister, Bell.

40

Emma
Sydney, 2024

Aunty Julia has broken out the champagne. Allie is visiting and the four of us are gathered together in Julia's apartment, celebrating my promotion. Allie clinks her glass briefly against mine. 'Congratulations, Em,' she says.

'Thank you.' I think Allie now knows that Hammer and Tongs won the Hot Rain contract on merit, and I think she believes that I honestly wasn't asking for any special favours from her. It might take a lifetime to truly understand one another, but I know that with this toast, we are agreeing to try. After all, we are family.

'I'm glad we're all together because I have something to show you,' Julia says, putting her glass down on a side table. She gets up and goes to the table in the hall. When she comes back, she is carrying an envelope. A very old, cream envelope with an address on it written in faded ink.

She passes it to Lauren, who passes it straight to me. I see it is addressed to Bellbird Procter, care of the Carrington, but has been redirected to Mayfields & Co. My hands shake as I take it from her.

'When I was incapacitated with my sodding knee, I decided to take a closer look at that memorabilia you brought down for me from upstairs,' Julia says. 'That's when I found this.'

I turn it over. The back of the envelope reads 'Mrs Walter Ryan', and a return address in Los Angeles.

I take the letter from the envelope, scan it briefly from the salutation to the signature. I can't believe what I'm seeing. 'It's from Rose to Bell,' I murmur.

Julia sits down again, with a nod and an expectant smile.

'Well, read it to us,' says Lauren.

I take it from its aged envelope and begin.

'My Darling Sister Bellbird . . . ' I have to stop and close my eyes for a moment. It is such a hopeful start.

Beverly Hills, Los Angeles
Thursday, 19th June 1924

My darling sister Bellbird,

Thank you for your letters. You must think me slow to respond but it is that I received them all at once, after returning from a trip to New York. Now that I have read them, I am replying straightaway, so that you don't mistake my silence for something it is not.

Please know that you have nothing to fear from me, darling Bell, whatever happened in the past, and whatever comes next, I hold no grudges. I only have the dearest of memories of the two of us. Working together, playing together, coming up with the wonderful creations you made for me.

Oh, how I miss you! Even more so now that I know you are my sister. I wish you had shared that information with me before, I'm so sorry that you never felt comfortable enough to tell me.

It all makes sense to me now, though, looking back. How alike we were in so many ways. Goodness, we even look alike – and yet, it never occurred to me that we might be sisters. How much like our mother you are too – why, you play the piano exactly like she did, with the same light and shade. I remember thinking it when I heard you play at Fairview. I wish you could have known her, Bell, I wish you could have met Dad.

I also know you had nothing to do with the attempts on my life. The thing that convinces me is the fact that you were in the warehouse on that fateful day, when the tank shattered. If you'd had any hand in it, you would not have been there. You would have made excuses, as Eddie did. I also know that you were coerced, perhaps even blackmailed into doing things you would never have done. I shudder to think of it now, and I am desperately sorry that you had to suffer the way you must have, knowing what you came to know about Eddie – I can hardly bear to write his name – and that you were forced into marriage with him! It is too awful, too horrible to even think about.

I so hope you are happy with Griff. He is a charming rogue, I will give him that. I think you will have a life of adventure with him and that is fitting, for haven't you and I had some adventures? And now you have a little stranger on the way. How beautiful, Bell, our heartiest congratulations. I will be an Aunt! Imagine that. It makes me smile to think that when we meet again, as surely we must – I will meet three of you.

And now for our news. We are back in Los Angeles. We have rented a house not far from Pickfair, Mary and Douglas' home. Oh, you should see it, Bell. They are making quite the renovations. And you wouldn't believe it, they have a swimming pool! The first in Los Angeles, they say.

Mary and I are friends now, and I've been swimming in that pool. Of course it is tiny compared to the baths I have swum in throughout my life, but oh, it is delicious, shaped like a kidney. And the visitors they have, you wouldn't believe. Hollywood royalty, and English aristocracy. Not that I'm surprised, Doug and Mary being the King and Queen of Hollywood and all.

I digress. We are back, but we have made a major decision which will affect the rest of our lives.

We have decided to exit show business. As I am sure you now must know, the film we made in New Zealand, The Sea Princess of the South Pacific, *is lost to us, its whereabouts completely unknown. The last we knew, the film and everything to do with it was in Eddie's possession. He was to take it back to the States on a boat due to sail out a week ahead of us. But despite our exhaustive efforts, we have found no trace of it. The authorities cannot help us. We have nothing to show for all that time, effort and expense in New Zealand.*

I should be heartbroken. It has cost us so dearly, financially and otherwise. We owed embarrassing amounts of money and although Walter has sorted out some of our financial difficulties, we have had to sell assets to pay our debts. But because we have paid our debts, he has managed to keep the worst of our troubles out of the papers and for that I am overwhelmingly grateful. If he had not, we would not be able to take the new direction we have now decided to take – and here it is.

Darling, you will know how much I admire our own sex and I do believe we are going into a new age for women. We have the vote now, so we are stronger than we have ever been before in more ways than one, if only we knew it. We are also the fairer sex, and as such, we are the champions of all that is beautiful. Who are the people longing for tickets to the ballet and the theatre and the movies? Why, women, of course.

My wonderful Walter has played such a key role in my success, so too did our Alec . . . but when I look back I know it was also due to you. Without you, how would I even have become who I am? Women are such wonderful supporters of each other. I know this because of how well they have supported me, right back to our beautiful mother, and you. Then there was dear Miss Lewis, who brought me back from the brink of a scandal that had the power to ruin us all, and even Bonnie Spark, who went against the grain to pen articles of praise for my efforts, rather than scorn. I am deeply grateful to all the women who have helped me along the way and so my plan is to enable others as much as I can.

Do you remember the book I wrote for women a few years ago on health and fitness? Well, I've decided to take it one step further. I've devised a fitness routine for the everyday woman. Eventually, I will have routines for every age of women and every level of fitness. My plan is to create a club for women, perhaps many clubs. And to make sure everyone knows about it, Walter and I will be filming some shorts, where I will be demonstrating simple routines. So you see, although my movie star days are over, I will still be on screens. We are working with companies here, and some of our movie star chums, to support our efforts so that we can provide the programs free to women who can't afford to pay. Oh, I can't tell you how excited I am by the idea, Bell! I wish you were here to enjoy it.

Now, my darling, I will send you back, under separate cover, the letters you wrote me, not because I no longer want them, but because I think of them as little bits of your poor broken heart. They will no doubt take longer than this letter to arrive, but I hope in returning them to you, you will come to understand that I blame you for nothing. You said you were returning to the Mountains and so I am sending everything care of the Carrington.

I love you, I trust you and if forgiveness is what you need, I forgive you.

Go well, sister, and please write again.

Love,

Rosella

A short silence follows. I feel almost overcome by emotion.

'I wonder why your family had this . . . but not Bell's letters,' I say finally.

'Rose said she was sending them back under separate cover,' Julia says. 'She said they might take longer to arrive.'

I nod. 'But the Carrington must have forwarded this letter on to her at Mayfields . . . why wouldn't they also have forwarded those?'

'Perhaps by the time they arrived the staff no longer had a forwarding address,' Lauren muses.

'They're not in any kind of packaging.' Julia observes.

'Perhaps the package they came in was damaged in transit,' I reason. 'Someone might have looked through the contents, searching for a return address.'

'But the only address on the letters was the Carrington,' Julia says.

I nod. 'I mean, we think it's also possible that Bell knew the box was at the Carrington but she didn't want it forwarded on. Her lover had died, her criminal husband had been shot dead, she wanted no reminders.'

'So everything was sent to the store room, where they were forgotten for the past hundred years,' Lauren says cheerfully. I still marvel that she bears me no grudge for effectively losing her inheritance.

I look at Julia. 'I don't understand why you didn't already know about Bell and Rose.'

She shrugs. 'We didn't know much about our father's family at all,' she says. 'He never talked about them. I sensed it was painful for him and so I didn't ask. I've looked through all the memorabilia, and there are no more letters, so I don't know any more about Rose and Bell than you. I don't know if they ever met or corresponded again.'

I nod, thinking about it. 'Well at least . . .' I look at the letter in my hands and then back at Julia. 'I mean, the fact that you have this letter in your possession means . . . Bell must have received it, right?' I find I desperately want this confirmed.

She looks at me with a gentle smile. 'Of course she did, dear Emma. Of course she did.'

I don't recognise the number on my phone, but I pick up anyway. 'Emma Quinn, Hammer and Tongs Productions,' I say, in my best General Manager voice.

'Ms Quinn? It's Luke Hamilton here from the National Film and Sound Archives.'

I freeze.

'I'm ringing about the film you found.'

'Oh,' I say, feigning disinterest, or surprise, though I don't think I'm fooling anyone.

The film has made it there, no doubt via the bomb squad. 'It's quite a find. Thank you, and congratulations. You've filled a gap we didn't even know existed in the Rose Carey collection.'

'Well, no problem. I'm glad it's where it needs to be.' I'm also glad it didn't set my apartment alight.

'Yes.' He goes on to chat to me at length about the film, including that it is an example of Prizma Color, an early motion picture colour process, before saying, 'I'm also calling to ask for your address.'

'Oh?'

'Yes, we can't house the rest of Ms Carey's, um . . . collection.' I suppose he's seen the naked photos, then. 'So, we thought we'd return some things to you. I understand your wife is a descendant.'

'That's right.' I give him my address. 'Can I ask what exactly you are shipping back to us?'

'Oh, yes, certainly. It's the, ah, photographs . . . some ah, newspaper clippings and . . . a camera.'

AUTHOR NOTE

When I first began dreaming about my next book, all I knew is that I wanted it to feature a heroine inspired by the audacious Australian Annette Kellerman: swimmer, aquatic performer, movie star, writer and entrepreneur. The character of Rose Carey is an homage to this trailblazing woman.

Annette achieved extraordinary things in her life. Suffering from weak legs as a child, her parents enrolled her in swimming classes, and not only did the therapy work, it led to her becoming a champion. She began giving diving demonstrations at pools and aquatic performances in a glass aquarium, before heading to England where she attempted to swim the English Channel three times. Although unsuccessful, she earned a place in history for being the first woman in the world to try.

Heading to America, she claimed to have been arrested for indecency on a Boston beach for daring to wear a one-piece swimming costume. Whether or not she was arrested is a moot point; the publicity helped popularise the one-piece, liberating women from heavy woollen costumes.

She became a performer, then set her sights on becoming a film star, and, in typical Annette fashion, she did.

Her performances included all kinds of stunts – jumping off cliffs (once into a pool of crocodiles), walking tightropes, riding horses. Underwater, she performed a kind of ballet that is said to have inspired the invention of what we now know as 'artistic swimming'. She is also credited as being the first woman to appear in a major motion picture naked.

I admire Annette for what might have been described in her day as her 'derring-do'. She marched through life, seizing opportunities, rising to meet challenges, reinventing herself at every turn and talking up her own achievements. But what I love most about her is the way she encouraged other women to be bold and strong – to be all that we are and all that we can be.

Although inspired by Annette's strength, bravery, intellect, and unquenchable passion for life, Rose Carey came to me as her own person, with her own voice and her own tale to tell. If not for the fact that she is, of course, fictional, I am certain she and Annette would have been friends, and I hope her story is just as inspiring.

ACKNOWLEDGEMENTS

Thank you to everyone who helped me, personally and professionally, as I brought the stories of Rose and Emma to life, and to you for reading this novel inspired by the amazing Annette Kellerman.

Thank you Dan Ruffino and Cassandra Di Bello from Simon & Schuster Australia for continuing to believe in me; to the brilliant S&S team who helped elevate my work, especially Anthea Bariamis and Rosie Outred, and to the sales, marketing and distribution teams that promote my books. I'm blessed to be enabled by such professionals.

Thank you to one of my favourite videographers Greg 'Swampy' Marsh. Also to Gary Schweikert, Big Hat Pictures (film producers). I worked with these professionals in a previous life, and they are as fabulous today as they were then, both sharing invaluable insights.

Thank you to my fabulous friends, Blue Kemball, and Gavin Kemball, consultant gynaecologist and fertility specialist. Thanks Gav, for so patiently answering my questions about IVF.

To Alice Almeida, Founder of The Amber Network, which connects and supports those experiencing infertility and/or fertility treatment – thank you for speaking so candidly about your personal IVF journey and for helping me to understand the experience.

Thanks also to the City of Sydney Assistant Curator for walking me through the Sydney Town Hall, sharing her knowledge of one of the city's most beautiful landmarks.

To Lorraine Stacker, retired librarian, author, and family historian, thanks for helping me understand the way in which genealogists provide services to clients.

At this point, I'd like to say that this book wouldn't be what it is without the help of these professionals, but any factual errors are all mine!

I stayed a night at the gorgeous Carrington Hotel in the Blue Mountains as I prepared to write this book and it was such a nostalgic experience. Special thanks to the hotel for responding to my follow-up questions and sharing photos.

Thank you Jo West for being not only a fantastic friend, but for giving me insights into the experience of genealogy from a user's perspective, and Mark West – you were one of the first people to talk with me about nitrate film. You also shared your insights into electricity and how far along it might have been in Australia in the 1920s. Thank you for also sharing experiences which helped better inform my characters.

I'd like to acknowledge the work of the countless professionals who chronicle and preserve history. The existence of their work means I have been able to study not only the life and times of Annette Kellerman and her peers, but also view surviving snippets of early films. Such work helps fiction authors bring historic tales to life. Trove (Australia), Papers Past (NZ), The National Film and Sound Archive of Australia and the many biographical and historical works I consulted deserve special mention.

A big thank you to the book communities who champion the work of authors, particularly readers, reviewers, and the media. A special shout-out to bookstores and libraries. They not only help books reach readers, but also generously provide venues to host events.

Thank you to the author community itself. In particular the Northern Beaches Readers Festival, which is so engaged in our author worlds, and my fellow writers – Mary-Lou Stephens, Tania Blanchard, Nina D Campbell and Sandie Docker; also Claudine Tinellis, Shelley Gardner, Robyn Haynes and many others who have treated me with such kindness. They have always been willing to share their own experiences and lend a compassionate ear, particularly when writer's block met struggle street.

Thanks to those who read my earliest draft and, without exception, encouraged me to go on. Mishell Currie (visit her at Bowral's Sweets & Treats, you won't be sorry), Margaret English-Aurisch, who is such a wonderful supporter not just of me, but of other authors, my unfailingly enthusiastic parents and of course my friend Penny McLaren, a talented sewing creative who also helped me better understand fabric, design, and the dressmaking process.

Julia Newbould - thank you for supporting me in so many ways, from reading a draft, to talking with me and others about my work, to steering me towards people who could help with my research, and for inspiring the character of 'Julia'. Most importantly, thank you for being my friend. It is wonderful to have you in my corner.

I would also like to thank Santina Porpiglia, who generously hosted me in her Redfern atelier salon, Collezione Santina, for my debut launch in 2022. This was when I first saw exquisite fabrics being expertly cut and sewn.

Special thanks to Holly Urzi for hosting a book event that was so wonderful I will remember it always and Belinda Nobbs Grube for your enduring friendship and for encouraging people to come along to support me at a regional NSW book talk. In fact, thank you to every friend who bought a book, hosted or came along to one of my events. I am fortunate to travel life with such wonderful people.

Thank you Trish Newie-Hunt, for sharing your personal story with me and thanks also to my extended family. A special mention to my husband's family – in particular, Clare and Kai, Jenny, Sally-Anne, and Marg. Your affection and encouragement warm my heart.

There are also communities of people who cheer me from the sidelines, including those from my professional life in financial services – clients, colleagues, friends, and associates – I hope you know how much I appreciate you.

Finally, thank you to those closest to me.

My sister, Reenie: I would be lost without you. You are treasured.

My husband, Bruce: the best home handyman I ever knew, thank you for your love, support, and belief in me, especially in our hard times.

My sons, Chris and Lachlan: thank you for always being on my team, for advice beyond your years, and for simply being you.

Love you all, always.

ABOUT THE AUTHOR

Julie Bennett fell in love with words at a very young age and soon after leaving school began a career in libraries. In her late twenties she decided to follow her dream to write for a living and, after graduating university, became a journalist. In 2004 she launched a public relations company, which she still manages today. Julie lives with her wonderful husband, Bruce, and their gorgeous kelpie cross cattle dog, Riley, within walking distance of the Sydney Opera House where she performed as a child extra back in 1973, the year it opened. *The Lost Letters of Rose Carey* is Julie's second novel. Her debut *The Understudy* was published by Simon & Schuster in 2022.